Devil's Knights Series
Book 2

Winter Travers

Amanda,

Enjoy Rigid & Cyn!

Copyright © 2015 Winter Travers

ISBN-13: 978-1514372678

ISBN-10: 1514372673

Finding Cyn: Devil's Knights Series

Editor: Brandi Beers

Cover Designer: Bonnie Trujillo at Bonnieriffic Covers

All rights reserved. Without limiting the rights under copyright reserved above, no part of this publication may be reproduction, stored in or introduced into a retrieval system, or transmitted, in any form, or by any means (electronic, mechanical, photocopying, recording, or otherwise) utilization of this work without written permission of both the copyright owner and the above publisher of this book.

This is a work of fiction. Names, characters, places, brands, media and incidents are either the products of the author's imagination or are used fictitiously. The author acknowledges the trademarked status and trademark owners of various products referenced in this work of fiction, which have been used without permission. The publication/use of these trademarks is not authorized, associated with, or sponsored by the trademark owners.

For questions or comments about this book, please contact the author at wintertravers84@gmail.com

Cover Images

Motorcycle on the road © Andrey Armyagov | Dollarphotoclub.com

Lovers - sensual couple making love in bed © Igor Mojzes | Dollarphotoclub.com

The Devil's Knights Series

Loving Lo

Finding Cyn

Gravel's Road (Coming Soon)

Dedication

To all the strong women in my life who have overcome all of life's diversities and came out stronger.

Acknowledgements

To my amazing hubby and phenomenal son. Thank you for being awesome during this whole writing journey. I'd like to tell you the craziness is over, but it's only just begun. I love you both.

To my family. Thanks for supporting me in every way possible.

Bonnie and Lizette. I seriously don't know where the hell the three of you came from but you better not leave. Ever.

To all the amazing authors I have met and have the pleasure of being friends with (There are way too many to name). You are all amazing and are making my TBR pile a mile high!

To my Wicked Women. You ladies are amazing and sure do know how to pimp a girl! Thank you for all the time you put in getting my name out there. You all rock!

Finding Cyn

Chapter 1

Cyn

I'm not dead.

My head was throbbing, and I felt like I was going to hurl.

If I were dead, I would feel nothing, at least, that's what I think being dead would feel like. All I feel is pain; dull, throbbing pain.

I groaned, feeling hands run over my body. They run over my stomach and I flinch. I lost count of how many times Nick had kicked me in the stomach. *You need to learn a lesson, Cyn. Who the fuck do you think you are? You should be thankful I fucked your fat ass. If I wanted to have a kid, I sure wouldn't do it with your ugly face.*

I had told Nick I was pregnant. He obviously wasn't happy with that bit of news as I was laid out on my living room floor, unable to get up.

I remember everything he did to me. Everywhere he touched me. I remember everything he said to me.

"Cyn. Cyn, are you awake. Can you hear me? Are you ok? Where does it hurt?" It's Meg. I had called her as soon as I knew Nick was gone. I had tried to stay on the phone with her, but the darkness I had been fighting off had finally enveloped me, and I blacked out.

"Yeah." I croaked out.

"Open your eyes, honey. I need to see your eyes." I could tell Meg was hanging on by a thread. I feel terrible for making her feel this way.

"Stop feeling me up, Meg." I groaned as her hands moved my arm I was cradling against my chest. It was throbbing, and I'm pretty sure broken.

The hands stopped moving but didn't leave my body. "I'm just trying to figure out where you're hurt." I hear growled. I crack my eyes open and see a blue Mohawk. Fuck, Rigid.

"Why don't you ask?" I snap at him. Why is he here? I can't deal with him right now. I can barely deal with him when I'm lucid and coherent. Right now, all of my energy was going to keeping my eyes open.

"Meg did ask, you didn't answer her," he snapped back. His hands left my arm and traveled back over my stomach. He lifted my shirt up, and I heard Meg gasp. I guess I must look pretty rough.

"Why the fuck are your pants undone?" Rigid thundered.

Oh, that. Fuck. I know it was hard to believe, but my pants being undone made things look a lot worse than what they were.

I turned my head away, closing my eyes again. I didn't need to deal with his shit. I had dealt with one raging lunatic tonight, I didn't need to deal with Rigid.

"Cyn, honey, tell me what happened," Meg whispered, her hand cradling my face. I squeezed my eyes shut tighter, not wanting to feel anything. It was taking everything in me to fight off the tears threatening to fall.

I feel the bile crawling up my throat, the words rattling around in my head. *You always liked this Cyn, you fucking whore. Fucking take it you, fat bitch.*

"Fucking answer me!" Rigid roared again.

My eyes snapped open, and I swung my head to look at Rigid. His eyes boring into me, waiting. Fuck him, he wanted to know, I'd fucking tell him. "I told him I was pregnant. He told me no fat bitch was going to have his kid.' I heard Meg gasp, but I didn't look at her. 'I tried to get away, but he shoved me down on the couch and ripped my pants down. Told me fat bitches were only good for fucking and throwing away. I managed to elbow him in the face, knocking him off me. He went fucking insane. I lost count how many times he kicked me in the stomach. Is that what you wanted to hear Rigid?' I sneered at him. 'Does that make you feel better knowing what happened to me?" He didn't look shocked, he looked pissed off. The motherfucker looked pissed off at me. I couldn't handle this.

I closed my eyes and laid my head back down. Everything fucking hurt. Everything. I just wanted them all to go away.

"Cyn," Meg sobbed. "I'm so sorry." I heard boots stomping towards the door, the screen door slapping shut. He left. Good.

"Stop crying, Meg, and help me off the floor," I ordered. I had to get a grip and get the fuck off the floor. I needed to get to the hospital to fix my arm and anything else that needed fixing then pass out for days. I didn't feel when I slept.

Strong arms lifted me off the floor, cradling me to their chest. I opened my eyes and looked up into King's eyes filled with concern and pity. Another thing I couldn't deal with, pity. "Hi, King. If this were all it took to get in your arms, I would have gotten beaten up a long time ago," I winked at him.

"How's the head, Cyn?" King rumbled at me. I guess he didn't like my joke.

"Throbbing. Now ask me about my arm."

"Sprained?" He guessed.

"Broke. Hurts like a bitch." He propped me up on the couch, my back against the armrest. Meg swung my legs up, and I winced. Fuck that hurt.

"Sorry," Meg mumbled.

"You didn't beat the shit out of me, Meg, don't be sorry."

"I'm going to kill him," she whispered, her voice laced with hate.

"Me too," I whispered. I lean my head back on the armrest, closing my eyes again.

"I'm sure Rigid is taking care of that right now," King mumbled as I heard him walk out of the room. My head hurt too much to think about whatever that meant. Something to file away for another time. Focus on the now.

"My house is a mess, Meg." I opened my eyes and looked around. My once cute, girly living room was now shattered and broken. My pretty teal and purple paisley rug was bunched up under my coffee table, a blood stain on the corner. That wasn't going to come out.

"It doesn't matter, Cyn, there's other things to worry about." Meg kneeled next to the couch. I finally really looked at her, and my heart hurt even more. Her eyes were bloodshot and puffy, her kick ass marooney purple hair piled on top of her head, her clothes rumpled and creased.

"Don't cry for me, Meg." I pleaded.

"How can I not?' she wailed. 'I should have come with you instead of going to Lo's."

"Meg, I'm only going to say this once; this was not your fault. If you had come with me, he might have beaten both of us. I'm glad you didn't come, I wouldn't be able to live with myself if he had hurt you. I'll be fine." As far as anyone would know.

"Cyn, you don't need to be strong right now, just let it go." She grabbed my hand and squeezed it.

"I'll be fine, Meg.' I pulled my hand from hers, resting it on my stomach. Fuck, I barely touched myself, and it felt like I had been kicked again. I took a deep breath, trying to silence the pain. 'Now, distract me from how much my arm hurts by telling me how your visit to King went. From the fact that he's here, I would guess it went well." I smirked, playing down the fact I was in agony.

"He loves me." Meg marveled like it was hard to believe.

Totally clueless about how awesome she was, that's my Meg. "He should," I replied. King was hot, no other way to put it. Meg thought she wasn't worthy of King, and he would get rid of her, yada, yada, yada. They were meant for each other, it had only been a matter of time before Meg realized it.

I heard sirens in the distance and breathed a sigh of relief. Thank God.

"Ambulance is almost here," King said, slamming back into the house, shoving his phone into his back pocket.

"Yay.' I sighed in relief. I never thought I would be happy about an ambulance ride. 'I hope they have the good drugs on board."

"What about the baby?" Meg asked.

I didn't want to think about the baby. I knew he didn't make it. I was only a month along, there was no way he made it after the twenty plus kicks Nick had landed to my stomach.

"There is no baby anymore, Meg. Nick made sure of that." Tears rolled down my cheeks. I lightly rubbed my stomach, saying goodbye to my baby. The same baby that hours ago I wasn't sure about, but I knew I wanted, now gone.

"You don't know that, Cyn," Meg whispered.

Fuck, I loved her. She was the best friend I had ever had. "Ok, Meg. I'll ask the doctor." I knew he was gone, but she was right, I needed to be checked out.

"Ambulance is here," some guy yelled through the screen door.

"Who was that?" I asked as I swung my legs off the couch. The room spun, making me drop my chin to my chest, willing the dizziness to go away.

"Gambler," King said. I opened my eyes and saw King walking toward me.

"Half the clubhouse came to make sure you were ok. They're all outside," Meg replied as King lifted me again and we headed to the door.

"I can probably walk," I told him as he turned sideways out the door and down the porch steps.

"Just because you can don't mean you have to," King stated.

"Whatever, Stud Muffin. I'm just going to enjoy my time in your arms.' Meg was walking behind us and giggled. 'I should probably stop flirting with you. You love my best friend."

We had reached the ambulance, and the two paramedics were scrambling to get the back doors open. "I'll let you borrow him," Meg chimed in.

"I think I'm out of commission for a while," I said, then saw Meg and King's face drop. Fuck. There's that pity again.

King set me on the gurney inside, and I winced. Pretty sure Nick must have broken a couple of ribs too. "You want me to ride with you?" Meg asked, hopeful.

"No, honey, I'm good." I wanted to be alone. I know it was shitty of me pushing her away, but I needed to close my eyes and not think.

"You sure?' She asked. I nodded my head, feeling the darkness coming closer again. Getting the shit beat out of you really takes it out of you. 'Ok, Lo and I will be right behind you. We'll meet you there.' I smiled at Meg, which was more of a wince, as the paramedic helped me lay down. I closed my eyes and heard the back doors slam shut.

"We'll be there in ten minutes." The paramedic said.

"I'm pregnant,' I told him. 'Or at least, I was." I felt the tears threatening again and prayed for the darkness to take me away again.

"Ok, we'll take care of you." I could hear compassion in his voice and it made me want to cry even more.

He started examining me, lifting my shirt, poking and prodding. "Anything else we should know?" The paramedic asked.

"He took my baby away," I whispered, realizing my baby was gone. I closed my eyes and felt the darkness seeping in. It was close, I needed it.

"Stay with me. No sleeping yet," The paramedic ordered. Except I didn't listen, I let the darkness take me. I didn't want to feel anything. I was done.

Gone.

Chapter 2

RIGID

"What's his name, Meg?" I demanded as soon as the ambulance doors slammed. Meg was wrapped up in King's arms, tears streaming down her face.

"Nick. I don't remember his last name. I didn't like him. I never really hung out with her when she was with him,' She quaked, 'I should have gone with her tonight."

"You couldn't have known this was going to happen," King murmured into her hair, soothing her.

I didn't have time for this shit. The longer this piece of shit was out there, the further he got away. "I need his last name. Find it out," I demanded.

"Chill the fuck out, Rigid. How the fuck is she supposed to figure out his last name? She told you she barely knew the guy," Lo barked.

"I can call Troy. He might remember it." Meg pulled her phone out, hands shaking.

"Give me the phone, babe, I'll call him." King grabbed the phone out of her hand and led her over to the front steps, depositing her on them and started barking into the phone.

I didn't care who the fuck gave me the fucker's last name, I just wanted it.

All that I could see was Cyn laying on the floor, motionless. The second I saw her, I thought she was dead. My whole world stopped at that moment. The only thing that snapped me out of it was King yelling she was breathing. I had to touch her, make sure for myself that she was ok. When her eyes snapped open, my world stopped again. She was alive.

When I saw her pants were open, I fucking lost it. Hearing that she had been able to fight him off was the only thing that had kept me from punching a hole in the god damn wall. Her words were meant to hurt and shock me. All they did was start a fire that burned deep in my stomach. A fire that I knew the only way it would be put out was to have the fucker in the ground and Cyn in my arms. Forever.

"Kratter. Nick Kratter. Troy said he lives out on Crosstown Rd. He's headed out here right now, said he'll show us which house," Lo hollered across the yard.

"How long will that fucking be? The longer we let this fucker go, the further he gets away from us." I fumed at King as I ran my hands through my Mohawk. "This is fucking bullshit!"

"Chill the fuck out, Rigid. You going off half-cocked isn't going to help. Troy will be here in ten minutes, not even," King ordered.

Chill out? Fuck, I wasn't going to be able to chill till I put this fucker behind bars or in the fucking ground. If I had my way, it would definitely be the fucking ground.

"I need to go to the hospital. I have to be there," Meg trembled from the steps. She was a fucking wreck, I really did need to chill out because yelling at Meg and King wasn't helping.

"I'll have Gravel drive you to the hospital, babe, and he'll stay with you till we get there. Rigid and I can drive with Troy. Hopefully, we won't be too long," King said.

"Be careful, Lo, you too, Rigid. I don't really know this guy, but from what I just saw of Cyn, he seems a little out of control," Meg said, rising up from the steps and walking into King's arms.

"Just take care of Cyn for me until I get there, Meg, don't worry about us," I said.

"What happens when you get there?" Meg trembled.

"Not a fucking clue. I was giving Cyn room, waiting for her to come to me. That's over. This changed everything." I stated as I looked down the road and saw headlights headed our way.

"I think you'll be good for Cyn, Rigid, just be careful. None of us knows how this will affect her. I can't imagine what she is thinking or feeling right now." Meg started crying again and buried her face in King's neck.

King crooned comforting words in Meg's hair, and I turned away. All I wanted was to hold Cyn right now and I couldn't. She was lying in an ambulance, broken, and I didn't know how I was going to fix her.

I watched a late model sports car approaching, hoping it was Troy, but it passed by slowly, the driver openly staring at all the bikes and bikers scattered around Cyn's lawn. Fucking rubber necker.

I heard another car approaching, clearly hauling ass down the road. A jacked up Ford truck careened into the driveway, spraying gravel in its wake.

Time to take the fucking garbage out.

<<<<<<<<

Cyn

I couldn't move. My arms felt like they weighed a hundred pounds and my chest felt like an anchor was sitting on it. The room was quiet except for insistent beeping from the machine I was hooked up to and a low rumble of what I was pretty sure was snoring.

I opened my eyes and groaned as the room tilted. I slammed my eyes shut, trying to will my rolling stomach to cease, and groaned. Ugh, fuck me. This was horrible.

"You awake, beautiful?"

My eyes snapped open, and I whipped my head to the right at the sound of Rigid's voice. I instantly regretted it when another wave of nausea hit me. I closed my eyes, willing myself not to throw up.

I heard a chair scrape across the floor, slamming into the wall, and Rigid was next to me instantly. "Talk to me, Cyn, what's wrong?" He asked concern laced in his gravelly voice from just waking up.

I still felt like I was going to throw up and couldn't speak. Rigid's hand brushed my hair out of my face, caressing my cheek. "Say something please, Cyn," he pleaded.

Weird, Rigid not his usual cocky self. The last time I had talked to him, he had demanded I come over to a bonfire Meg was having. After Nick's bullshit, I really didn't deal well with demands. "Why are you here?" I croaked out. I barely recognized my own voice. It sounded like I had been gargling gravel.

"I needed to know if you were ok."

"I'm fine. You can go," I whimpered as another wave of nausea hit me. I groaned, knowing it was only a matter of time before I lost my dinner.

"I'm not leaving. Someone needs to take care of you, protect you."

"I'm pretty sure I'm in a hospital, and I am going to have a huge ass bill telling me someone was taking care of me. You can go. Please." He had to leave, I was losing the battle of keeping my stomach from doing somersaults.

"I'm not leaving. Bitch all you want, I-"

But I didn't hear what the rest of what he said because that's when I lost the battle of my rolling stomach all over Rigid's boots, then proceeded to pass out.

Chapter 3

RIGID

"I can see if I can get you some pants, maybe find some boots in the lost and found." A nurse fluttered around Cyn, trying to get me to talk to her while she barely looked at Cyn.

Bitch was fucking insane if she thought she had a chance in hell with me. It was pretty fucking obvious I was with Cyn. Well as much as Cyn would let me be with her, but the nurse kept fluttering her eyes at me and shaking her ass as she walked around, trying to get my attention.

"It's really not a big deal. I'm sure I can-."

"Leave. Now." Rude, I know, but effective. The nurse huffed at me and stormed out of the room. I seriously didn't know what was wrong with some bitches these days.

"Now you can leave too." Cyn rasped, eyes still shut, not moving.

The nurse had told me before she started flirting with me and ignoring Cyn, that Cyn had a nasty concussion which was most likely causing nausea and the reason she had decided to leave her dinner on my boots.

"Is that how you talk to the guy you threw up on?' I asked, smirking as she groaned, rolling her head in my direction. 'Take it easy, Cyn, no quick movements," I warned.

"Ugh, I kind of figured that out after puking all over you." Her face was pointed at me, but her eyes were still closed. She had a bad cut above her left eye, close to swelling shut and the right side of her face was already turning purple and puffy.

"You need anything?" I asked as I dragged the chair closer to the side of the bed and eased into it. I bumped the bed with my knee, and Cyn groaned. Fuck.

"I need for you to never do that again," she whined.

"Sorry, beautiful." I gently brushed her hair to the side and felt my stomach clench seeing her battered face up close. The motherfucker who had done this to her was going to die.

We had swung by his house, but he was nowhere to be found. Gambler, Demon, and Troy were doing everything to find the fucker, but they still hadn't found a trace of him. It was like the fucker just up and disappeared.

"Liar." She gulped.

"What? I promise I won't bump the bed again, I'm sorry." Geeze she was really bad off.

"No, I mean you lied when you called me beautiful. I don't need a mirror to tell me what I look like. I can feel it. I feel like shit, so I know I'm not beautiful, I'm shit." She wheezed and coughed.

My blood boiled as I heard Cyn talk. Even beaten and bruised she was still the most beautiful woman I had ever seen. All I saw when I looked at her was a strong-willed, tough as nails woman who had been through so much and was still fighting. She was beautiful. All she was seeing was the surface, there was so much more to her than what was on top.

"Open your eyes," I ordered.

"Rigid, please leave. I don't want to see anyone right now. I just want to sleep and not feel anything.' She finally opened her eyes and looked at me. 'Get that nurse back in here who was trying to get in your pants and sweet talk her to make her give me some pain medicine then you can go."

"You got some pain meds in your IV. That bitch doesn't need to come back in here, you don't need her for anything. You need something, I'll get it for you."

"I just don't know why you are here. No one else is, why are you?" She pleaded.

She had no fucking clue. Half the fucking club had been camped out in the waiting room since she got here. "Get some sleep, Cyn, you're going to need it. Doctor said you can leave tomorrow if everything checks out ok."

"How many days have I been here?" she asked.

"It's early, Monday morning. So three days. You've been knocked out of it," I replied as I made my way to the door, planning on letting everyone know she was awake.

"Wait, why did the doctor talk to you? I thought you had to be family," she asked as she laid her head down, closing her eyes. It was only a matter of time before the meds kicked in, knocking her out again.

"You do have to be family, I told them I was your husband." It was the only way for the doctor to tell me anything. Meg told me Cyn's parents were on vacation, and we had no idea how to get in touch with them. Meg had said she could say she was her sister, but I knew I wouldn't be allowed to stay in the room if she did that.

"I must have been knocked out for a while since I missed the wedding,' she said sarcastically. Suddenly Cyn whipped her eyes to me, opened wide. 'Oh my god, they don't think you did this to me, do they?"

All I could do was shake my head. Here she was laying broken and bruised in the hospital, and she was worried I was getting blamed. Crazy. "Naw, babe. If they thought I did this to you, I sure as shit wouldn't be sitting in your room alone with you."

"Oh, yeah. I guess you're right.' She laid her head back down, sighing in relief. 'I need to sleep." She said, deflated.

By the time I made it to the door and looked back at her, I knew she was already asleep. Even asleep, I could tell she was broken. So broken that I had no idea how to put her back together.

<<<<<<<<

RIGID

"I want to see her! She's my best friend!" Meg screamed at me.

I had finally made it to the waiting room after getting my shit together after talking to Cyn. Seeing her so beaten down and hopeless had ripped my heart in two.

"She's sleeping. There's nothing you can do for her right now," I grunted out.

"I can sit with her, hold her hand. Be there when she wakes up. Anything other than just sitting here doing nothing!" Meg was damn near hysterical. I looked at King, who looked a little freaked and not sure what to do.

"I'm sorry Meg. She just needs to rest. Please," I pleaded. Cyn really did just need to rest.

"Fine! But I need something to do!" She exclaimed.

"We need to figure out where she is going to go when she is released tomorrow. I don't know where she is going to want to go, but I know wherever she goes she shouldn't be alone. At least not until we catch Nick."

"Asshat!" Meg said venomously.

"Babe, calm down. Rigid is just trying to help," King tried soothing her, folding her into his chest.

"No, not Rigid, Nick. Cyn and I renamed him Asshat after she found out he was cheating on her. His name is Asshat. Plus I could never remember his real name," Meg explained as she buried her head in King's neck.

King and I just shook our heads, silently laughing at Meg.

Meg was like a pit bull, ready to protect Cyn. 'So, back to what I was saying, Cyn can't be alone until we find *Asshat*," I said, using his new name Meg and Cyn had given him.

"She can stay with me. I can ask Remy if he can stay with his dad till we figure everything out," Meg offered.

"Babe, no. Your house is small, and you're not home at night. She can stay at the clubhouse. There's always, at least, five people there so she'll never be alone," King stated.

"No fucking way! Not with all those skank whores you have wandering around. Hell to the no!" Meg protested, pushing away from King, huffing, as she propped her hands on her hips, pure pissed.

"Babe, those chicks aren't there all the time, you know. Just when there's a party going on. We do run a business Monday thru Friday," King said, running his fingers through his hair.

Meg had left King because of the pussy hanging around the house, and they had just gotten back together less than 72 hours ago. Club pussy was really going to be an issue for them if Meg's attitude was anything to go by. King hadn't touched any of the pussy since he had met Meg, but I think just the fact that they were around drove Meg crazy.

"Bullshit, King!' She sneered at him. 'All you have to do is snap your fingers, and anyone of them will suck your dick! Cyn is not going to be around that while she is recovering."

"The only fucking person I'm going to snap my fucking fingers at is you, Meg. Get that through your head and we'll get along a hell of a lot better. And you know what happens when you call me King!" King thundered. There were only two people that called King by his real name; Meg and his mom. From what I had gathered, King had grown quite fond of Meg calling him Lo and got pissed when she called him King.

King and Meg stared each other down, neither one giving.

"Jesus Christ! You both fucking love each other, knock it the fuck off. He isn't going to fuck around on you, Meg, and, King, you need to fucking tell the pussy to fuck off, or they're all gone. Problem solved. Can we get back to Cyn now?' I asked, fucking annoyed. 'She can fucking stay at her house. It just needs to get cleaned up and then I can stay with her.' I was fucking irritated. Cyn was lying in a fucking hospital bed, and here these two were arguing about rancid pussy. 'I'm going back to Cyn. Get her house cleaned up by this afternoon."

"Fine! But the only reason I'm going to put up with the club pussy is because I can't fucking breath without you, Lo. Remember that the next time one of them tries to touch you," Meg ranted as King reached for her.

"Noted, babe. How about I take you home to get a couple hours of sleep and then we can head to Cyn's to clean up?" He stroked her hair, nuzzling her neck. One minute these two were going at each other and the next they were all lovey and shit. Fucking crazy.

"See you guys tomorrow. I'll text when I know what time I'm springing her out of here." I was ready to get back to Cyn, even if she was sleeping.

"All right brother, try to get some sleep. Text if you need anything," King ordered as he gathered Meg in his arms and steered her toward the exit. Meg threw a wave over her shoulder to me, and they disappeared out the sliding doors.

I watched King talk to the rest of the guys who had come to the hospital to make sure Cyn was ok. After King had talked to them, they all got on their bikes and headed out except for Mickey, who I'm sure King had told to stay behind to be on watch at the hospital.

I walked back into Cyn's room, lightly closing the door behind me. I walked to her bed and just looked at her.

Her left eye was swollen shut, the cut that went to her eye and down her cheek had taken ten stitches and would most likely leave a scar. She had a soft cast on her right arm that would be getting a hard cast tomorrow. She had the blanket drawn up to her chest, but I knew what was underneath the blanket. Both of her knees had cuts and bruises, and her stomach was black and blue from where the fucking bastard had kicked her.

Cyn had lost her baby. The doctor had told me, thinking that she had been pregnant with my baby. I couldn't believe someone's reaction to learning they were going to be a dad was to beat the shit out of the mother and tell her how worthless she was. I grasped the rail of her bed, my knuckles turning white, trying to calm myself down. I couldn't wait to get my hands on the fucker who had done this to her.

She whimpered in her sleep, her legs thrashing. "Shhh, beautiful, you're ok,' I caressed her cheek, careful of her stitches. She leaned into my hand, turning her body towards me. 'I got you Cyn. Nothing bad will ever happen to you again."

She sighed contently, wrapping her hand around my arm and pulling it to her chest. "Don't leave," she whispered in her sleep.

I pulled the chair closer to the bed, careful to not move my hand from her and sat. My arm completely stretched out, not comfortable at all, but I would sit like this forever if Cyn wanted me to.

"I'll never leave," I confided to the dark room.

Never.

Chapter 4

Cyn

"You'll need to come back in seven days to get your stitches out, and we'll check to see how your arm is healing. After that, check up in five more weeks to get the cast-off, then hopefully you should be all healed. Good as new." The doctor recited off, not even looking at me. His eyes were glued to his clipboard, furiously writing.

"Is there, um, anything I should know or do about, um, you know…" I trailed off, not really wanting to ask my question since Rigid hadn't left my side all day yesterday and today, no matter how many times I had asked him to leave. I tried to block him out as he helped me to the bathroom this morning or when he insisted he needed to help me eat, cut my food, feed me.

I couldn't do it anymore. He needed to leave so I could talk to the doctor. I needed to know how I was after losing the baby if I would ever be able to get pregnant again.

I shot a glare at Rigid, silently pleading for him to leave the room. All the fucker did was smirk at me. What a douche.

"Can you please leave the room Rigid? I want to talk to the doctor privately," I sneered.

"Oh, sweetie, you know you can say anything in front of your husband,' Rigid stated. 'You can go ahead and ask the doctor whatever you want. We don't have any secrets," he said, smiling at the doctor who had finally looked up from his clipboard, now staring at Rigid. He paled as he took in Rigid's blue Mohawk and never ending tattoos. Intimidating didn't even scratch the surface on what Rigid was. Right now, all he was is an annoyance to me.

"Please, dear, it's rather personal," I pleaded, playing along with his husband and wife charade.

Rigid moved from the foot of the bed, and I breathed a sigh of relief. Thank God.

"So, Doctor, what I want to know is if-." The door clicked shut, and then I saw Rigid walking to the chair that was pulled up next to the bed.

"Go ahead, beautiful, I just shut the door to give you more privacy," Rigid mocked as he sat in the chair, cocking his long legs open and leaning back in the chair.

"I hate you," I whispered.

"No, you don't," Rigid shot back.

"Um, Mrs. Meyers, did you have any questions or am I ok to leave?" The doctor asked, anxious to leave.

I looked at Rigid, hoping he would leave, but no, he just sat there, waiting right along with the doctor.

Fuck it. "I lost my baby," I blurted out. Rigid stiffened next to me, but I ignored him. I asked the fucker to leave so he can sit there and be uncomfortable.

"Yes," the Doctor replied matter of fact.

"This was my first pregnancy. He used my stomach like a punching bag. I wanted to know if everything was ok, you know, on the inside?" I glanced at Rigid, and he didn't look so smug anymore about staying when I asked him to leave.

"Well, from what we can tell, you should heal completely. Hopefully no permanent damage."

"What do you mean hopefully?" Rigid barked.

That was going to be my next question, but Rigid beat me to it.

"Well, like you said Ms. Meyers, you were severely beaten. It's hard to tell right now what, if any, lasting damage has been done. I would recommend you check with your normal doctor in a month or two and have him do a thorough exam. He should be able to give you all the answers you need. Right now, you are ok to be discharged. Just take it easy at home and no strenuous exercise for at least three weeks." The doctor flipped his clipboard shut and looked at me expectantly, waiting to be dismissed.

"Um, thank you, Doctor. I guess I'll save the rest of my questions for later then," I mumbled, stunned by the fact that on the surface I will heal, but underneath I could be damaged forever.

"Thanks, Doc." Rigid got up and walked the doctor out the door. He shut the door tight and looked at me.

"Why didn't you leave when I asked you to? That was private." I demanded.

"I didn't leave because you shouldn't have to do this alone."

"Yes, I do have to do this alone. I want to be alone, but you just won't leave. Take me home and then leave," I stood up from the bed, grabbing onto the side rail, losing my balance.

Rigid reached out, easily steadying me, wrapping his arms around me. "Careful, beautiful, you don't want to hurt yourself."

"Too late for that," I said as I waved my cast in his face. I was very much past hurt.

"You ready to get home? Meg and some of the guys have been over there most of the day fixing things up," Rigid asked, helping me put my coat on and grabbing the bag that had been dropped off this morning, most likely thanks to Meg.

"Yup, take me home, pour a *stiff* drink and then pass out. Those are the only plans I have for today." I grabbed my sunglasses, jammed them on my face, ready to get the hell out of here.

<<<<<<<<

RIGID

Cyn was silent the whole ride home. I tried to talk to her, asking her if she had tried Head's BBQ or seen the new 007 movie and all I got was, no. The closer we got to her house, the more I could sense her drawing into herself.

When we pulled up to her house, Meg bounded out the front door towards us, but Cyn made no move to get out. I hit the lock button and turned in my seat toward her.

Meg got to Cyn's door and almost yanked the door off its hinges trying to open it. "Open the door, Rigid!" She yelled at me, looking like she wanted to rip my head off.

"Give us five minutes, Meg. Go back to the house and we'll be right there." I yelled back, not taking my eyes off Cyn.

"Cyn, open the door," Meg pleaded through the glass.

Cyn looked out the window, just staring at Meg.

"Meg, go in the house. You're scaring the shit out of Cyn," I barked.

Meg looked at the house, seeing King standing on the front porch, waving her to him. She looked back in the truck, running her hand down the window and headed back to the house.

"I can't do this," Cyn whispered. Her hands were clamped together in her lap, her head bent down, and tears streaming down her cheeks.

"Look at me, Cyn," I ordered softly.

"I don't feel anything. Nothing. All I want is to lay down and never wake up," Cyn pleaded.

I slid across the seat, wrapping my arm around the back of her neck, pulling her to me. She wound her arms around my neck and crawled into my lap. "Cyn, I, jeez, fuck me,' She was falling apart in my arms, and I had no idea how to stop it. She wouldn't look at me, so I tipped her chin up and took her sunglasses off. She had her eyes closed, with tear tracks running down her cheeks. 'Open your eyes beautiful."

"Please don't lie to me,' she whispered as she opened her eyes. 'I have a huge gash on half of my face and the other half is black and blue. Just please don't lie. I'm anything but beautiful."

"I'm not lying.' She huffed and buried her head in my neck. 'You're the most beautiful woman I know. Dry your tears, walk in your house, let Meg fawn all over you, and I'll make you a drink. Just try, baby."

"Please don't tell her anything. I don't want her to worry."

"She knows what happened," I reasoned.

"No, I mean that I might be ruined on the inside. Please don't tell her. That's mine. It's mine to worry about."

"She's your best friend, Cyn, you should tell her. She can help you."

She ripped herself out of my arms, backing up against the door of the truck. "No one will know, Rigid. If you tell her, I'll never talk to you again. I promise you tell her, I leave."

"Cyn, you need to talk to someone. You don't want me to tell Meg, fine, I won't. But then you need to talk to me. It's not good to stay in your head. Promise me that?" I asked. Cyn hadn't had any reaction to what had happened to her. She hadn't broken down, screamed, raged, anything. On the outside, she acted like nothing had happened, but on the inside, I knew that she was going crazy. She needed to let it out.

"Fine, I promise. If I want to talk, I'll talk to you. Now let me out," She pleaded, looking like a caged animal who couldn't get away from me fast enough.

I hit the button to unlock the door, and she scrambled out as fast as a broken arm and ribs would let her. She slammed the door, looking relieved there was something between us. She twisted away from the truck, making her way to the house.

I watched her till she was shut away in the house, a broken woman who I was going to help find her way again.

<<<<<<<<

Cyn

"Meg, I can't breathe," I wheezed out. The second I had walked through the door, Meg had grabbed me and hadn't let go.

"Babe, loosen up," King ordered softly from behind Meg.

Meg's arms loosened, but she still held me. "Are you ok?" She whispered.

"Um, I guess as good as can be expected. Just sore." My ribs were throbbing where she had squeezed me and my head was starting to throb also. "I think I need to go get my prescriptions filled."

"We got them for you,' Meg replied. Relief ran through me, thankful I didn't need to run to the pharmacy. 'Lo, can you get Cyn her pain pill?" Meg asked. I slipped from her arms and walked over to the couch.

Everything had been put back in its place. It didn't even look like I had been attacked in my own house. Just like as soon as the outside healed on me, you'd never be able to tell I was still damaged on the inside. Maybe forever.

I looked down at my feet, resting on the rug. I remember there had been blood on the edge of the carpet, but it was gone now.

"I brought my carpet cleaner over and cleaned all your rugs. The guys helped move the furniture back in place and actually helped clean up. Good as new." Meg chirped at me as she handed me two white pills and a glass of water.

"Thanks," I replied as I popped the pills into my mouth and took a swig of water.

The front door opened, and Rigid walked in, carrying the small bag that had been packed for me while I was in the hospital. He tossed it next to the couch and walked into the kitchen.

He started rummaging through my cabinets, looking for Lord knows what. I couldn't remember the last time that I had grocery shopped. I hoped he wasn't looking for food.

"What's he doing?" Meg whispered as she sat down next to me.

"Not a fucking clue," I whispered back.

We both sat back, watching as King walked into the kitchen, helping Rigid search. "I don't have any food. I'm pretty sure all I have is the makings for a ketchup sandwich."

Meg scrunched up her nose, "Ew. I brought some groceries over. Lo knows that," she mumbled

Rigid finally got to the cabinet over my sink, and it finally clicked when he opened my liquor cabinet. He was making me a drink, just like I wanted.

He pulled down my bottle of Southern Comfort and four shot glasses. I guess we were all doing shots.

"You up for a shot, beautiful?" Rigid asked, his back to me as he opened the bottle, sloshing the four shot glasses full.

"Definitely," I answered. No reason not to drink now that I wasn't pregnant.

Rigid grabbed two glasses, and King followed him with the other two. Meg and I both grabbed a glass and clinked them together. King and Rigid nodded at us, and I tossed mine back, waiting for the burn in the back of my throat. I needed to feel something other than the nothing.

"Whew! I want another one," Meg said, grimacing.

"Babe, we're trying to help Cyn relax, not get rip roaring drunk," King chided.

"One more won't hurt," Meg reasoned.

"You can have one more, Meg, but Cyn's done. She shouldn't even be drinking with the pills she just took. One is it," Rigid said, grabbing my glass and headed back to the kitchen.

"What!' I screeched. 'I can drink however many I want! It's not like I'm pregnant or anything!" I scoffed.

"Jesus Christ," King muttered under his breath. Meg gasped, her face going pale.

"Fuck me, Cyn. I'm just trying to look out for you. Everyone knows you shouldn't drink when you're on medication," Rigid bellowed as he dropped the glasses in the sink.

"Well, Rigid,' I sneered, 'the last time I checked, I was twenty-nine years old and didn't need a fucking babysitter telling me what to do!"

"Cyn, honey, he's right. I shouldn't have said anything. Once you're feeling better we can go out," Meg reasoned.

"Oh, trust me, we are sure as shit going out when my face doesn't scare small children and dogs whether or not Rigid thinks it's a good idea," I ranted. Seriously, I knew I shouldn't be drinking when I was taking pain medicine, but what was going to happen after two shots except taking away the pain a little bit faster.

"I'm not the bad guy in this, Cyn. No need to get pissed off at me," Rigid snapped.

"We all know who the bad guy is in this Rigid. He left his footprint on my ribs if you want to go track him down," I shrieked.

"We all know what happened to you Cyn, no need to throw it our faces," he barked back at me.

"Oh, I'm sorry, Rigid, did I shock you? Hurt you? Well, I'm so sorry I didn't ask for your fucking help, I didn't ask for anyone's help!" I spun around, seeing the shocked faces of King and Meg and stormed to my bedroom.

I slammed the door, leaned against it, and slid down on my ass.

Tears were streaming down my face, and I couldn't stop them. I don't know why I snapped at Rigid. He was trying to be nice, but I didn't want nice right now. Not that I had a fucking clue as to what I did want, but I knew nice wasn't it.

I heard footsteps headed to my door and quickly reached up and twisted the lock on my door.

"Cyn? Can I come in?" Meg asked as she timidly knocked on the door.

"I'm sorry, Meg," I sobbed out.

"Let me in, honey. You don't need to be sorry," she pleaded.

"I just want to sleep, Meg."

"And I just want to make sure you're ok." Concern and pity laced her voice as she talked.

Pity. The one thing I did not want.

"I'm ok. I'm just going to change and get some sleep. I think those pills are starting to kick in." My eyes were starting to get droopy. The floor looking like a comfortable alternative to getting up and sleeping in my bed.

"Ok. Get some sleep.' Footsteps moved away from the door but stopped. 'I love you, Cyn." She called through the door.

I didn't say anything. I was silently sobbing too much to get any words out. How could she still love me after what had happened to me? I didn't even know if I loved myself anymore.

I leaned over, curling up on the floor. I closed my eyes, hearing the darkness calling to me again. The darkness didn't tell me what to do or feel sorry for me. It was nothingness, just like me.

<<<<<<<

Chapter 5

RIGID

Meg was quietly sobbing into King's chest while I gripped the kitchen counter, trying not to storm into Cyn's room and demand she fall apart in my arms, not alone.

I wasn't trying to tell her what to do, but fuck me, she shouldn't be drinking while taking those fucking pills.

"We're going to head out, man. Meg hasn't gotten much sleep. We both need to crash for a bit," King called from the living room.

I loosened my grip off the counter and turned to King. "Yeah, brother. I'm going to crash on the couch till Cyn wakes up." I had tried to sleep in the chair at the hospital, but a nurse came in every half an hour to check on Cyn, so I didn't get more than a couple minutes of uninterrupted sleep.

"Text me when she wakes up? I can come over if you want so you don't need to stay." Meg sniffed as she wiped her eyes with the back of her hand.

"I'm not leaving, Meg. You're more than welcome to come over, but I'm not leaving her right now," I insisted.

I needed to be with Cyn for my own piece of mind. I had almost lost her before I even had her.

"Alright, brother. Get some sleep." King ushered Meg out the door, shutting it behind him.

I ran my hands down my face, trying to wipe the fatigue out of my eyes. I looked around Cyn's living room, trying to see any traces of what happened last night. It was amazing. Walking in, not knowing what happened to Cyn, there was no way you would be able to tell. It was all cleaned away. The only way you would be able to tell is if you walked into her bedroom and saw the broken woman lying on the bed.

I walked to her door and listened to hear if she was awake.

I tried turning the handle when I didn't hear her moving around, but it didn't turn. She had locked me out. Son of a bitch.

I thought about picking the lock but decided not to. She had been violated enough already, she didn't need me breaking into her room when she obviously didn't want me to come in.

Walking back into the living room, I collapsed on the couch. I laid out, propping her girly throw pillows behind my head.

I had no idea what to do. I was out here, and Cyn was in her room.

Locked away, broken.

<<<<<<<<

Cyn

I woke up sprawled out on my bedroom floor, my head squished against the door. Lovely.

Stretching my arms above my head, I clunked my broken arm on the door, pain shot through my arm, radiating up into my shoulder. I hoisted myself up, slumping against the door.

Taking stock of my body, the pain was screaming at me from everywhere. My face felt tight from all the swelling, and my ribs hurt just from breathing. Time for another magic pill. I hauled myself off the floor, checking my balance, leaning against the wall. Fuck this hurt. If anyone asked, I would not recommend getting beaten.

I laughed, thinking how absurd it was that I had thought that. I winced holding my ribs, trying to control my crazy laughing.

I unlocked the door and walked out, my mission finding those magic pills that took away my pain.

I listened as I walked down the hall for any noise or talking. I heard nothing and made my way to the kitchen.

Thankfully King, Meg, and Rigid had left. I couldn't handle their pitiful glances right now.

Limping towards the kitchen, I walked past the living room, glancing at the couch and froze. Someone was sleeping on my couch. Fuck.

I couldn't tell who it was and hoped they would continue to sleep and not wake up. I tiptoed to the sink, hoping Meg had left my pills next to my Midol and Tylenol. Thankfully, I glimpsed the telltale prescription bottle and grabbed it. I quietly twisted the cap off, mindful of whoever the fuck was sleeping on the couch and shook two pills into my hand. Twisting the top back on, I opened my cupboard, grabbing a glass down.

"Hurting?" Rigid rumbled from the living room. I jumped, surprised to hear Rigid and lost my grip on the glass, dropping it on the floor. It shattered into a million pieces all around my feet.

"Son of a bitch! You scared the living shit out of me!" I shrilled at Rigid. I looked around trying to figure out where I could step without cutting a toe off.

"Don't move,' Rigid ordered. 'Where's your broom, beautiful?"

"Hall closet," I muttered, still trying to find an escape route. If I could quick grab a glass, I could motor it to the bathroom and fill my glass up there.

Before I could even make one step, Rigid was back, broom in hand. "Why is your shirt off?" I asked, entranced by all the colorful tattoos all over his body.

"I normally sleep naked. I thought taking all my clothes off and sleeping on your couch naked might not be the best idea right now," Rigid said, sweeping up the glass.

"Probably for the best," I mumbled, ripping my gaze from his massive chest, watching to make sure he got all the glass.

"You in a lot of pain, beautiful?" Rigid asked as he started sweeping the shards into the dustpan.

"Yes, and could you stop calling me that?" I retorted. I wasn't beautiful before I had gotten beaten to a pulp and I sure as shit wasn't now.

"No." No? No, was all he had to say. Really?

"Um, yes. I asked you to stop. I'm not beautiful. You'd be better off calling me butt face than beautiful."

Rigid threw his head back laughing. I cocked my head to the side and looked at him. If either of us was beautiful, it was Rigid. Sweeping my floor in the middle of the night, shirtless, and laughing was a sight to see. Even with a bright blue Mohawk, Rigid could turn the head of any woman. Add in the colorful tattoos and, wait, was that a nipple piercing? Wait, holy shit, both nipples pierced? Well, slap me silly and call me Sally, Rigid just catapulted off the charts.

"I'm not going to call you buttface," Rigid said, which sent him off into more laughter.

I smiled, realizing how handsome he was. "Well, I'm definitely more of a butt face right now than beautiful."

"No, babe, not when you smile like that," Rigid smirked as he dumped the full dustpan in the garbage.

"I think we need to get your eyes checked." I rolled my eyes and made it back over to the cupboard to grab another glass.

"You get your pills already?" Rigid asked as I popped them into my mouth while filling up my glass. I opened my mouth to show him my tongue. He shook his head at me and moved to the hall closet to put away the broom.

I swallowed the pills, emptying my glass and setting it in the sink.

"You hungry?" Rigid asked as he walked back to the kitchen. He opened the fridge, surveying what I had to eat.

My stomach promptly rumbled. "What time is it?" I asked.

"One AM. We both slept like the dead apparently. We missed dinner."

My stomach growled again at the mention of dinner. "I could eat," I replied.

"Well, I'm fucking starved, babe. How about omelets and bagels?" Rigid started pulling things out of my fridge that I don't think I had ever had in there before.

"How much is in there?" I asked as he piled fresh veggies, cheese, milk, eggs, butter and bagels onto the counter.

"A fridge full."

"Fucking Meg. Now I'm going to have to pay her back. She didn't need to do that," I huffed, irked that Meg had to go grocery shopping for me. I felt so helpless.

"You don't need to pay her back," Rigid replied as he grabbed an apple, ripping a huge chunk out of it with his teeth.

"Um, yes I do," I countered.

"Um, no you don't. She didn't pay for them," Rigid shot back while he dug through my cupboards.

"Then who bought them and what are you looking for?"

"I did and a frying pan," Rigid mumbled, his head stuck in my cabinet.

"Wait, what?" I asked, shocked.

"I need a frying pan, babe. You know, most of them are nonstick, round, have a handle. You stick them on the stove and cook stuff in them." Rigid joked.

"I know what a fucking frying pan is. It's in that cabinet,' I pointed to the one cabinet he hadn't looked in yet. 'I meant what do you mean you paid for my groceries?"

"I gave Meg money, and she went to the store and bought groceries." Rigid pulled my frying pan out, setting it on the stove.

"Why would you do that?"

"Because you need to eat and so do I," Rigid grabbed a bowl down and started cracking eggs into it.

"Well, then how much did you spend? I'll pay you back." I moved to the door where I dropped my purse.

"Nope, not going to happen. How many eggs do you want?" Rigid asked.

"How much did you spend?" I demanded, grabbing my checkbook out of my purse.

"I said no, Cyn. I'm going to eat more than half of this food so you don't need to pay me back. Now, how many eggs do you want?"

"Fine, then I'll pay you for half. Tell me how much." I grabbed a pen off the counter and waited with my checkbook open for an answer.

Rigid spun around from the stove and plucked the pen and checkbook out of my hand and sailed them across the kitchen and into the living room.

"Hey!" I shrilled as I watched them land on the couch.

"How. Many. Eggs. Do. You. Want?" Rigid demanded.

"Three you… you… Caveman!" I screamed.

"Now was that so fucking hard?" Rigid jeered.

"I hate you!"

"Good, at least, you feel something," Rigid said as he walked back to the bowl and cracked two more eggs in.

"What does that mean? Of course, I feel. Right now I feel pissed!"

"It means if you have me to be pissed off at, you don't have time to become a zombie, feeling sorry for yourself. I want you to tell me how you feel, not shut yourself in your room and lock the door like you did before."

"I told you what I wanted before I locked the door. I don't want any help. I'm not a cripple who can't do anything! I can buy my own groceries and pick up my own prescription! I don't need you or Meg doing those things for me!" I shouted. He wanted to know what I was feeling, well he was going to fucking find out!

"What the fuck do you have friends for then? That's what we are here for, to help you and listen. We all just want to know that you are ok! You got beaten, Cyn, we all know that. Now we want to know that you are ok on the inside. Just tell me what you are feeling!" He roared at me.

"You want to know what I feel. Really know?"

"Yes! If I didn't want to know, I wouldn't fucking ask!"

"I feel nothing, Rigid! Not a god damn thing. I was beaten, and all I feel is nothing. I want to sleep and never wake up. There's a darkness that just calls to me. It doesn't judge me. I'm going to heal on the outside, but my insides will never be the same. You heard the doctor, I might never be able to get pregnant again. I might never know what it feels like to hold my baby in my arms, knowing that I carried him for nine months and get to watch him grow for the rest of my life. He beat me so badly that every day I will think of him and know what he took from me. Every day I will relive that day, knowing it changed me forever. Is that what you wanted to hear? Does that make you feel better?!" Tears were streaming down my face, and I was gasping for breath.

My vision was blurred from my tears. One second Rigid was standing across the kitchen from me and the next he was wrapping me up in his arms. Crushing me to him.

"Son of a bitch, Cyn. I'm here baby. I'm here." He picked me up, and I wrapped my arms and legs around him.

He carried me over to the couch and sat down. I was sprawled out on top of him, straddling him. He stroked my back, murmuring comforting words, making me cry even harder. Rigid, this hard as nails, gorgeous man, was wrapped up on my couch with me, trying to make me feel better.

"I'm sorry, beautiful. Don't cry. I just don't want you getting lost in your own head, not telling anyone what you're thinking."

"I'm so broken, Rigid. I don't even know where all the pieces of me went, let alone how I am going to put them back together." I whimpered.

"Let me help, Cyn. Let me find the pieces and we'll put them back together," He whispered.

"I'm never going to be the same. I just-."

"Cyn,' Rigid cut me off. 'You are the strongest person I know. We'll get you through this. You just have to let me in. Let me help." He pleaded.

I buried my face in his neck, enjoying the feel of Rigid wrapped around me. My sobs and tears slowing.

"You still hungry, beautiful?" Rigid asked, kissing the top of my head.

"Yeah. But I can cook. You paid for the groceries, the least I can do is cook them for you," I reasoned, leaning back to look at him.

"How about we do it together?" He asked, looking wary of my cooking skills.

"Just because I didn't have food in my house doesn't mean I can't cook. I just don't see the point of buying and making so much food when it's just me." I clambered off Rigid's lap, standing in between his legs. "Man you're hot." I slapped my hand over my mouth. Apparently even in the middle of a breakdown, my mind couldn't completely ignore the physical pull I had toward Rigid.

"Glad you like the package, babe, even with a blue mohawk,' he said, running a hand through his mohawk. 'I'm quite the fan of you, too," he smirked at me, rising from the couch.

"That's it, tomorrow we are going to get your eyes checked. I seriously think you are going blind," I huffed.

Rigid stepped closer, wrapping his arms around me. "I got 20/20 vision babe. I see you for exactly what you are. It's you who needs to adjust the way you see yourself."

Rigid leaned in, his lips inches away from mine. I closed my eyes, waiting for him to close the distance, and saw Nick, standing above me. The second his lips touched mine, I flinched and jumped away. Fuck. Fuck fuck.

"You ok?" He whispered.

I opened my eyes, breathing in, not knowing I had been holding my breath. "I'm sorry. I just, I closed my eyes, and I saw... I saw him."

"No worries, beautiful.' Rigid stepped back, putting more distance between us. 'You ready to make some food with me?" He asked.

"Um, yeah. Just let me run to the bathroom quick." I muttered, running out of the room.

I threw open the door and slammed it shut behind me. I leaned against the sink, arms braced, hanging my head down, panting.

Son of a bitch. One second I was ready for Rigid to kiss me and the next fucking second Nick popped in my thoughts.

There was no way Rigid would ever want to be with me if every time he tried to kiss me I jumped away like I was on fire. I looked in the mirror, reminding myself of what I looked like. Beaten and bruised. Broken. Never to be whole again.

Never to be Rigid's.

Chapter 6

RIGID

Why the fuck did I try to kiss her? Fucking idiot!

Fucking beaten four days ago and what the fuck do I do, try to fucking kiss her.

I slammed the bowl on the counter, pissed the fuck off that I was such a fucking idiot. She looked so beautiful when she smiled. Even bruised and swollen she was the most beautiful thing I had ever seen.

Waiting to hear the bathroom door open, I checked to make sure she had ran to the bathroom and not her bedroom after she had sprinted out of the room.

Pulling a knife from the drawer, I started chopping peppers and mushrooms, trying to calm myself down.

Hearing the toilet flush, I counted the seconds until the bathroom door opened.

Ninety seconds and half a pepper chopped I heard her walk in the kitchen.

"Um, you want me to chop up the mushrooms?" She timidly asked.

I did that to her, made her afraid of me. Fucking idiot for trying to kiss her. "You actually want to crack a couple more eggs? I planned on just making a huge omelet and splitting it." I tried to keep my tone even, not to send her running.

"Sure," she whispered.

We worked in silence. Cyn cracking and whisking as I chopped all the veggies up. While she started cooking the omelet, I stuck the bagels in the toaster.

"You don't want any meat in this?" Cyn asked as she dumped all the veggies in.

"Naw. I'm good unless you wanted some. I saw a pack of bacon in the fridge."

"No, I love veggies with my eggs. This is perfect," she claimed.

"Whatever you want, Cyn." I stared at the toaster, willing it to pop up so it would give me something to do with my hands other than grabbing Cyn and pledging to her she was going to be ok.

"Please don't do that, Rigid."

Her words, right next to me, caught me off guard. She had moved away from the stove and was standing next to me. "Don't do what?" I asked, balling my fists up, trying to resist touching her.

"Feel sorry for me, I don't want it. I'm sorry I flinched when you kissed me," she trembled.

"Beautiful, you don't need to apologize. I should have kept my hands to myself, it's too soon. I want you more than anything, but I know that's not what you need right now. I'm the one who's sorry."

"Just let it go, ok? Why shouldn't you kiss me, you've done it before? I just, I guess I'm not ready for that. Not yet." Her eyes were filling with tears threatening to fall.

"Fuck. Ok, beautiful. Just don't cry again, please." I knew the second I saw a tear fall from her beautiful eyes that I wouldn't be able to control myself. I would have to touch her.

She wiped her eyes, smirking at me. "Not into crying girls?"

"Just you. I could give a flying fuck if anyone else cries. I don't want to see you cry, not over that stupid fuck."

"OK," she whispered, walking back over to the stove.

The bagel popped up, finally. I grabbed it out, sticking the other one in. I slathered both sides with butter.

Cyn sprinkled a shit ton of cheese on the omelet then folded it over onto itself.

"Put enough cheese in it, babe?" I laughed as I grabbed two plates down from the cabinet next to her.

"We live in Wisconsin, Rigid. There is never enough cheese."

"Duly noted," I chuckled.

By the time I had both bagels done, Cyn was flipping the omelet out of the pan, cutting off a third of it off for her and sliding the rest onto my plate.

"I'm going to grab the milk. You want some?" She asked, walking to the fridge.

"Yeah, babe." I grabbed both plates and headed to her little table she had tucked in the corner. I sat down, glancing at her as she reached up, grabbing two glasses down. I saw a bright blue and purple tattooed feathers peeking out from under the waistband of her pants. Fuck, Cyn had a fucking tattoo. Just that little peak had made me want to rip her pants off and see what it was. I adjusted my dick, trying not to let her see how turned on I was just by watching her grab a glass.

We ate in silence, both of us famished from not eating all day.

"We can just leave the dishes for tomorrow. I think my pills are starting to kick in. They make me really sleepy."

Cyn grabbed both plates, placing them in the sink along with all the other dirty dishes.

"You can head back to bed, beautiful. I can clean this up." Having slept most of the day, I wasn't tired.

"You sure?" She asked, smothering a yawn with the back of her hand.

"Yeah."

"K. Night, Rigid." She whispered and headed to her room.

I finished clearing the table, stacking the dishes in the sink. I turned off all the lights, shutting the house down again for the night.

Grabbing the pillows off the couch, I shoved them behind my back, sprawling out on the couch. I listened to hear Cyn moving from the bathroom into her room. I waited to hear her door shut and the lock being thrown.

After waiting ten minutes, I got up, quietly creeping towards her room. Her door was cracked open, the light turned off. Pushing the door open, I saw Cyn with her back to the door, curled up under the covers. Her hair was fanned out on the pillow, begging for me to touch it.

I shut the door, leaving it opened a crack and walked back to the couch. Laying back down, I grabbed the blanket she had draped on the back of the couch and covered myself.

I was so lost on what to do. One minute Cyn was the carefree woman I had met at the bar weeks ago, then the next second she was moments away from breaking. Shattering right before my eyes.

I needed to help her, I just had to figure out how.

<<<<<<<

Chapter 7

RIGID

My eyes popped open, my head coming from the pillow. Something wasn't right. I looked at the clock on the DVD player realizing I had only been asleep for two hours. I listened to the sounds of the house, trying to figure out what had woken me up.

Then I heard it, Cyn whimpering.

I whipped the blanket off me, sprinting to Cyn's room. I pushed the door open and a blood-curdling scream ripped from her lips. The blanket was twisted around her legs, and her arms were flailing, fighting someone who wasn't there.

Son of a bitch.

"Cyn, beautiful, wake up. You're OK," I softly called as I walked over to the bed. I didn't want to wake her up and surprise her. Her struggling and whimpering became more urgent, fighting off whatever nightmare was haunting her.

I couldn't watch her struggle through this. I grabbed both her wrists, firmly tugging them down to her sides. "Cyn, it's Rigid. I'm not going to hurt you."

She struggled harder, trying to break out of my grasp. I leaned down my mouth right next to her ear. "Wake up, beautiful, open those pretty eyes for me," I whispered.

Her eyes popped open, and her body stilled.

"Rigid," she croaked out.

"You're ok, honey. Bad dream?" I asked, her eyes on me.

"Um, yeah. Why are you holding my arms?" She twisted her wrists, trying to break free. I released her, stepping back.

"You were pretty frantic in your sleep. I was just trying to help." I missed being close to her. I craved being with her.

"Oh, I'm sorry. I didn't mean to wake you up." She whispered. She straightened the blanket, tucking her arms underneath, her head the only thing peeking out.

"Cyn, stop apologizing. You can't help that you had a nightmare."

"I know, it's just … I …" She trailed off, not finishing her sentence. I wish I knew what was going on in her head.

"You going to be ok?"

"I think so. You can go back to sleep."

"It's almost five, I don't think I can sleep anymore. I got some shit I need to take care of." I ran my hand through my hair, my fingers getting caught in my bent Mohawk. I normally slathered it full of gunk to get it to stay in place, but it had been over a day since I had put anything in it. I needed a fucking shower.

"Oh, ok. Just lock the door on the way out," Cyn trembled.

"I'm not leaving you, Cyn. I just meant I got some phone calls to make and take a shower." She actually thought that I would leave her alone.

"Oh, I thought maybe you had to get back to the clubhouse or something…" Cyn trailed off.

"Babe, what the hell would I have to do at the clubhouse at 5 o'clock in the morning?"

"Well, you know. I, um, well, kind of heard from Cyn how the clubhouse is, you know, and well I didn't know if you might, well, you know, have someone waiting for you or something," Cyn stuttered.

I dropped my hands to my sides, just staring at Cyn. She actually thought that I would be here with her and then leave to go be with some pussy from the club? So fucked up. I didn't need to wonder anymore what she thought of me. "I don't have anyone waiting for me anywhere. I don't do relationships, babe."

"Oh, ok. Gotcha. Well, I guess you can go shower or whatever. I'm just going to try to pass out again."

She looked so afraid and lost lying in her big bed by herself. I wanted to crawl in with her and just wrap myself around her. "Alright, beautiful. Just yell if you need me." I needed to get the fuck out of there before I lost my control.

"Ok," she whispered.

I backed out of her room, leaving the door cracked open. "Thank you, Rigid." I heard quietly through the door.

Fuck, she was destroying me with every word she spoke. "Anytime, beautiful."

I walked out the front door and grabbed my bag that Gambler had dropped off while we were sleeping.

I looked at the sky, the early light of morning coming through and sighed. I shouldn't have waited for Cyn. If I hadn't been such a dick to her the last time we spoke, things would be so different right now.

I just couldn't wrap my head around being with one person. I enjoyed the freedom that came with the club. I definitely responsibilities, but they didn't feel like they were tying me down. At the time, when I thought of being with only Cyn, it made me want to jump on my bike and never come back. Now, the thought of never seeing or touching her made my chest hurt, like my air was being taken away.

I knew she thought that I wasn't the type of guy to stick around, but that wasn't the case anymore. I wasn't going anywhere until I found the Cyn, who had captured my breath and became my air. I needed her.

Forever.

<<<<<<<<<<

Cyn

I heard Rigid walk out the front, the screen door slapping shut behind him. I closed my eyes, wishing for the darkness to come.

When Rigid told me he wasn't leaving, I hated to admit it, but I was relieved. I doubted that Nick would come back but, of course, I never thought that he would hurt me either.

My arm was starting to throb, the pain medication not lasting as long as it should. I had so much pain it probably couldn't take it all away. I didn't want to get out of bed to get more, though. Rigid walking around with his shirt off was driving me crazy.

His tattoos just called to me, wanting me to reach out and run my fingers over them and demand he tell me what they all meant. Some of them were obvious, like his back that was covered with the Devil's Knights insignia of a skeleton knight riding a motorcycle. The words Devil's Knights in big block letters arching across his shoulders.

It was the stars tattooed on his knees, the full sleeve of bright, colorful flowers he had on his left and his right arm that was covered with skulls and crosses that I wanted to know what they meant. I wanted to know why flowers, why skulls, why stars, and why the hell were they on his knees? It was such a strange array tattoos that somehow went together.

I heard the front door shut, the loud clicking of the lock sliding into place, and Rigid making his way to the bathroom. He passed by my door, not hesitating. The bathroom door clicked shut, shutting Rigid away.

I curled up in a ball, wishing that things could be different. Wishing that I could feel something besides this sickening feeling of nothing. I felt so alone even though I had Rigid and Meg. I knew even Troy would be here in a second if I wanted him. Except nothing was going to help.

I don't know how long I laid there, just wishing for things to change when I heard the bathroom door open.

Rigid pushed my door open, looking in, not saying a word.

He must have thought I was asleep. He leaned against the door jam and crossed his arms over his bare chest. It was like the man didn't own a shirt anymore. Jeeze.

"Will you come lay with me till I fall asleep?" I whispered.

I didn't think he heard me. He stayed leaning against the door, not moving.

"If I get in the bed beautiful, I'm not going to be able to keep my hands off you." Rigid quietly said.

"Can you just hold me? Please,' I pleaded. 'Just until I fall asleep." I didn't want to be alone, at least not until the darkness pulled me under.

"Fuck," he murmured, pushing away from the door, walking away.

Tears fell down my cheeks, soaking the pillow. I felt more alone than ever. I couldn't give Rigid what he wanted. I was so broken that I doubted I would ever be able to. I rolled over, facing away from the door.

"Sit up." Rigid boomed.

I shot up from the bed, surprised he was back. He thrust a glass of water in my hand and two pills.

"Take 'em. I know you got to be hurting again. I broke four ribs one time. I was sore for weeks."

I swallowed the pills and handed the glass back to him. "How'd you break four ribs? I can't imagine you losing a fight."

"Laid my bike down when I was nineteen. I'm lucky to be alive. I'll be right back," Rigid rumbled, walking out the door.

I laid back down. I peeked under the covers, trying to remember what pajamas I had thrown on. Black tank and shorts. Not sexy at all. Thank god I was under the blanket so Rigid wouldn't be able to see all the bruises on my knees and legs

Rigid walked back in the room and just stared at me. "You don't have to stay, Rigid, I'll be fine." He looked extremely annoyed and slightly frustrated.

"I just don't want to hurt you." His words had a double meaning. I know he meant physically, but I couldn't help thinking that it was also a warning. Rigid could hurt me so easily.

"You won't," I reasoned.

"Scoot over," he ordered.

I gingerly scooted to the left side of the bed, keeping the covers up to my chin. The blanket was my shield for the time being.

Rigid pulled back the covers, slipping beneath them, "Can you sleep on your side, beautiful?"

"Um, yeah. It's actually more comfy that way." I had a big bruise on my shoulder blades from when Nick had slammed me on the coffee table.

"Turn away from me," Rigid ordered his voice tense.

I rolled on my side, tucking my hands under my head. I felt tears building in my eyes, realizing Rigid didn't want to see me. I scooted closer to the edge of the bed, curling up into a ball.

"Careful, beautiful, I don't want you to fall off the bed." Rigid wrapped his arm around me, pulling my back to his front. He nestled his nose in my hair, inhaling deeply.

"Did you just smell my hair?"

"Fuck yeah. Now go to sleep." He rested his hand on my stomach, careful not to hurt me.

"That's kind of weird, Rigid," I stated.

"Your hair smells like fucking heaven. I want to bury my face in it and never come out." Even weirder, but strangely awesome.

"Oh," I whispered.

"Yeah, oh. Now sleep." He insisted. He hooked his legs through mine, wrapping himself fully around me.

"We're spooning."

"You going to tell me everything I'm doing after I do it?" Rigid rumbled.

"Sorry. You're just kind of surprising me. You know, being nice and all."

"You keep that nice shit to yourself. As far as all those fuckers in the clubhouse know, I'm an asshole. Sleep."

"Is your name really Rigid?" I asked. Apparently, I wasn't as tired as I thought.

"No."

"What is it?"

"No one knows, babe. I mean no one," He snarled.

"Will you tell me? I won't tell anyone," I promised.

"No."

"Really? If I guess it, will you tell me?" I begged.

"If you guess it, I'll tell you, but you'll never guess it," he replied flatly.

"I'm assuming it's embarrassing. Let's go with, Martin."

"Nope."

"Clarence."

"Nope."

"Bob."

"Do I look like a fucking Bob to you?" Rigid shot back.

"No, but I don't have a fucking clue. How about a hint. What does it start with?" I pleaded.

"Beautiful, you are not going to guess it."

"Just one hint. That's all I ask."

I started to roll over, to plead with Rigid face to face, but he held me firmly but gently in place. "Stay still, beautiful. I'll give you the first letter, but only if you promise to go to sleep. No more talking, you need to rest."

It felt like all I had been doing was sleep, but I would agree to pretty much anything for Rigid to tell me the letter of his first name. "Promise."

"Fuck me. I've never told this to anyone. Both my parents are dead, and I don't have any other family.' That made me sad. Rigid didn't have anyone. 'It starts with an A."

"Ooo, A. Let me think," I pondered.

"No. No thinking. You promised if I told you, you would sleep."

"Humph, fine," I pouted. I could feel my pills starting to kick in any way. The darkness was calling to me again.

I nestled into Rigid, his arms flexing around me. "Fuck me,' he groaned, 'babe, you rub that sweet ass against me anymore, neither of us are going to get any sleep."

I immediately froze. Oops.

"Just sleep and for fucks sake, don't do that again."

"Ok, sorry," I mumbled.

I felt my eyes get droopy, the darkness getting closer. "Allan," I whispered.

Rigid chuckled, his body shaking against me. "No, babe. Not Allan."

Damn. My brain was getting foggy. Oh well, there was always tomorrow, or I guess later today to figure out his name.

I fell asleep, tucked into Rigid's arms, safe, dreaming of the letter A.

<<<<<<<<<

RIGID

It didn't take long for Cyn to fall asleep. Those pills the doctor had prescribed knocked her out in no time. She was nestled in my front, and I was fighting a raging hard on.

There were times that I would forget what she had gone through, where I would see glimpses of the Cyn she used to be. But then something would dull the brightness of her eyes, sealing off the carefree woman she used to be.

I wanted to take away the darkness she craved so badly. I wanted to be the light that made her happy.

I just wanted to be something for her.

Chapter 8

Cyn

I woke up sore and alone.

Turning over gently, I looked at Rigid's pillow, still indented from where he laid his head and buried my face in it. I inhaled his clean, fresh scent, wishing he was still lying next to me.

I heard voices through the house and listened closely to hear them.

"She can't sleep all day, Lo. She needs to eat and take her pill. You heard Rigid when he left, she needed a pill, but he didn't want to wake her up. He left over an hour ago!" Meg shrilled.

I couldn't hear anything but rumbling when King talked. I swear the bastard gargled gravel in the morning. "I'm waking her up!" Meg exclaimed.

"Babe!" King called, but I heard Meg's hurried steps walking down the hall than my bedroom door was thrown open.

"Jesus Christ, Meg! Slow the fuck down!" King ordered.

"No! She's mine! My friend! You're not going to tell me what to do, King!" She sneered at him. I still had my nose buried in Rigid's pillow, unable to see either Meg or King.

"Don't cross that line, babe, you're not going to like the consequences," King warned. Apparently, King still didn't want Meg to call him King. Men.

"Try me, babe!" She snapped back.

"She's ok, King," I mumbled into the pillow.

"What the fuck did she say?" King asked.

I lifted my head from the pillow and looked at King and Meg. "She's fine," I repeated.

"Told ya so!" Meg bragged at King.

King grabbed Meg in his arms, pulling her into his body, and buried his face in her hair. Meg held herself stiff in King's arm, trying to resist him. He whispered what I'm assuming was sweet words and she slowly wrapped her arms around him.

"Do you guys want my bed?" I asked sarcastically.

"No, we used your guest bedroom already," King rumbled at me.

"Lo!' Meg screeched. 'What the fuck! Who tells people that?"

"I do. Stop acting like you don't like what we did in that bed, babe. I know you like where my tongue-"

"Oh my God, King! Shut the fuck up!" I screeched this time. I swung my legs over the side of the bed and sat up. I slowly stood, testing my balance, pleased to find I wasn't dizzy anymore.

"I can't let you out in public if this is how you're going to act," Meg scolded.

I grabbed my robe I had hanging off the back of my desk chair and slipped it on. "I'm going to hit the shower," I replied as I turned to my dresser. I grabbed clean panties and debated on putting on a bra. I hadn't worn one last night around Rigid because I was knocked out from pain meds ninety percent of the time. I grabbed a sports bra that was loose for me, hoping it wouldn't rub against the huge bruise I knew I had on my back. I grabbed my favorite gray yoga pants and flowing black tank top and headed for the door.

"You need any help?" Meg asked.

"Naw, I should be ok. Where did Rigid go?"

"Had some shit to take care of. He texted a little bit ago saying he would be back soon." King answered as he gathered Meg in his arms again.

She willingly went into his arms, forgetting the argument they had not even two minutes ago. "Do you want me to make you something to eat?' Meg asked. 'I can have it ready for you by the time you get out of the shower."

"Sure." I didn't know how many hours it had been since the omelet Rigid and I had eaten, but I knew it had to have been awhile.

"What are you in the mood for, honey?" Meg asked as she followed me to the bathroom and stood in the door frame.

"Um, I don't even know what time it is, Meg. Just a sandwich or something." I didn't want Meg to slave over me. A sandwich was easy enough to make.

"Perfect, it's only one o'clock. Lunch time! I can make turkey club sandwiches!" Meg sang out. Geez, only Meg would make a sandwich into something awesome.

"Sounds good, Meg. I'll be out in a bit," I said as I shut the bathroom door. I heard her retreat down the hall, King scolding her.

I gingerly stripped my clothes off, leaving them in a pile on the floor. I twisted the water on, turning it to the hottest it would go. I looked in the mirror and flinched. I don't know how Meg and King had been able to look at me. My face was varying shades of yellow, blue, and purple, all puffy and swollen. My stomach had turned angry shades of purple, with an obvious outline of Asshat's boot stamped right over my belly button.

I turned to the side, noticing my peacock tattoo I had on my hip blended in with the huge bruise I had from when I landed on my side. I had gotten the tattoo a year ago. Growing up, my grandmother had believed if you had a peacock feather on you, the eye on the feather represented the evil eye. By wearing the feather, you were giving the evil eye to any harm coming your way, warding off all harm. I took this to heart and had had the colorful bird permanently etched into my skin. Apparently, Nick had been immune to my peacock.

I turned around, glancing back into the mirror, seeing I was right about the bruise on my back. It spanned both shoulder blades, a dark purple band, easily identifying where I had landed.

Looking down at my feet, I saw various bruises from when I had tried to fight Nick off. I was basically one big bruise. I reached under the sink, grabbing a small garbage bag and wrapped it around my cast. I twisted a hair tie up my arm, sealing the bag to my cast so no water would get in, ruining the cast.

I pulled the curtain back and climbed in under the steaming water. It burned my skin, turning what little flesh that hadn't been bruised, bright, angry red.

Wetting my hair back, I let the tears fall. Tears that I had been holding in for too long. I had broken down in front of Rigid last night, but this was different. I was alone, and I could finally let the last broken pieces fall loose.

Chapter 9

RIGID

I couldn't find the fucking piece of shit anywhere. The fucker was like a goddamn ghost. I had Edge digging up every single piece of info he could find on the fucker. All he had found so far was general shit that anyone could find.

I had left Cyn this morning when King and Meg had shown up. She slept tucked in my arms for hours, not moving, just the steady beat of her heart against my arm. I hadn't slept. I wanted to be awake every second she was in my arms. I didn't know that next time she would let me touch her, so I needed to treasure the time she gave me.

Meg had stormed through Cyn's door, threw it open, and stopped in her tracks like she had hit a brick wall when she saw me in Cyn's bed. I quickly scooted out of the bed, careful not to wake Cyn, and ushered Meg back out the door without a word.

"You make quick work, brother," Lo smirked at me as he saw Meg and me walking out of Cyn's room.

"She had a fucking nightmare. She asked me to hold her till she fell asleep," I explained, even though I didn't need to.

"When did she have a nightmare? Recently?" Meg asked.

"Uh, about four AM," I mumbled, realizing I was busted. I could have easily waited for Cyn to fall asleep and then leave her, but I didn't.

Lo gave me a knowing look while Meg looked at me like I had run over her dog. "You really think this is the best time to try and get with Cyn? She's been through a lot. She doesn't need you to make things worse," She stated.

I knew Meg was right. This probably wasn't the best time to pursue Cyn, but I needed to be with her. "I just slept next to her Meg. Nothing happened. She asked me to."

Meg huffed and walked into King. He wrapped his arms around her, tucking her into his side. "Just tread lightly with her, brother," King warned.

"I am, brother. Hurting Cyn is the last thing I want to do."

"Alright. So what were your plans for today?" King asked.

"I want to find the fucker who did this to her. Think you guys could stay here with her till I get back?" I asked.

"Of course. I planned on spending the day with her even if you were here," Meg replied.

"Alright, I'm going to head out. Cyn needs her meds as soon as she wakes up. I don't imagine she'll sleep for much longer." I grabbed my boots from by the couch and slipped them on, lacing them up.

"You need help, just ask any of the brothers. They all want a shot at this guy once we catch him. Me included," King grunted, his eyes locking with mine. This was why I loved Devil's Knights and all my brothers. No matter what, we all had each other's backs.

"I'm going to give Edge a call and see what he had found out. I'm going to see if Demon wants to check around with me and see if I can find anything out." I grabbed my shirt and cut off the back of the couch and threw them on. The weight of my leather cut settling on my shoulders reminded me of who I was and what I will always be, a Devil's Knight.

"Holler if you need more help," King reminded me.

I walked out the door with a quick nod to Meg and headed to my bike Gambler had dropped off when he dropped my bag.

I swung my leg over her, straddling it, feeling at home. My ride was the only place that felt like home to me.

Or at least, it used to be. Looking back at Cyn's house, I could feel the pull of her, begging for me to stay and never leave.

I cranked her up and headed out to look for Asshat, which leads me to now.

I was sitting in front of his house, praying that the fucker is here, but I knew he wasn't. This had been my first stop, and he wasn't there then. I glanced at the neighbor's house and saw the curtains in their front window flutter, watching me.

I glanced at shithead's house, then back at the neighbors. I swung off my bike and headed to the house next door.

I knocked and waited. I heard no movement in the house, but I knew that they were in there. I knocked again, more persistent. I heard steps toward the door and stepped back.

The door swung open, a middle-aged man stepping forward.

"Like I told the other guys that stopped here two days ago, I haven't seen anyone at that house in days." The guy shot off before I could even ask. His eyes shifted to my cut and he stepped back a step.

"We don't want any trouble, man. Think if I give you my number you can give me a call if you see anyone go to the house? I'd appreciate." The guy pulled out his phone, and I rattled off my number as he punched it into his phone.

"I see anyone I'll let you know."

"Thanks, man," I replied. I walked over to the other neighbor's house, but no one answered.

Climbing back onto my bike, I sent a text off to King that I would be home within the hour and headed back to Cyn's.

I hadn't found anything new about asshat beside he had fucking vanished. Now I just had to find out where he vanished to and fucking end him.

<<<<<<<<<<

Cyn

The water washed over me. I couldn't tell if it was hot or cold anymore.

I felt nothing.

I stared at the tile by the shower head, counting them. I couldn't tell if I was crying anymore. My tears mingled with the water, making them disappear.

I heard pounding on the door but ignored it. I didn't want to get out of the shower. I didn't want to leave the bathroom. I crouched down in the water, resting my back against the wall. I closed my eyes and drowned out the pounding on the door and waited for the darkness to take me.

<<<<<<<<<<

Chapter 10

RIGID

"Break the fucking door down, Lo!" Meg bellowed as I walked through the front door.

"I'm not breaking down the fucking door. She could be fine," King rumbled at her.

I tore down the hall and saw Meg and King standing outside the bathroom door. "What the fuck is going on?" I bellowed.

"Cyn has been in the shower for 40 minutes. She locked the door, and Lo won't break the fucker down!" Meg screeched.

"We don't need to break it down. We just have to pick the lock," Lo boomed at Meg.

"Get the fuck out of my way," I ordered as I grabbed my lock pick set out of my vest pocket. I made quick work of the lock and threw the door open.

Steam bellowed out the door, curling around us. "Cyn!" Meg screamed over my shoulder.

I grabbed a towel off the counter and threw the curtain back.

My heart dropped at what I saw. Cyn was curled up in a ball on the floor, the water beating down on her. I couldn't tell if she was awake or passed out. I twisted the water off and climbed in next to her.

Meg crouched down next to the tub and brushed the hair out of Cyn's face. Her eyes fluttered opened, and I breathed a sigh of relief. I wrapped the towel around her and moved her into my arms. I sat down in the tub and just held her. She wrapped her arms around my neck and buried her nose in my neck. "Rigid," she whispered.

"Beautiful, I'm here," I whispered back.

"Are you ok, Cyn?" Meg asked.

"Yeah. I was just trying to get clean," Cyn muttered.

Meg's eyes locked with mine and tears started streaming down her face. King walked into the room and threw another towel to me. "Let's give Cyn a minute, babe." King raised Meg off the floor, tucking her under his arm.

"I don't want to leave, Lo," she stuttered as he walked her out the door.

"We're not," he rumbled as they walked down the hall.

I threw my head back and closed my eyes. Cyn shivered in my arms, and I wrapped my arms around her tighter. She nestled further into me, almost like she was trying to crawl into my skin.

"I'm sorry, Rigid."

"Nothing to be sorry about, beautiful. Just scared me a little," I replied, trying to play down the fact that she had scared the absolute living shit out of me. As I was picking the lock, I thought of all the horrible things I might have found. I was afraid she might have hurt herself, and I didn't know what I would have done.

"I still feel dirty. I can't get clean."

"You don't need to try to get clean beautiful, you are clean," I promised into her ear.

"I wish you were right," she croaked.

"I am, Cyn. You just need to realize it," I reasoned.

I held her close and prayed to God that I could help fix her. If I couldn't put all her broken pieces back together, I was going to break, too.

<<<<<

Cyn

I held on to Rigid like my life depended on it. I didn't want to let go.

He laid me on my bed, keeping the towels wrapped around me. He walked to my dresser and pulled out a pair of black cotton panties and an oversized sleep shirt.

Throwing the clothes on the bed, he grabbed my casted arm and removed the hair ties I had wrapped around the plastic bag to keep the water out.

He tossed the bag by the door and grabbed my panties. He worked them up to my knees and looked at me. "Lift your hips, beautiful," he ordered.

"I can do it," I croaked out. My throat was raw from sobbing in the shower. I was out of it in the bathroom and didn't care about Rigid seeing me. Now I was embarrassed. I can't believe I let Rigid see me like that.

"Never doubted that you could. I'm just trying to help, babe. Now, lift."

I lifted my hips and Rigid slid the panties on. "Normally I'm taking these off, not putting them on," Rigid joked.

"Asshole," I whispered.

"Definitely not my name, babe," Rigid smirked.

A grin spread across my face, remembering I still needed to guess Rigid's name. "Just calling 'em like I see 'em."

"Humph, wrong, beautiful.' Rigid grabbed the shirt off the bed and moved closer to me. 'Arms up," he ordered again.

"Nice try, buddy. That isn't happening. Give me the shirt." No way was I going to put myself on display. All I needed was a little help getting it over my cast, and I should be able to slip it on.

"I'll close my eyes. Promise." Rigid said. Humph. Remembering his insistence at the hospital about staying with me the whole time, I decided to just give in.

"Fine, eyes closed. No peeking," I ordered.

He held the shirt out and closed his eyes. "This is kind of hard with my eyes shut. I feel like a hanger," Rigid joked.

His arms were stretched out towards me, holding the shirt up by the seams on the shoulders. "You're going to have to do more than that," I said.

He opened his eyes and smirked. "Damn, I was hoping you would have already dropped the towel."

"No such luck, perv. Scrunch it up so I can put my head through the hole, then close your eyes." He helped get it over my head and closed his eyes. I got my left arm through no problem, but my cast on the other arm was giving me problems. Rigid stood in front of me, eyes closed while I struggled into my shirt. I let out a giggle at the absurdity of what was happening.

"You got it on yet?" Rigid asked.

"Um, halfway." I pulled the neck over my head, half covering my face, hoping the new angle would help to get it on. No such luck.

"Fuck. I need help." This was ridiculous. I couldn't even get my shirt on.

Rigid opened one eye and looked at me. "Can I open my eyes?"

"Yea, but one glance at my boobs, then I get a glance at your junk."

"You can look even if I don't look at your tits, babe."

"Ass," I grumbled.

"Not my name either. Take your arm out. You're doing it wrong."

"Obviously." I took my arm out, leaving the shirt hanging around my neck.

"You need to put your cast arm in first." He worked the shirt over my cast, putting me in a weird looking sling.

"How did you know that would work?" I asked as contorted my good arm into the other arm hole.

"Broke my arm when I was 8. I remember how shitty it was."

I had my head and both arms in the shirt. "Turn around," I ordered.

He shook his head and spun around, shaking his head. "Babe, I've seen you without your shirt on before."

"I know, but that was when I didn't look like a punching bag." I whipped the towel off and threw it on Rigid's head, pulling the shirt over my body.

I giggled as he took the towel off his head and buried his nose in it. "Fuck you smell good."

"So strange."

"Not strange, just the truth, babe. You ready to eat? I think Ethel came over with some of her world famous chicken and dumplings."

I walked over to my dresser and grabbed my brush. "Who's Ethel?" I asked as I ripped my brush through my hair. I didn't manage to condition my hair before my breakdown in the shower. Brushing it was going to be a bitch.

"Beautiful, you're going to rip all your hair out the way you're going. Let me." He snatched the brush out of my hand and pushed me into my desk chair.

"You're going to brush my hair?" I ask, astonished.

"Yeah. Hush." He worked the brush through my hair, managing to get snagged only a couple of times.

"Alec," I blurted out.

"Who the fuck is Alec?" He asked. He had worked out most of the knots in my hair but was still brushing it. It was really soothing.

"You are Alec."

"Nope."

"Alvin."

"Do I look like a chipmunk to you, babe?" Rigid joked.

"Abbot."

"What the fuck type of name is that?" Rigid snapped.

"Possibly yours?"

"Fuck no," Rigid replied venomously.

"Abe."

"No. You're done. Let's eat." Rigid threw the brush on my dresser and headed for the door.

I looked in the mirror on my dresser and saw my jet black hair was no longer a rat's nest and was now laying flatly down my shoulders and back. I grabbed a hair tie and started to tie it back.

"Leave it down," Rigid ordered.

"No, it's too long. I need to get it cut. It gets in the way all the time." I was twisting the band around my hair when Rigid stalked over and tugged the tie from my hair.

"I want it down. Please," Rigid asked, his eyes connecting with mine in the mirror.

I couldn't rip my eyes from his. It was like I was in a trance. "Why?"

"I like knowing I can bury my face in your silky hair whenever I want; inhale your scent."

"I never know what's going to come out of your mouth. One minute you're big, hulking Rigid and the next you're this caring, sweet Rigid who contradicts everything I thought I knew about you."

"Just go with it, babe."

He grabbed my hand and tugged me to the door. "Wait!' I bellowed, 'I don't have pants on."

"That fucking shirt goes to your god damn knees. You're more covered than half the women I know."

"I'm not sure I want to know what women you know if they think meeting someone in a t-shirt is acceptable."

"Probably not. Grab some pants and let's go." Rigid leaned against the doorframe, arms crossed over his chest.

I pulled a pair of black yoga pants out and shimmied them up my legs. "You can go. I know the way to the kitchen. I do live here."

"Such a smart ass." Rigid shook his head and ran his fingers through his hair.

"Just go with it," I parroted Rigid's words back to him.

"See, smart ass," Rigid laughed.

"You like it," I shot back.

"Maybe. Now let me feed you, beautiful, and then we are going to talk."

"Yes to eating, no to talking, Arnold."

"Arnold? Really?" Rigid laughed as he grabbed my hand and hauled me to the kitchen.

"You're not giving me any hints other than it starts with an A, so yes, Arnold."

"Not Arnold, babe."

"Who's Arnold?" Meg asked as we reached the kitchen table.

A big pot sat in the middle of the table, with a loaf fresh baked bread next to it. My mouth started watering at the smells that were swirling around me.

"Not Rigid," I stated as I sat down.

"Cyn's trying to guess my name," Rigid rumbled as he grabbed a beer out of the fridge.

"Rigid's not very helpful. He only told me it starts with an A." Rigid pulled a chair next to me, sitting down and throwing his arm over the back of mine.

"Oh, fun! I want to guess! Let's see, Anakin!" Meg chirped in.

Rigid spewed beer out of his mouth and nose, choking on the words Meg had just said.

I snickered at Meg. Fuck she was funny.

"Really, babe?" King asked as he pulled her into his arms.

"What? Maybe the force is with Rigid." Meg smirked.

"My name is not Anakin," Rigid said, wiping his face off with the bottom of his shirt. I saw his abs peeking out, covered in ink and felt my face get hot. I needed to get a grip. How many times had I seen Rigid with his shirt off these past couple of days and now, with just a glance, I get all hot and bothered? Get. A. Grip. Cyn.

"Oh, I love that show. Live long and prosper and stuff," an older lady said, walking in the front door.

"That's Star Trek, Ma," King replied, pressing a kiss to Meg's forehead. So this was Ethel. Also known as the beginning of a chain reaction that had thrown Meg and King together.

"Oh, whatever. They're all a bunch of men dressed up, lost in outer space. Should have had GPS,' Ethel threw a wink at me and started rummaging through my cabinets. 'I need a pie tin."

"Uh, I don't think I have one," I replied.

"Ok. I'll have to get you one. Everyone needs a pie tin. I'll just make it in a 9x9 pan," Ethel said as she grabbed the pan out and shut the cabinet.

"Ma, this is Cyn," King rumbled as he pulled a stool out from under the island and settled into it, pulling Meg into his lap.

"Hi, honey. Meg has told me all about you," Ethel replied as she pulled a gallon of milk out of the fridge.

"Hey. It's nice to meet you, Ethel. I honestly haven't heard much about you besides you're the reason Meg and Lo met."

"You've had more to worry about than me. How are you feeling?" She asked.

All eyes turned to me, waiting for my response. Honestly, I was feeling fine, almost normal, till that question. It was like I had forgotten everything that had happened. Until now. Fuck. "Um, you know, just sore," I said as I lifted the lid off the pot. The savory smell wafted out, making my stomach growl.

"Eat, beautiful," Rigid rumbled next to me.

I glanced over at him. His gorgeous blue eyes were staring me down, lazy and relaxed. I smiled and lifted the ladle to the pot and spooned out delicious chicken and dumplings into both our bowls.

"So what are you going to do about this shit head that hurt Cyn?" Ethel asked.

I choked on the spoonful I had just put in my mouth. "Hot, sweetie?' Ethel asked, not knowing it was her words had choked me. 'Hate when I burn my mouth. Nothing tastes good for days."

Meg giggled on King's lap and buried her head in his neck. "I don't think it's the food that choked her," Rigid replied.

"Well, I hope it wasn't my question. You better be doing something about that shithead, Rigid. I know what kind of man you are and letting this go is not who you are." Ethel said as she shook her finger at Rigid. She turned away from the table and started taking things out of bags she had on the island.

"Ma, Meg just went shopping. You didn't need to buy anything," King informed her.

"Well, how was I supposed to know? Now stop distracting me. I want to know how Rigid is going to fix this," Ethel ordered King, shushing him.

"Not much to tell, Ethel. We went looking for him right after it happened but couldn't find a trace of him. I hit up the neighbors again, thinking that might have remembered something from the last time I had talked to them, but they didn't. The guy is like a ghost right now."

"Asshat," Meg bit out.

"Asshat is too nice of a name now," I said as I devoured my lunch.

"Yeah, it is. We need to think of something better," Meg thought out loud.

"Douche monkey," I replied.

"Naw, cocksucker?"

"Too nice. He might like it," I giggled.

"You want a drink, babe?" Rigid asked.

"Um, can I have a beer or something?" The last time I had a drink, Rigid got pissed. I was in a good mood and didn't want to ruin it. I really wanted a beer, though.

"I bought you those wine coolers you like, Jamaican Me Happy," Meg piped in.

"One," Rigid said as he walked to the fridge.

"Dickbreath!" Meg yelled.

"Babe, he said she could have one," King scolded Meg.

"No. Not Rigid, asshat! Total dick breath."

"Babe," King rumbled as he nuzzled his nose into her hair, chuckling. I loved how they interacted. King couldn't keep his hands of Meg. She deserved that.

"You ok, beautiful?" Rigid asked.

My eyes snapped to Rigid, realizing I was staring at King and Meg. His eyes were studying me, and he was holding the wine cooler out to me.

"Yup. Just fine," I chirped as I grabbed the bottle.

Rigid had opened it for me, and I chugged half of it. So good. Watermelon with a kick.

"I'm making roast chicken and mashed tators for dinner with brownies for dessert. Sound ok?" Ethel asked as she began chopping garlic and celery.

"Fuck yeah." Rigid answered as he scraped the bottom of his bowl.

"Sounds good, ma," King said.

"Time for another pill, beautiful," Rigid said.

"I can get it, Allister," Meg cracked.

I burst out laughing. I mean, Allister, really? "Holy fuck, Meg. I'm going to need you to make a list of names," I gasped out.

"Never should have told you," Rigid mumbled under his breath as he walked past Meg, who was keeled over, laughing her ass off.

"Oh, come on, Rigid. You could just tell me, and you wouldn't need to put up with Allister or Anakin anymore." Meg burst out laughing even louder, holding on to King so she didn't fall over.

"Just remember this shit. Here, take these.' He shook out two of my pills and handed it to me. "Paybacks a bitch." Rigid winked at me and put the pills back.

I looked around, seeing Meg holding on to King, Rigid with his back to me talking to Ethel and I felt a sense of calm. I still felt the darkness calling to me, wanting to me to sink into it, but being with Meg and Rigid, they quieted the calling.

"Come on, Cyn. Let's go watch a movie. We never did get to Ryan Reynold's ass the other night." Meg grabbed my hand and pulled me to the couch.

"Really, babe? Can't we watch some shit blow up or something? Fucking chick flicks." King grumbled as he sat in my big ass recliner.

"No. Cyn and I want to see Ryan Reynold's ass. Not some bus blow up."

"Keep talking about another man's ass and I'm going to bend you over and spank yours," King threatened.

Meg stuck her tongue out at him but scooted closer to me. "Savage," Meg mumbled under her breath.

"Mmhm.' King popped the foot rest up on the chair and kicked back. 'Remember, you love this savage."

"I may love you, but it doesn't mean I like you," Meg shot back.

"I'm going to put the movie in," I mumbled as I walked to the TV cabinet to find *The Proposal.*

"Son of a bitch!" Meg screamed.

I glanced over my shoulder and saw King had grabbed Meg and pulled her in the chair with him. She was sprawled out on top of him, yelling about savages and spankings.

I turned back to my searching when King's hands slid to her ass, and she stopped fighting him.

"Need help, beautiful?" Rigid asked as he walked into the living room.

"I got it, thanks," I replied as I spotted the DVD case and popped it into the player.

I grabbed the remote and headed back to the couch. Rigid had sprawled out, his hands thrown behind his head. Meg and King were cuddled up on the chair, whispering to each other. Looked like I was sitting on the floor.

"Come here, beautiful," Rigid called as he held his hand out to me.

"I can sit on the floor." I grabbed two throw pillows and tossed them next to the couch. I bent over when two hands gently wrapped around my waist and pulled me on the couch.

"Sit," Rigid ordered.

"I'm not a dog, Rigid."

"I know, beautiful. Now, stay," Rigid cracked, chuckling.

"You're such a dumbass," I said shaking my head.

"Just relax, please."

"Where am I supposed to sit with you sprawled all over?" I asked.

"Babe, lay down with me."

I was nestled into Rigid's stomach right now as he laid on his side. "Can't you sit up?"

"Are ya'll going to argue about where the fuck you are going to sit the whole movie?" King rumbled from the recliner.

"Fuck off, brother. Worry about your own woman," Rigid growled back.

The opening scene of Sandra Bullock started playing, and I really wanted to watch. This was one of my favorite movies. I laid down next to Rigid, hugging the edge of the couch.

"Really?" Rigid asked before his arm wrapped around me and pulled me flush with his front. He tangled his legs with mine and threw a blanket over us.

He was comfy and warm. I focused my eyes on the screen and tried not to think about the hot as hell man behind me.

I felt my eyes growing heavy and cursed those damn pills. All I seemed to do was sleep. I couldn't even keep track of what day it was, let alone the time.

Rigid nestled his face in my hair and inhaled. "Love your smell, beautiful." Rigid whispered in my ear.

I relaxed even more into Rigid's body, enjoying this man, even though it made no sense why he was still there with me.

"It's just shampoo," I mumbled, my eyes closing involuntarily.

"No, it's just you, beautiful. I've never smelled anything like it before," he said as he inhaled again.

"You're so full of shit, Archie," I giggled, guessing.

"You're so whacked, babe," Rigid chuckled.

"Am I right?" I whispered before I passed out.

"No, babe, not Archie." I heard Rigid say before I passed out.

<<<<<<

RIGID

I held Cyn, waiting for her breathing to even out, telling me she had fallen asleep. I glanced at the TV. She had only made it through ten minutes of the movie before she passed out. Now I was stuck watching a fucking chick flick unless I wanted to wake Cyn up and change it. That wasn't going to fucking happen.

"She asleep?" Ethel yelled from the kitchen.

"Yeah." I quietly yelled, not wanting to wake her.

"She's hurt Rigid," Ethel stated, walking into the living room.

"That's pretty obvious, Ma," King said.

"Not talking about physical, Lo. I meant inside. You can see it in her eyes," Ethel said sadly.

She was right. I knew the light that had normally shined from her eyes was gone. Every now and then I thought I could see the light flicker, but no sooner than I thought I saw it, it was gone. "I know, Ethel," I said.

"Can you help fix her?" She asked.

I didn't know the answer. I wanted to help her. I wanted to see that light shine in her eyes again, but I didn't know if I was the one to bring it out. "I'm going to try."

"Try hard, Rigid. She deserves you," Ethel said and walked back to the kitchen.

Cyn needed me? More like I needed Cyn.

I squeezed my arms around her tighter and prayed I would be able to fix her.

Chapter 11

Cyn

I was nestled in a warm cocoon, a blanket tucked around me and a pillow nudged under my head.

"Who the fuck is that?" I heard Rigid spit out.

"Troy, brother," King replied.

"Why the fuck is he here?"

"Because he is one of my best friends, dipshit," Meg sneered at Rigid.

I heard the front screen door slam shut. I assumed Meg walked out to see Troy. "You need to chill, brother. Troy isn't a fucking threat," King stated to Rigid.

"Yeah, you know he isn't into Meg, but how do you know that he isn't into Cyn?" Rigid shot back.

"Cause I tried. Hard," I said as I peeked out of my cocoon.

"What the fuck do you mean you tried?" Rigid yelled.

"It means, five years ago when I started working at the factory, I went after Troy."

"So you fucking slept with him?" Rigid's fist was clenched at his sides, his face turning red.

"No. Just because I went after him, doesn't mean he felt the same way. He shot me down." I sat up, stretching my arms over my head. I had no idea why the hell Rigid was so upset about Troy. It was years ago, and nothing happened.

"Why the hell did he shoot you down?" He demanded.

Now he was pissed that I didn't sleep with Troy? Jesus, I swear this man was bi-polar. "Because he didn't like me that way? I don't know. Ask him."

"Ask me what?" Troy said as he walked in the door with Meg on his heels.

"Rigid wants to know why we didn't sleep together," I said, standing up from the couch. I folded up the blanket and threw it at the end of the couch.

"Uh, I guess I didn't see you like that back then," Troy replied.

"See, he doesn't like me," I said to Rigid.

"I said back then I didn't like you," Troy said as he walked over to me.

"Same thing," I said, rolling my eyes.

"No, it's not," Troy and Rigid said at the same time.

"Whatever. Just shut up," Meg said, annoyed.

"Jeez, he really fucked you up," Troy said, standing in front of me.

"Such a charmer, Troy," I joked, rolling my eyes.

"You know me, ladies just fall all over me."

"More like just fall down," I laughed.

"Into fire pits," Meg added. We broke out into laughter, remembering Troy's date that ended up in the emergency room.

"She didn't fall in the fire pit. She just fell," Troy huffed.

"Same thing," Meg giggled.

"Can we not talk about my dating life and focus on something more important?" Troy asked, annoyed we were teasing him.

"Like what?" I asked.

"You." He took two more steps to me and wrapped his arms around me.

I froze. Troy had never hugged me. Let alone touched me voluntarily. We were friends but not as close as Meg and he were. "I'm so sorry," he whispered in my ear.

"You don't need to be sorry," I whispered back. I was getting choked up. I had never really seen Troy show any emotion other than indifference to me. I always felt he saw me as someone he had to put up with for the sake of Meg.

"You can let her go," Rigid barked.

I wrapped my arms around Troy, holding on. I didn't like Troy like that anymore. I really saw him as just a friend, and is was why I am letting him hold me. He didn't want anything from me like Rigid. I knew he didn't want to sleep with me or want my heart. I was safe with him.

I peeked over Troy's shoulder and saw Rigid fuming at me. I didn't know how to deal with him. I know what he wants from me, but I'm afraid he'll just break me even more. I swear I heard Rigid growl and decided this was enough hugging time with Troy.

I pulled away from Troy, unwrapping my arms from his shoulders. "Thanks, Troy," I whispered. I tucked my hair behind my ear and looked at Rigid.

God, he looked mad. "You find anything out?" Rigid bit out.

I glanced at Troy, realizing Rigid wasn't talking to me. I sat back down on the couch, tucking my legs underneath me. Meg plopped down on the couch next to me, throwing her arm over my shoulder.

"What the hell was that?" She whispered.

"Nothing. I don't know. He's my friend." Gah, even Meg wondered what the hell that was between Troy and me.

"We're talking later, sister," Meg said.

"Ok." All three men were looking at us, waiting expectantly.

"Oh, sorry. Proceed," Meg said to King.

He shook his head at her and smiled. She giggled and blushed. Apparently, I must have missed something.

"Still remember that first phone call, babe." King murmured.

Totally missed something.

"Enough with the sappy shit," Troy said.

"What did you find out about shit for brains?" Rigid asked.

I giggled. Shit for brains. So fitting.

Troy scowled at me. "He's got connections to the Assassins."

"How the fuck did you find that out?" Rigid snapped.

"I asked around."

"So did I," Rigid barked.

"Yeah, well, I don't look like a punk ass biker on steroids. If you showed up with a blue mohawk and riding a motorcycle to my front door, I'm pretty sure I wouldn't talk to you either. I'm a little bit more approachable." Troy sneered.

"I'm going to beat the fucking shit out of you," Rigid bellowed, bunching his fists at his sides.

"Knock it the fuck off.' King barked, 'Rigid, reel it the fuck in, brother. Troy, spit it the fuck out whatever you know."

They both stared each other down, sizing the other up.

"Big A is his fucking cousin," Troy bit out, breaking his stare down with Rigid.

"Son of a bitch," King snapped.

"Who's Big A and the Assassins?" Meg asked, sounding just as confused as I was.

"Trouble, babe," King said.

"You know he had connections with Big A?" Rigid asked me.

"Uh, no. I don't even know who Big A is, let alone who the Assassins are," I said.

"This isn't fucking good. We just got shit all squared away with the Assassins and now this bullshit? I guess we figured out who Big A's eyes were in town." Rigid snarled as he ran his hands through his mohawk.

"Who the fuck is Big A?" Meg asked again. She apparently wasn't happy with King's answer of trouble. I wasn't really either.

"We just handed part of the club business over to him. We thought we had washed our hands of him. Apparently not," King explained.

"What kind of business?" Meg asked.

"Babe, it's club shit. Nothing for you to worry about." King said, trying to sooth Meg over.

"Um, no," she shot back.

"Babe, not now."

"Fine. But we are so discussing this later, and you are so not going to put me in the Lo daze to make me forget," Meg fumed.

"Fuck me," King mumbled under his breath.

"Not till we talk," Meg jeered.

"Can we get back on track here? We need to figure out what the fuck we are going to do," Rigid snapped, annoyed.

"Church," King said as he pulled his phone out of his pocket.

"Church?" I asked, confused.

"Meeting," Meg said.

I looked at her, wondering how the hell she knew what they were talking about. "How the hell did you know that?" I asked.

"Sons of Anarchy," she said.

"You watch too much TV," I said.

"Oh, hell no. You must watch Sons. Everyone loves Jax, but Opie has my heart." She sighed.

"Who?" I asked, even more confused.

"Don't worry sweetie, I'll educate you. We'll watch it while the boys are gone," Meg said, patting my arm.

"It's a movie?"

"Jesus Christ! You're hanging out with a god damn motorcycle club, and you've never seen Sons?" Troy asked.

"You know Sons?" I asked surprised Troy had watched it.

"It's a TV show, and yes, I've seen it," Troy said.

I added watching Son's to my to-do list. According to Troy and Meg, I was missing out.

"Alright, Mickey and Turtle are headed over here. Demon is rounding up all the other guys for church. Troy, you come with us," King ordered.

"Why are Mickey and Turtle coming?" Meg asked.

"To stay with you two till we get back," King said as he sat on the couch next to Meg and pulled his boots on.

"We don't need a babysitter. We'll lock the door. All we are going to do is watch Son's. I need to educate Cyn on Jax and Opie," Meg giggled.

"Locking the door isn't enough. Mickey and Turtle will stay outside if you want them to. It's for your protection. Shit for brains is still out there and with the info Troy just gave us, I doubt he's just going to go away." King stood up and looked down at Meg and me.

"We are so talking later," Meg said as she looked up at King.

"I know,' He grabbed Meg's arm and pulled her into his arms. 'Walk me to my bike, babe."

"I'll be back." She shot at me over her shoulder as King walked them out the front door.

"I've got to make a stop before I go to the clubhouse," Troy said.

"Ok," I said, still in shock from all that had happened in the last ten minutes.

"Call me if you need anything, Cyn. Doesn't matter the time or day," Troy said as he wrapped me in his arms for another hug. This one was quicker, and only half pissed off Rigid. Men.

Troy nodded at Rigid and headed out the door. The screen door slammed shut, and I looked at Rigid. I seriously had no idea where to begin.

"You going to be ok while I'm gone?" He asked, walking to me and wrapping me in his arms.

"I think so. I guess Meg is going to educate me on all things Sons of Anarchy," I mumbled into his shoulder.

"That'll take a while. That show has seven seasons."

"You've seen it?" I asked, amazed another person had seen it, and I had never even heard of it before.

"Yeah, beautiful. It's good. You'll like it," he said as he kissed the side of my head.

"Meg mentioned something about Jax and Opie. Hopefully, there's some good eye candy in it. That way if I don't like it, I'll, at least, have something nice to look at."

"You're crazy, babe. I'll see you when I get back, ok? Mickey and Turtle will take good care of you two."

I snuggled closer to Rigid, not wanting to let go. It was nice when Troy had hugged me, but Rigid's hugs were different. "You smell good," I said as I inhaled his scent. He smelled like leather and sandalwood.

"You smell better, beautiful," Rigid chuckled at me as I sniffed him.

I heard King's bike crank up and pulled away from Rigid. "You better go. King's waiting."

"I'll be back soon." He kissed me on the forehead and headed out the door. I heard his bike crank up and then they both took off.

Meg walked back in the door and grabbed the remote from the coffee table. Ethel walked out of the kitchen and sat in the recliner King and Meg were sitting in before. I didn't even realize she was still here.

"I heard Son's mentioned," Ethel said as she popped open the recliner and threw her feet up.

"Yup. You like it too?" Meg asked.

"Oh, yeah. Love me some Happy. That man may be deadly, but he sure is something to look at," Ethel chuckled.

"Oh, I'm all about Opie," Meg said as she pulled up Netflix and started the show. I sat next to Meg, grabbing the blanket and throwing it over us.

King, Rigid, and Troy were on the way to deal with my shitty life, and I was camped out on the couch with Meg and Ethel.

I heard two bikes pull in the driveway. "That's Turtle and Mickey. I bet they will want to watch with us," Meg said.

Ten minutes later I was enthralled in all things Sons, not even thinking about Asshat. Rigid, on the other hand, was a different story. I don't think anything could keep me from thinking about him.

Chapter 12

RIGID

King and I pulled up to the clubhouse with bikes littering the parking lot. It was Wednesday, and there were also people off the street bringing their cars and trucks in to be fixed at the garage.

I should be working in the body shop, painting, but Cyn was more important. King had told me I could take off for however long it took to take care of the Cyn situation.

We swung off our bikes and headed into church.

"Troy's going to be pulling up soon. Bring him back to church when he gets here," King ordered Crowbar as we passed by the bar.

Crowbar nodded and headed to the front door.

We walked into the room, and most of the brothers were already there waiting for us. What fuckface did to Cyn didn't sit well with any of the brothers.

I took my seat to King's left and waited for Troy. Most of the brothers were somber, waiting in silence.

Troy walked in and took a seat at the other end of the table. Civilians were never allowed in church, but we were making an exception for Troy since he had information we needed.

"Alright, brothers. We got info that the fucker who attacked Cyn has affiliations with the Assassins. He's gone underground, and we don't know where. Troy here was able to get some info for us," King addressed us.

"Nick is cousins with Big A. It isn't a well-known fact around town. He kept it on the down low because he was to keep tabs on the going ons around town and report back to Big A." Troy said.

"That's how that fucker knew about Meg, brother," Demon spit out.

"I know. Meg said she never liked the fucker. She's got a good fucking instinct," King said, pride in his voice.

"I didn't get a good feel for the guy either. Meg and Cyn had it out about the fuck face a while ago. Meg backed off when Cyn told us she had it under control. Obviously, she was wrong." Troy took his hat off and ran his fingers through his hair.

"What else did you find out?" I asked.

"I was talking to a couple of people from work, and one of them lives by Nick. He said he saw three Escalades roll up to his house the night Cyn got attacked. He saw them take a bunch of shit from the house, and Nick followed them when they left. He hasn't seen him at the house since."

"Alright. We, at least, know he's more than likely up by Fall's City. Who wants to head up there and see what they can find?" King asked.

"I'm fucking going. I don't care if none of you other fuckers what to go, I'm still going," I retorted.

"We all got your back, brother. I'll head up there with you, too," Demon replied.

"I want a piece of this shit, too." Slider chimed in.

"I'm in," Gambler and Crowbar said at the same time.

"Alright. Rigid, you head up the Fall's City with Demon. Gravel, Gambler, and Turtle see what you can dig up. Try to keep it on the down low. Edge, I want you still trying to find out as much as you can about this fucker," King ordered.

"I want in on this, too," Troy said.

"Keep doing what you're doing, Troy. Ask anyone you can think of that might have a connection to fuck face if they have seen him lately. I'm going to stay at the house with Meg and Cyn while you're out of town Rigid," King said.

"I'm hoping this won't take long, and I won't be gone for long from her." I really didn't want to leave Cyn at all, but I need to take care of this fucker.

"I think we should wait and let this fucker think we aren't looking for him. Give him a false sense of hope," Gravel said.

"I'm not letting this fuck face get away with this!" I thundered at Gravel.

"I'm not saying you let him go, Rigid. I'm just saying wait. He'll see us coming from a mile away right now. The longer we wait, the more comfortable he gets," Gravel reasoned.

I gritted my teeth and clenched my fists, trying to control the pure hate rolling through me. "No," I bit out.

"He's kind of got a point," Troy said.

"No one asked for your god damn opinion," I sneered at Troy.

"He's right, Rigid. And since you're right, you get to be the one who goes up there now and keeps an eye on things. You are the one who said you can get more info because of the way you look." King said to Troy.

"Good thing I got a shit ton of vacation coming to me," Troy smirked.

"Alright, it's decided. Troy, you head up now and keep your ear to the ground about the Assassins. Rigid, you stick home for the next week and then we make our move."

"What happens if something goes down in that week I'm just sitting around with my goddamn thumb up my ass?" I barked. This was fucking bullshit!

"If anything happens, Troy will tell us, and we'll take care of it. Stay home and take care of Cyn. Got me?" King asked, staring me down.

"Fine." I shoved my chair back and stormed out of the room.

I walked to the bar pouring three shots and threw them back one right after the other. I threw the last shot glass against the wall, watching it shatter into a million pieces.

"Your temper isn't going to help her," Gravel rumbled as he sat down next to me and poured himself a shot.

"Yeah, well, I don't think sitting around doing nothing is going to do much better."

"It's time to plan, Rigid. We go in there with a plan, we'll take this fucker down in no time. You walk in there guns blazing, he could run, and we'll never find him," Gravel reasoned.

"I get it. I just don't fucking like it," I bit out.

"You going to head back to Cyn's or stick around here?" King asked as he walked out of church and snagged a stool next to Gravel.

"I plan on heading back there for a bit." I poured another shot and threw it back. It burned down my throat, matching the burn I felt in my heart for Cyn.

"Why don't we play a couple games of pool before you head back?" King asked as he grabbed the bottle and headed to the pool table.

"I'm surprised you're not running back to Meg," Gravel said as he threw another shot back and ambled to the pool table.

"She wants time to spend with Cyn. Don't mean I like it, but I'll give it to her. Get your ass over here, Rigid, and play a couple games of fucking pool with me," King shouted at me.

"Fine. I'm going to whip your ass, and then I can head back to Cyn."

"Yeah, we'll see about that, asswipe," King jeered at me.

"Best two out of three, then I'm heading back to my girl." I grabbed the triangle and started racking the balls. Gravel pulled a stool up to the table and sat back to watch me beat King's ass.

"She your girl now?" King asked.

"Yeah. She may not know it yet, but she is."

"That mean you are done with all the random pussy wandering around the club?" King asked as he took the first shot, sinking the seven ball.

"I've been done with that since I met Cyn."

"Bullshit! That night of the bonfire at Meg's you came back to the clubhouse and got your dick sucked," King yelled as he missed the three ball, almost sinking the eight ball. King fucking sucked at pool. This was going to be like taking candy from a baby.

"Haven't touched the club pussy, brother. Swear." I lined up my shot and sunk the striped four and two ball.

"Humph, we'll see how long that lasts,' Gravel said, disbelieving, as he lined up three shot glasses on the side of the pool table and filled them up. 'Bottoms up fuckers. May God help you with these bitches you keep tying yourselves to."

We all picked up a shot and threw them back. "Alright, time for me to beat your ass," I said.

The sooner I beat King's ass, the sooner I could get back to Cyn. I missed her.

Chapter 13

Cyn

"I want my own Jax," I said after watching the first four episodes of Sons of Anarchy. King and Rigid weren't home yet, and Meg and I were camped out on the couch with junk food surrounding us while Ethel was in the kitchen popping popcorn. We ate roasted chicken and tators, as Ethel liked to call them, during episode three and now Ethel said we needed snacks.

Meg and I didn't really argue because you just didn't argue with Ethel.

"Ready for the next episode?" Meg asked as the next one started playing.

"Hell yeah. More Jax, please," I said as I burrowed into my blanket.

"How you feeling?" Meg asked as the opening credits played.

"Good. Better than I look, I think."

"Good. So what was with you and Troy today?" Meg asked.

"I don't know. That's the first time Troy has ever intentionally touched me. It was weird but nice."

"Nice as in ripping my clothes off and take me or nice as in you see Troy as a brother?" Meg asked.

"Um, more like a brother. I'm over Troy."

"So, then Rigid?"

"I don't really think that's a question," I said.

"Ok, so you want Rigid's man meat?"

"Meg! Really!" I yelled, throwing a pillow at Meg.

"Answer the question," Meg giggled as she threw the pillow back at me.

"I swear you're ten sometimes,' I shoved the pillow behind my back and looked at Meg. 'I don't know, I guess. He's hot."

"He likes you." Defiantly acting like a ten-year-old. Next thing she would start signing, 'Cyn and Rigid sitting in a tree…'

"I don't know why. He must be into punching bags," I joked.

"You're not going to look like a punching bag forever. Plus, he liked you before all this."

"Humph, he wanted in my pants before, Meg. Get it straight."

"He likes you, Cyn. I can tell just by the way he looks at you."

"And how the hell is he looking at me?" I scoffed.

"Like he will die before something bad ever happens to you again. Lo looks at me the same way. It's sweet, at least, when Rigid looks at you like that. When Lo does it, I get all hot and bothered and then I-"

"Ok!' I yelled, interrupting Meg. 'I get the freaking point. Jesus. I do not need a play by play of all the things King does to you."

"I call it the 'Lo Daze,'" She said blissfully.

"How are you and stud muffin doing?" I asked, not wanting to discuss Rigid or anything about the way he looked at me.

"Wonderful. But…" She trailed off. She played with the seam on the blanket, not looking at me.

"But what, Meg?" I asked, throwing my arm over her shoulder.

"He wants to meet Remy." She looked at me, terrified.

"So?"

"Cyn! Remy and Lo meeting will make Lo and me official. Once he meets Remy, he'll more than likely meet Hunter! That would be a freaking disaster!" Meg screeched.

"OK. One thing at a time. Aren't you and Lo official?" Last I knew, Meg was head over heels in love with Lo.

"Yes, but Lo meeting Remy just makes it official."

Ok. I'm was just going to leave that one alone. "Who cares if King meets Hunter?"

"Uh, because then Lo will see the horrible mistake I made and think differently about me. Plus, I'm pretty sure Lo would try to kick Hunter's ass. He's not really a fan of him." Meg said.

"Not many people are, Meg. He was a douche lord to you." I replied. Don't even get me started on Hunter. The asshole made Meg cry too many times to count.

"I know! That's why I don't want him to meet Lo."

"Then don't have him meet Hunter. It's not like Remy is a little kid and Hunter needs to see who Remy is with. You barely see Hunter anymore." Ever since Remy got his license and car, he drove back and forth between his parent's houses.

"You're right. I'm just freaking out. I know Lo will like Remy, I just hope that Remy likes him."

"Remy is one awesome kid, Meg. You raised him. You have nothing to worry about. Although, I wouldn't mind watching King kick Hunter's ass," I reassured her.

"Whose ass is King kicking?" Rigid asked as he walked through the front door with King right behind him.

"Hunter," I said. Rigid flipped his boots off, threw his cut on the back of the couch and plopped down next to me.

King pulled Meg off the couch and wrapped her in his arms. "Missed you, babe." I heard him whisper in her ear.

"Hey, beautiful," Rigid said, throwing his arm over my shoulders.

"Hi," I whispered back.

"Feeling ok?"

"Surprisingly, yes."

"Meg get you hooked on Sons?" Rigid asked as he looked at the TV.

"Just a little." I lied. I was completely addicted.

"Mmhm," Rigid hummed, smirking at me.

"She wants her own Jax," Meg chirped in.

"Meg!" I bellowed at her.

"What? You totally do," She laughed.

"Jax? Really, babe?" Rigid laughed.

"What? He's hot and stuff." I felt my face burn with embarrassment. Telling the guy you like about a fictional character you like was a little embarrassing.

"You're crazy, babe. Plus, everyone knows Otto is the shit in this show," Rigid said as he pulled me into his arms and relaxed back into the couch.

"Otto is not hot," Meg said as she walked into the kitchen.

"I didn't say he was hot, I said he was the shit," Rigid shot back.

"Did you find anything out about asshat?" Meg asked, walking back into the living room with two beers and handing them to the guys.

King took a long pull of his, pulled Meg to him and fell back into the recliner. "We more than likely know where he is. We got a plan all set up."

"That's it?" Meg asked.

"Yeah, babe. That's it. I'll tell you later," King said, laying his head on the back of the recliner.

"You have an awful lot of things to tell me later," Meg pouted.

"I know, babe," King said, exhausted.

"You hungry?" Ethel asked walking back into the living room carrying two huge bowls of popcorn.

"Got any chicken left?" Rigid asked.

"I can get you some," I replied, standing up.

Rigid tugged me back in his arms. "Relax, beautiful."

"I'm good. I've been either sitting or lying down all day. No worries." I leaned down and placed a kiss on Rigid's cheek.

Rigid and I both froze. "Sorry," I whispered and ran to the kitchen.

I leaned against the counter, trying to calm my racing heart. I just kissed Rigid. It was just a peck, but still. I just kissed Rigid.

Holy shit.

"You ok, hun?" Ethel asked as she walked back to the kitchen.

"Uh, yeah. Rigid wants some dinner, so I thought I would warm some up some up for him," I mumbled as I walked to the fridge and rummaged through it.

"You pull it out, and I'll put it on a plate for you," Ethel said, pulling two plates out.

I took out all the containers of leftovers and piled them on the counter. Ethel scooped out enough to feed an army when she was really only feeding King and Rigid.

She popped one plate in the microwave, turned, and looked at me. "Rigid is a good man, sweetie."

My eyes bugged out, and I stared at Ethel. "Um, yeah, I know, kind of, you know, that," I stuttered.

Ethel chuckled. "I don't mean to be so straight forward with you, honey, but I think that's what you need. I think that you could get lost in all the things that happened to you and not see what is right in front of you."

"OK." I had no idea what else to say.

"I know you are broken, honey, but that man out there on the couch is going to be the one to fix you. I can see it when he looks at you," Ethel said.

Another person who thought Rigid looked at me like, well like I don't know what, but I didn't see it. "I don't really know what to say," I mumbled.

"Don't need to say anything, hun. Just don't shut Rigid out," Ethel said. The microwave dinged, and she took the first plate out and set the other one in.

"You can take that one to King if you want. I can grab Rigid's when it's done," I said.

Ethel gave me a smile, grabbed the plate and headed for the living room.

I watched the plate spin around the microwave and thought about what Ethel said. Was I shutting Rigid out? I couldn't figure out what I felt anymore. I had liked Rigid before everything happened with Nick, but I knew back then, he was only in it for sex.

Now? I had no idea what Rigid wanted from me. He treated me with such gentleness and acted like I would break at any second.

Would I break, though? I had been through so much in the past few days, and I was still standing. I may be physically broken, but inside, was I really that frail that I couldn't make it through this?

The microwave dinged, and I grabbed the plate out, sticking a fork into the tators. I grabbed two more beers and two Jamaican Me Happy's for Meg and me and headed back to the living room.

I handed out the drinks and food and sat back down next to Rigid.

Meg was curled up in King's lap, his hand stroking her back while he ate with the other hand. Rigid was sitting forward, resting his elbows on his knees and shoveling food into his mouth.

"You're going to get the hiccups eating that fast," I chided.

Rigid glanced at me, smiled and shoveled more food into his mouth.

"Bikers don't get the hiccups, they're too badass," Meg joked.

"Babe," King smirked at her.

"What? It's the truth. You badasses are pretty intimidating," Meg said as she snuggled into King.

"Yeah, he looks pretty intimidating wrapped around you. He looks like a fucking marshmallow." Rigid shoveled the last bite of his food in his mouth and clattered his plate on the end table.

"Well kids, I'm off. Thanks for the Jax candy ladies," Ethel said, walking out of the bathroom. I never knew where she was half the time.

"Thanks for making dinner, Ma," King said as he and Meg got up out of the chair. He hugged his mom and kissed her on the cheek.

"Welcome, Lo. Call if you two need anything. I want to meet that Rem of yours, too, Meg," Ethel said to Meg.

Meg blushed and dropped her eyes to the floor. "Sure thing Ethel. Maybe Rem and I can come over one day for lunch."

"Count me in too, Ma," King said.

"You have work, Lo," Meg said. King gave her 'what the fuck' look.

I giggled, knowing what Meg was thinking. She was still terrified of King meeting Remy.

"You all three can come," Ethel said as she slid her shoes on.

"Alright, Ma. I'll let you know a day," King said as he walked her to the door.

"Bye, Cyn. See you, Rigid." She yelled over her shoulder.

Rigid and I shouted out goodbyes as she slammed out the screen door.

"Meg, he's going to have to meet Remy. It's inevitable," I laughed. She was so ridiculous about this.

"I know." She grumped, sitting back in the recliner.

"Hey, where did Turtle and Mickey go?" I asked. They had gone out to smoke right before Rigid had come back but had never come back inside.

"They went back to the clubhouse. King has some shit he needed them to do." Rigid said as he grabbed his empty plate and head into the kitchen.

"You ready, babe?" King asked as he walked back into the house.

"Can't we just stay the night here?" Meg asked.

"Naw, babe. Rigid is here, we don't need to be. Plus, I got a couple things on my list I want to check off," Rigid smirked.

"No, handsome. Nothing is getting checked off your list until you tell me all the shit you told me you would tell me later. Guess what? It's later," Meg said as she slipped her shoes one.

"We'll see about that, babe.' King grabbed his keys out of his pocket and twirled them around his finger.

"I'll be over before work tomorrow. Ok, Cyn?" Meg asked.

"Yeah, I'll be here. I don't plan on leaving the house till my face stops scaring small children," I joked.

"You're beautiful. I'll see you tomorrow." Meg and King walked out the door and shortly after I heard King's motorcycle crank up and take off.

"You want to watch anymore?" Rigid asked, plucking the controller out of my hand.

"Maybe a couple more?" I asked.

"Sure, babe. Can we watch it in your room, though?" Rigid asked.

"I guess." I covered a yawn with the back of my hand. The thought of heading to bed instantly made me tired.

"Go ahead and get changed babe, I'll lock up the house."

"OK," I whispered. Rigid pulled me up, kissed me on the forehead, and flipped off the TV.

I hightailed it to the bathroom, shutting the door behind me. I leaned against the door and closed my eyes.

I liked Rigid. When he kissed me on the forehead, I felt butterflies in my stomach. I couldn't remember the last time, if ever, that I had butterflies in my stomach. What the hell was going on?

I was beaten five days ago. Or was it six? I couldn't keep track of the days anymore.

I shouldn't have feelings for someone right now. It was crazy feeling this right now.

Shaking my head, I quickly brushed my teeth and hair and cracked the door open, looking to see where Rigid was. The kitchen and living room lights were turned off, but I saw the outside light streaming in through the front window. Rigid must have gone outside.

I heard the front door slam shut, and the lock clicked into place. I opened the door all the way and made my way to my room. I flipped the light on and looked around. Everything looked the same since Rigid had slept with me last night.

I don't know why but it felt like it should look different. The blue paisley comforter I normally had on my bed was still there, bed not made (definitely normal) and three pillows at the head of the bed. Nothing had changed, but it still felt different.

I peeled off my clothes and grabbed a pair of blue sleep shorts and a black tank top and threw them on before Rigid walked in. He had seen all of me in the shower, but that was different. Now I was shy around him. Don't ask me how that made sense.

I grabbed the comforter, semi making the bed and crawled under the covers.

Rigid walked in when my head hit the pillow, and I watched him. He pulled his shirt over his and threw it over the back of the desk chair. He toed off his boots, setting them next to the desk and grabbed the TV remote and threw it on the bed next to me.

Unsnapping the button on his jeans, I inhaled and held my breath. He slid them down his legs, slowly revealing all the ink he had. Pulling them off, he threw them on the chair on top of his shirt.

"Why do you have stars on your knees?" I asked. His tattoos were so stunning, I never knew where to look when he didn't have clothes on. His knee tattoos were the ones that drew the most wonder from me, though.

"Means I don't kneel to any authority. I'm King's Sgt. at Arms, beautiful. I'm basically there to make sure shit gets done. No matter how..." He trailed off.

"Oh." Totally not the explanation I was expecting, but it made sense.

"Why a peacock?" Rigid asked as he slid into bed next to me.

"Evil eye," I said.

Rigid looked at me like I was crazy and I laughed. "Babe?"

"The feathers of a peacock are believed to be the evil eye. If you wear them, they protect you from evil. My grandma told me that." Rigid pulled me into his side and flipped the TV on.

"Makes sense, beautiful," Rigid mumbled.

"Why all the flowers?" I asked, running my fingertips up his arm. His left tattoo sleeve was a vibrant array of beautiful flowers. It was stunning.

Rigid didn't say anything, just concentrated on getting Sons of Anarchy playing.

"Rigid?"

"Yeah, babe," he said.

"Are you going to answer my question? You don't have to if you don't want to," I said, waiting for him to say something.

"My mom always had flowers around. That is the only thing I can remember about her anymore. She loved flowers." I could hear the sadness in Rigid's voice talking about his mom, my heart hurt for him.

"They're beautiful," I whispered. He finally got Sons playing and laid the remote on the nightstand. He turned to me, face to face, wrapping both arms around me.

"I seriously cannot remember anything about her. I try all the time, but all I see are flowers. I started the sleeve when I turned eighteen. Every extra dime I had gone to getting it done. If all I could remember about her was flowers, I was determined to have them on me." Rigid said, opening up to me.

"How did she die?" I asked, whispering.

"Her and my dad were on vacation. The first fucking vacation they ever went on. They decided to go on a road trip. I was staying at my grandma's when we got the phone call they had gotten in a car accident. I was only five. They were both killed instantly."

"I'm so sorry, Rigid." I sniffed, a tear running down my cheek. I couldn't imagine not having my parents, let alone losing them at such a young age.

"Don't cry for me, beautiful. It was a long time ago." Rigid rumbled, gently wiping the tear off my cheek.

I burrowed my face in Rigid's neck and wrapped my arms around him. "Your tattoos are beautiful," I whispered.

"Even the skulls and the devil on my back?" Rigid chuckled.

"Yeah, even those," I smiled into his chest.

"You ever think of getting any other tattoos, beautiful?" Rigid asked.

"All the time. But then I think of something else to get and then I forget about all the other ones I wanted. It's a vicious cycle," I laughed.

"Tattoo you would get right now?"

"A lotus flower," I whispered.

"Why?"

"Google it." I giggled.

"Really? Google it?" He scoffed.

"Yeah. You won't tell me your name, I'm not going to tell you why I want a lotus flower, Aaron," I guessed.

Rigid laughed and buried his nose in my hair. I could hear him breathe in and burrow even further into me. "Not Aaron," he whispered.

Dammit. I was never going to guess his name the way this was going. "Not fair," I pouted.

"Not much in life is fair, beautiful." Rigid propped his head up on his hand and looked down at me.

"That's sad," I said.

"You think life was fair when Nick hurt you?" He asked.

"No. But I think a better assessment of life is that it isn't perfect. I had a really good life before Nick, and I'm going to have a really good life after Nick. I'm not going to let him take away my life. He took away my baby and a part of me that I'll never get back, but I think I'll come out stronger."

"I don't know how you can say that. It's only been six days, and you are over it. But I don't think that you really are over it."

"I'm not. Not by a long shot. There are times I completely forget about it and then it comes raging at me like a freight train, threatening to run me over and ruin me."

"I won't let it ruin you, Cyn. I'll die before anything hurts you again."

I reached up, cradling his cheek in my hand. I ran my thumb over his lips. "Will you kiss me, Rigid?"

"I said I don't want to hurt you, beautiful. I don't think you are ready for that," he said, pulling away from me.

"Please, Rigid. Just one." I pleaded. I had to feel his lips on mine, knowing it was my choice to have him there. I needed this.

"Cyn. I just... I don't want to hurt you."

"I heard you the first time, Rigid, and I believe you. This is my choice. Please." I don't know what came over me, but I knew this was something I had to do. It might be too soon, but how would I know when the time was right unless I tried.

Rigid looked like he was about to bolt at any second. I did the only thing I could think of. I threw the comforter back, shot up over him, and straddled his hips.

"Cyn! What the fuck?" He boomed at me.

I placed my good hand on his chest, leaning into him. "Just one kiss. That's all I want."

"No."

I leaned closer to him, my face a foot away from his. His eyes frantically darted left to right, looking for an escape. "What do you want from me, Rigid?"

"What do you mean?"

"I mean, if you don't want to kiss me, what are you doing here. If you don't want to kiss me, then I'm positive you don't want to have sex with me. What. Do. You. Want?" I punctuated each word by leaning inch by inch closer to him till I was just a breath away from him.

"I don't want to hurt you," he pleaded.

"You won't." I leaned in, pressing my lips against his and waited for the panic to hit me. I moved my lips, lightly kissing him, and felt butterflies in my stomach. Rigid stayed solid as stone, not moving.

"Please, Rigid," I begged.

"One kiss, Cyn. That's it," he bargained.

I nodded my head and waited for him to move. He slowly lifted his head from the pillow and lightly pressed his lips against mine. I moaned, enjoying the feel of his lips on mine.

"Rigid," I whispered against his lips. I framed his face with my hands and leaned into him more, praying he would keep kissing me.

He finally moved his hands from his side and cradled my hips, holding me in place. I parted my lips, and his tongue hesitantly licked my lips. He growled as I pressed my hips into his growing cock, wanting to feel more.

His hands ran up my back and wrapped around my shoulders, pulling my body flush against his.

"I shouldn't be doing this," he whispered against my lips.

"Yes, you should. I'll tell you if I want you to stop," I promised.

"Just one word, Cyn, and I'll stop." He pressed his lips against mine again and sucked my bottom lip into his mouth. I ground my hips against him, wishing we didn't have any clothes on.

He swatted my ass, making me moan. "Just kissing, Cyn. You promised,' he groaned in agony. 'Stop moving, you're killing me."

"It feels so good," I whimpered, running my hands down his body.

Rigid let out a low growl and flipped me over on my back, our lips still connected. I closed my eyes, enjoying the kiss. His lips moved from mine, raining little kisses over the cuts and bruises on my face.

"I'm so sorry he hurt you," Rigid whispered in between kisses.

"Me too," I whispered. Sweet Rigid was firmly in place, and it was one of the best things I had ever known. His little kisses and his hands caressing my arms and face were heaven.

"I'll never let him hurt you again," he promised venomously.

"I know. I believe you," I whispered as I lifted his face to look at me. My eyes were filled with tears, and my cheeks had tear tracks running down them. I know I looked a mess, but I had to see him.

"Don't cry, beautiful," he said, wiping away the tears.

"I think I'm ready for bed now, Antonio," I whispered, a smile tugging at my lips.

"Crazy." Rigid pressed one more kiss to my lips and gently lifted off me. He laid down on his back next to me, both of us staring at the ceiling.

"Artois?"

"Is that even a name?" Rigid asked.

"It is if it's your name," I giggled.

"Not my name, babe."

"Damn."

"You want me to get you a pill? Are you sore?" He asked getting up from the bed. His boxers were tented, his cock straining to get out.

"Wow." I gulped, my eyes bugging out from the sheer size.

"Ugh, yeah. You have that effect on me, beautiful," Rigid said, adjusting himself. He pulled his jeans on, maneuvering his cock in. He zipped the fly up and looked at me.

"What was the question?" I asked, my eyes still glued to his fly.

Rigid chuckled and ran his hand through his hair. "Pill, babe. You need one?"

"Oh, um, yeah. My arm is hurting." I replied, tearing my eyes away from his crotch to look at his face.

Rigid shook his head and headed out the door.

I pulled a pillow over my face and screamed into it.

Jesus Christ! I just about jumped Rigid. What the hell was going on? Whenever I was with him, he made me forget everything that happened. I felt so safe with him. He kept telling me he would never hurt me, and I completely believed him.

"Up," Rigid said, walking back into the room. He handed me a pill and a glass of water. I popped the pill in my mouth and swallowed it down.

I handed the glass back to him. He took the glass but didn't move. He looked down at me like he couldn't believe what he was seeing. "Is something wrong?" I asked, looking up at him.

"No. I just... Fuck. I don't even know," he bit out and walked out of the room.

I laid back down, not sure what the hell just happened. I had just had the most phenomenal kiss of my life and Rigid seemed like he couldn't get away from me fast enough.

Fuck.

=======

RIGID

Fuck. Shit. God Dammit. I ran my hands through my hair and leaned against the kitchen sink, looking out the window into the backyard.

I finally had Cyn in my arms, and I ran like a fucking kid out of the room. The last time I had tried to kiss her, she froze up and ran away.

Now she literally threw herself at me, and I gave into her for a little bit, but in the back of my mind all I could think about what had happened to her. Looking down at her after the best kiss of my life, I saw her trust in me shining through her eyes. It scared the living shit out of me.

I wanted her, but I was so afraid of hurting her and messing everything up. I had never wanted something so bad in my whole life.

On the flip side, I had never been more terrified of something in my life. I was the badass of the club who didn't let anyone or anything push me around.

They'd all laugh their asses off if they knew a 5'6" woman was making me consider running for the hills.

I flipped the kitchen light off and headed to the bathroom. I walked past Cyn's door and saw her leaning up against the head of the bed, watching Sons.

I took a quick cold shower to get my dick under control and made it back into her room.

She was curled up on her side, her hands folded under head. Her eyes were closed, and I thanked God that she was sleeping.

I slid under the covers and pulled her to me. She curled into me, resting her head on my shoulder. I turned the TV down, not wanting to wake her up, and waited for sleep to take me.

It took a long fucking time till I slept.

Chapter 14

RIGID

I woke up, and Cyn was gone. I glanced at the clock she had sitting on the night stand seeing it was passed ten already.

It had been a little over two weeks since Troy had left for Fall's City. He checked in with King daily, but he said there wasn't much going on up there. He had seen Nick three times, and each time he was surrounded by Assassins. It still wasn't time for us to make a move.

I was getting more restless with each day that passed. I was spending a lot of time with Cyn, but the fact Nick was walking around, free, drove me insane.

I pulled a pair of sweatpants out of the bag I had packed and followed the smell of coffee and bacon.

As I walked into the kitchen, I saw Cyn dancing her ass off to an old Bon Jovi song on the radio.

I leaned against the wall and watched the show she was putting on. She was flipping bacon in a skillet in between using the spatula as a microphone. Her arms were flailing, her casted arm stiffly swinging.

She had on a pair of cutoff shorts and a green t-shirt with a huge neck that made it hang off one shoulder. Her neon green bra strap showing.

She was barefoot, and her jet black hair was swinging down her back as she danced. She looked like fucking heaven.

I cleared my throat, wanting to see her face. She jumped, tossing the spatula into the air and it landed with a splat at her feet.

"Jesus Christ, Rigid! Fucking scared the shit out of me!" She cussed at me. Picking up the spatula, she threw it in the sink and grabbed a new one from the drawer.

"Sorry, beautiful," I said and walked to the coffee pot. I didn't take my eyes off her, I couldn't.

"Hungry?" She asked, her back turned to me as she continued to turn the bacon. I turned down the radio by the coffee pot and grabbed a cup down from the cabinet.

"Starving," I reply as I fill my cup.

"Good. I'm making waffles and bacon," she said as she grabbed the waffle iron down from the cabinet.

"Need help?" I asked taking a sip of coffee.

"No, you can just set the table if you want. Shouldn't be no more than ten minutes till it's ready."

I grabbed plates and silverware and set them on the table. Milk, butter, juice, and syrup joined the table after I inspected the fridge and grabbed what we needed.

I pulled up a chair and sat at the table.

"How'd you sleep, beautiful?" I asked, draining my coffee cup.

"Good. I didn't wake up once.' She flipped a huge waffle out of the iron onto the plate and grabbed the bacon and set both plates in front of me. 'Eat." Cyn smiled at me and turned back to the waffle iron. She filled it with batter and snapped the lid shut.

"I'll wait till you can eat too, babe," I said, pushing the plate away from me.

"That's crazy, eat. It's nice and hot. You'll hurt my feelings if you don't eat, Armando." She threw a wink over her shoulder at me and turned back to check on the waffle iron.

"Not Armando, babe," I smirk as I slathered my waffle with butter.

"Then what is it?" She asked.

"Nice try," I chuckled as I poured syrup all over my waffle, filling every crevices and hole till they are overflowing.

"Holy shit, Rigid. You want some waffle with your syrup," she joked seeing the swimming pool of syrup I have going on.

Setting her plate in front of her chair, I see she only has half a waffle and one piece of bacon. "That all you going to eat, babe?" I asked as I shovel a quarter of the waffle in my mouth. I moan around the sweet goodness. Cyn can definitely cook.

"Yeah, why?' She asked as she cut a small piece off and held her fork up in front of her mouth.

"Because that is not going to fill you up." I pointed out.

"Yeah, it will if I eat it slow enough." She insisted, taking a small bite.

My fork froze halfway to my mouth, and I shook my head. What the fuck did she say? "Come again, babe."

"The slower you eat, the fuller you get. If you wolf down your food, your stomach can't catch up and tell your brain you're full."

"Babe, that's the biggest crock of shit I've ever heard. Just fucking eat. You hungry?" I asked.

"Um, yeah. That's why I have a plate of food in front of me. I can't eat as much as you, Rigid. I would have hips the size of a Cadillac." Cutting off another piece of waffle, she slowly chews it and swallows. This is almost fucking comical.

"You haven't eaten like this the past two weeks. What's with the change?" I shovel another quarter of waffle in my mouth followed with half a piece of bacon.

"I always eat like this. I was too doped up on pain pills the last two weeks to care. I need to lose a couple pounds," she explained as though what she is said made sense.

Cyn lose weight? Was she fucking out of her mind? Her body was fucking perfect. She had curves in all the right places, and my hands were itching to follow each and every one.

"Excuse me?" I asked, wondering if she maybe took one too many pain pills this morning.

"Ok! Fifteen pounds," she grumbled, cutting her waffle into tiny pieces. She is completely out of her fucking mind.

"Babe," I growled.

She kept her eyes glued to her plate, basically massacring her waffle.

"Eyes. Now," I demanded.

She kept her face to the plate, but her eyes moved to me. "What?" she sassed.

"If you lose a fucking ounce of you, I will put you over my knee and spank the living shit out of you."

She rolled her eyes at me and mumbled something under her breath about Fatty McFat pants and living in a donut house and snorted.

Even pissing me off, thinking she needed to lose weight, she still made me laugh. This is the carefree woman I saw that first night I met her. "No fucking clue what you said, babe, but I'll come live in that donut house with you," I smirk.

"Nope. Only fatties get to live in the donut house. You're too hard and muscly to even think about living there. The donut house is mine."

"Are we really talking about a donut house right now?" I asked. I couldn't believe this is the conversation were having.

"You brought up living there with me," She said as though we were having a normal conversation.

"Fucking crazy," I muttered under my breath.

She shrugged her shoulders at me, and we finished eating in silence.

As I was loading the dishwasher, I heard a car door slam and Meg walked in seconds later.

"Aw man, I missed waffles," she said in greeting as she tossed her purse next to the couch.

"I saved you some," Cyn said as she grabbed the other half of her waffle from the fridge and popped it in the toaster.

"Score!" Meg said as she grabbed the syrup out of the fridge.

"Meg, Rigid wants to live in the donut house with us." Cyn grabbed the waffle from the toaster, lying it on a plate and took it to Meg who took a seat at the table.

"Bullshit. He's way too hard and stuff," Meg said as she slathered butter and syrup on her waffle.

"See, told you," Cyn said smugly, crossing her arms over her chest.

"Dude, if Lo can't live in the donut house, you can't either." Meg cut into her waffle, shoveling half of it in, in one bit. At least, Meg wasn't afraid to eat.

"I swear to God, it's like you two chicks are in a different world. What the fuck are you two talking about?" I asked, annoyed with this whole conversation.

"Cyn and I are fat," Meg said as if that explained everything.

"What the fuck! Neither of you are fat!"

"He's so sweet," Meg cooed to Cyn, shoveling the last of the waffle into her mouth.

"He is.' Cyn agreed, sitting across from Meg at the table. 'But don't tell anyone. He needs to keep the tough guy act up."

Meg threw her head back and laughed. "Lo is the same way. Sweet with me and then a jackass whenever he's around the club."

"What the fuck is a donut house?" I asked, annoyed Meg and Cyn were talking about how sweet Lo and I were.

"The place Meg and I are going to live so we can be surrounded by donuts and eat the living shit out of them and not have to worry about anyone judging us," Meg explained.

"You're fucking crazy," I countered.

"You can't come because you wouldn't eat donuts all day. You'd end up eating one and lose weight. Cyn and I gain weight just looking at them. It's not fair." Meg pouted as though this whole crazy conversation was going to happen.

"I can't even wrap my head around this shit right now. I'm going to tell you again Cyn, you lose any weight, and we are going to have a problem. I like you the way you are. Meg,' I looked at her, a big grin on her face, 'King thinks the same thing about you. You both need to get that twisted bullshit out of your heads that you need to lose weight or diet." I couldn't take this anymore. They were both fucking crazy.

"Ok, Anakin," Meg giggled, as she stood up and took her plate to the dishwasher and dropped it in. I slammed it shut, twisting the knobs to start it up.

"Time for Sons!" Meg shouted. She walked into the living room and flipped on the TV and started pulling up Netflix.

"What the fuck just happened?" I asked Cyn who is still sitting at the table.

She shrugged her shoulder and giggled. "Meg," she said as if that's all the explanation needed.

"You want to watch TV or do something else?" I asked, done with the ridiculous conversation.

"TV is good for now. Maybe we can have a bonfire tonight or something?" She suggested.

"Fuck yeah. We can have a cookout. I'm sure the brothers from the clubhouse will be down with that." I pulled my phone out, shooting off a text to Demon to spread the word.

"Did you just invite all of the Devil's Knights to my house tonight?" Cyn asked, her mouth hanging open.

"Yeah, babe. They live for a good party." The fuckers honestly did. Plus it would be good for Cyn to be around more people. She was becoming a hermit sitting in the house all day.

"Rigid, I don't have enough food to feed that many people."

"So then we hit the store up, or I can text Turtle a list of shit you want and he can pick it up."

"Are you two coming to watch Sons with me or am I going to have to drool over Jax all by myself, Cyn?"

"What the fuck is she talking about?" I asked Cyn.

She turned bright red and hightailed it to the living room. I followed behind just in time to see her dive into Meg, who was sprawled out on the couch.

"You bitch!" Meg shrieked when Cyn boob punched her.

"Would you shut up? I'm going to tell King all about your Opie obsession."

"Gah, go ahead. He gets all sexy mad and thinks he has to show me how much hotter he is than Opie. Be my guest, Cyn," Meg said, rubbing her hands together.

Cyn screwed her face up in a grimace and stuck her tongue out at Meg. "Can we please have one conversation that doesn't involve King and his prowess in the bedroom?"

"I can't promise anything, but I'll try." Meg winked.

"You want to go to the store or have Turtle bring you the shit?" I asked.

"What are we going to the store for?" Meg asked.

"Rigid invited all the guys over for a cookout and a bonfire tonight. You need to come." Cyn demanded.

"No can do, chica. Troy took off from work so I have to be there. I can swing by after if it's still going on, but I'll help you shop for food. You'd be surprised at how much a group of hungry bikers can eat."

"That sucks. Why the hell does Troy need off?" Cyn asked.

Meg looked at me, unsure if she could tell Cyn what I'm sure King told her. "He's helping out with some club business. Get dressed so we can hit up the store."

"Wait, what is Troy doing? Does it have to do with Asshat?" Cyn asked.

"Yeah. Now get dressed," I ordered.

"Really, that's all the info I get? This totally has to do with me. I should know what's going on," Cyn said, stomping her foot, refusing to move until I told her what was going on.

"Troy's up in Fall's City keeping an eye on the Assassins and fuck face, making sure they don't leave till I head up there in a week or so. Dressed. Now," I ordered. I had managed to make it this far without telling Cyn what was going on. She had enough shit to deal with, she didn't need to worry about anything that had to do with Nick.

"He's not going to get hurt, is he?" Cyn asked, concern lacing her voice.

It pissed me off she was worried about Troy. The fucker could handle himself, Cyn had nothing to worry about. "He's fine. They have no idea who he is," I promised.

"You better be right," Cyn said as she stormed out of the room.

I looked at Meg, who had a shit eating grin on her face. "What?"

"You like her," Meg sang out.

Fuck. Now I was going to have to deal with Meg's crazy ass alone. "Yeah. So?"

"I wouldn't be worried about Troy. I asked her if she like him again and she said no. She sees him as a brother."

"Good to know, but I'm not worried about that fucker."

"Mmhm," Meg hummed.

I grabbed my boots, sliding my feet into the. "You might want to put a shirt on," Meg giggled from the couch.

I looked down, realizing I had only jeans and boots on, no shirt.

Fuck me.

======

Chapter 15

Cyn

I was trying to find a shirt that would cover the bruises that kept popping up on my arms. Thankfully it was spring and spring in Wisconsin was never really warm.

I found an old Badger long sleeve tee I hadn't worn in ages. I tried sliding my casted arm through the sleeve and only made it halfway before I got stuck. I ripped it off and sailed it across the room into the growing pile of clothes that didn't work with a broken arm.

I finally grabbed a short sleeve shirt that fit over my cast and grabbed my leather jacket, putting my good arm in and let the other sleeve hang loosely. Shoving my feet into a pair of flip flops, I headed back out to the living room.

Rigid passed me in the hallway and headed for my room.

"This is as good as it's going to get," I said to Meg, pulling my hair out from under my jacket.

"You look like a hot motorcycle chick. All you need is a pair of kick ass boots. Oh! We should hit up the Harley store on the way to the grocery store!" Meg exclaimed. She clapped her hands and jumped up and down.

"I don't have the money for boots, Meg. Lord knows how long I'm going to be off work."

"I'll buy you boots, beautiful. You'll need them for when you're on the back of my bike," Rigid said as he walked out, pulling his cut on over his shirt he finally put on.

"You're not buying me boots. I don't need them."

"Yeah, you do," he insisted.

"You can't make me buy boots. I won't try any on! You can't buy them if you don't know what size I am! Ha!" I shouted.

"I know her size! Lo wanted me to pick up some new boots, too. Oh yeah! Shoe shopping! I'll drive!" Meg chirped and headed out the door to her truck.

"You can't buy me boots," I repeated.

"I can and I will." Rigid walked out the door, leaving me with my mouth hanging open.

What the hell just happened? I thought we were just going to the grocery store to get shit for the cookout and now we were going shoe shopping?

He wasn't going to buy me shoes. I would just refuse. Simple as that.

======

RIGID

"Oh my god! Look at these!" Meg squealed as she grabbed a pair of boots off the shelf that had purple and orange flames on the toe.

Cyn had a pair of kick ass black pair of boots with a couple inch heel that laced up the back. She looked amazing in them.

"This is too much, Rigid. Meg is buying her own boots, why can't I buy mine?"

"I'm buying both pairs right now, and King is paying me back for Meg's. Find another excuse for me not to buy them for you," I smirked.

"I hate you, but I love these," she purred, lifting her foot up to admire them.

"That mean I get to buy them for you?"

"Humph, I wouldn't be so smug about it. You haven't seen the price tag yet," she giggled.

"You love them, they're worth it." I grabbed her empty box and Meg's and headed to the cash register.

"Hey! I need that!" Cyn yelled at me as I walked away.

"Wear those home. They look a fuck of a lot better." I dropped the boxes at the register and paid the cashier.

After throwing the girls old shoes into the boxes, we headed out to the grocery store, Meg behind the wheel. Cyn was sitting in the middle pressed up against me, my arm was thrown over her shoulder.

"Lo is going to flip when he sees these boots. Now I definitely feel like an ol' lady." Meg beamed as we pulled into the parking lot.

"I still can't believe you got purple flames on your boots." Cyn giggled as she slid out of the truck.

"Hey, these kick ass. I've never seen a pair like them before.'

"I'd believe that the fucking box had dust on it. They probably sat on the shelf for years." I mumbled under my breath.

Cyn giggled and covered her mouth with her hand.

Meg grabbed a cart, put her foot on the bottom rack, and pushed off with the other, rocketing herself through the parking lot to the front door.

"This is going to be interesting, isn't it, beautiful?" I laughed, watching Meg careening towards a parked car.

"It's always interesting when Meg is around," Cyn laughed and ran to catch up to Meg.

King was going to owe me big for spending the day with his ol' lady.

Fuck me.

======

Cyn

"We really need ten pounds of brats? That seems like a shit ton," I muttered, watching Meg load the cart up. We already had three packs of hot dogs, five pounds each of potato salad and cole slaw. Plus a bunch of baking shit because Meg was going to whip up some bars before she headed off to work.

"Buns!" Meg shouted and headed off to the other side of the store.

"Are you sure you can afford all this?" I asked, surveying the ever growing mountain of food. I had given up insisting I would pay for the food when Rigid went to get a second cart.

"Yeah, all the brothers will chip in. No worries, beautiful," he said, reassuring me.

"Cyn! A little help!" Meg boomed from across the store.

"Better go help your girl," Rigid chuckled, heading the opposite direction of Meg.

"Traitor," I mumbled under my breath.

I made my way to Meg, starting to regret Rigid's brilliant idea for a cookout. I was fucking exhausted and in desperate need of a nap.

I counted down the hours till Meg would leave for work and planned to slip out of the party shortly after dinner. I was feeling better, but I still wasn't one hundred percent.

Help Meg bake, man the grill, eat, then crash. I just hope it worked out that way.

======

Chapter 16

Cyn

"I've got to run, or I'll be late for work. I promise to head back over after to work. I'm sure the guys will still be here. King said they were in need of letting off steam," Meg rambled as she shoved her feet into her new boots and grabbed her keys off the counter.

After unloading the groceries, Meg and I set about making banana cream bars and Snickers bars. Rigid cleaned up the backyard and set up the grill. Gravel and Gambler came over with a load of chairs and tables and worked on setting them up then headed back to the clubhouse.

I had put the brats to boil in beer and the potato salad and cole slaw were set in bowls, chilling in the fridge.

"Thanks for all the help, Meg. I wish you could be here," I confessed, worried about tonight. I was getting a little anxious thinking about all the people who were about to invade my house.

Meg sensed the panic in my eyes and hugged me close. "You'll be ok. Just breathe, Cyn. Rigid won't let anything happen to you. Call if you need me." She squeezed me one last time and ducked out the front door.

"Meg off to work?" Rigid rumbled walking in the back door.

"Uh, yeah. She said she'll try to make it back over after," I muttered. I rubbed my eyes, heavy with sleep, and yawned.

"Go take a nap, beautiful. They guys won't be here until 6 after the garage closes," Rigid rumbled, opening the fridge and pulling a beer out. He popped the top and drank half of it.

"I need to keep an eye on the brats." They still had an hour of simmering left.

"Tell you what, get a movie going and we can watch it in the living room. That way you can relax and still keep an eye on the food.' Rigid grabbed my hand and pulled me to the couch. 'Sit,' he ordered.

I collapsed on the couch, too exhausted to even argue with him.

He flipped on the TV and started up Jackass. "Really?" I asked, half asleep.

"Quiet, beautiful. You're going to be asleep in half a minute. I shouldn't have dragged you around the grocery store. Half way through I could tell you were about to fall over. I'm sorry." Rigid apologized, sitting next to me. He twisted my body, resting my back on the arm of the couch and swung my feet into his lap. He rubbed my feet, lulling me even further to sleep.

"I'm a big girl, Rigid. It was my decision to go shopping. I'm just a little worn out." I mumbled, smothering a yawn.

"Sleep. I'll wake you before everyone shows up."

"Promise?" I asked, sleep quickly overtaking me.

"Promise, beautiful," Rigid whispered.

I fell asleep before the opening credits rolled, Rigid's strong hands relaxing me.

======

RIGID

The movie was over, and Cyn was sprawled out on the couch, her head in my lap. I had shut off the brats when the timer she had set went off and fired up the charcoal grill. King had just sent me a message letting me know they would be rolling in any time.

I needed to wake Cyn up, but I didn't want to. She had overdone it today and needed to rest. A bunch of bikers invading her house was not the best way to relax. She had curled up in my lap after I came back in the house and hadn't moved since.

"Beautiful, you need to wake up." I brushed the hair from her face, caressing her cheek.

She mumbled in her sleep and snuggled even further into me. I traced the cut on her face with my fingertip. It was already healing and should be gone within a week. The rest of the bruises on her body and face were fading into yellow. In a week, the only thing that wouldn't be healed would be her arm. I clenched my fists, remembering what she looked like after we had found her lying on the floor. The fucker was going to pay for what he had done.

Cyn was acting like she was over it, but I was afraid that she was just putting on a front in front of everyone.

"Cyn, you need to get up, babe," I said, louder this time. I ran my thumb over her lips, feeling how soft they were.

"Just point them in the direction of the back yard and let me sleep," she mumbled.

"As good as that sounds, beautiful, you need to get up, eat, and take a pill. If you're still tired after you can head to your room," I promised.

"Hmm, I got sweet Rigid," Cyn cooed, lifting her head from my lap.

"Only you get him, beautiful."

I heard a group of motorcycles pull up the drive and knew my alone time with Cyn was over. Time to share her.

"Ugh, I need to pee. Let me up," she bossed.

I lifted my arm I had wrapped around her waist and let her get up. She stumbled off to the bathroom, rubbing the sleep out of her eyes.

"You gonna sit on the couch all night or cook me my fucking meal?" Speed boomed as he walked in the front door.

"Fuck you. I'd make you man the fucking grill, but you'd probably light Cyn's fucking house on fire," I shot back, getting up from the couch.

"You tell anyone how you lit the end of your finger on fire the other night?" Gambler joked, setting two cases of beer on the table.

"Shut the fuck up. It was only for two seconds. Ain't nothing to tell," Speed said, ripping open a bag of chips, shoving a handful in his mouth.

"I don't know how you have all your hair, Speed. It seems like you're setting something on fire at least once a week," King smirked as he brought in a six pack of wine coolers and a bottle of Southern Comfort.

"You hitting the soft stuff tonight, King?" I asked, eyeing the wine colors.

"They're for Cyn, you dipshit," King shot back.

"He's grumpier than a bear shitting in the woods because Meg isn't here," Hammer said.

"That don't make sense, Ham. Try again, fuckwad," Gravel grumped, walking through the front door.

All the brothers laughed at Ham. Fucker never could get a saying right. It was amazing some days he could put two words together that made sense.

"Grab the brats and hot dogs, Turtle. You're helping me cook," I said, grabbing a pair of tongs and a beer. Turtle was a prospect, and I was his sponsor. He had been a prospect for almost a year now. His probationary period was almost up, and he would more than likely become a full member in the next month or so.

Turtle followed me out the door with all the brothers following us out.

"Cyn up?" King asked taking a seat at the picnic table. All the other brothers spread out on the picnic table and chairs that had been set up. King, Hammer, Gravel, Speed, Gambler, and Turtle were the first brothers to show up. It was only a matter of time till more showed up.

"She woke up right before ya'll showed up. She should be out anytime," I replied, filling the grill up with brats. Cyn might have been right, maybe ten pounds of brats was too many.

"How she doing?" Gravel asked, sitting down.

"As far as I can tell, well. She had nightmares that first night home but hasn't had any lately." I shut the lid on the grill, taking a long pull of my beer. The fucking grill was hot. Dinner would be made in no time.

"Good. Keep an eye on her, Rigid, that girl has gone through hell," Gravel said, leaning back in his chair, stretching his legs out.

"I'm on it, Gravel,' I said, nodding at him. 'Keep an eye on the grill, Turtle." I handed the tongs off and headed back to the house to see what Cyn was up.

"You checking up on me?" Cyn asked as I shut the patio door behind me.

"Just making sure you were ok, beautiful. You want me to grab you something to drink? King brought more of that girly shit you and Meg like to drink." I opened the fridge and grabbed another beer for me and drink for Cyn.

I turned around, waiting for Cyn to answer. She was standing at the entrance of the kitchen, wringing her hands together.

"What's wrong?" I asked, setting the drinks down. I moved closer to her, not liking the distance between us.

"Um, just a little nervous. I know we went to the store and all today but this is kind of the first time I've been around people since... you know." She wiped her hands on her thighs and wrapped her arms around her middle.

I moved to her and wrapped my arms around her. She melted into me, breathing a sigh of relief. "I'm sorry, beautiful. I didn't think of that when I came up with the idea of a barbecue. I'll tell the fuckers to leave." I ran my hands up and down her back, trying to soothe her. I can't believe I didn't think it was too soon for Cyn. Fucking idiot.

"No, no.' Cyn said, shaking her head. 'It's fine. I need to do this. Just, um... stay with me?" She ended on a whisper.

"You didn't even need to ask, Cyn."

<<<<<<<<<<

Cyn

I was wrapped up in Rigid's arms and all the anxiety I was feeling disappeared.

I had walked out of the bathroom and headed to the kitchen. I almost had been to the patio door open when my panic hit me. I saw Rigid and all the guys sprawled on my lawn, and I froze.

I knew I couldn't do it. I was headed back to my room, planning to fake being in pain when Rigid walked through the door. I tried to put on a brave face, but I just couldn't.

"I'm not going to go anywhere, Cyn," Rigid whispered into my hair.

"Promise me," I pleaded. Rigid's arms were the only place I felt safe. If he ever left, I didn't know what I would do.

"I promise." Rigid pulled back and looked me in the eyes. He cupped my face in his hands and brushed back my hair. He wiped my tears from my cheeks that I didn't even know I had shed.

"I'm sorry. I'm such a mess. One minute I'm fine and then the next I can't breathe. I was doing so good these past couple of days," I confessed.

"You're still doing good, beautiful. Just a bad day," Rigid said. He leaned down, pressing his lips to my forehead.

Rigid was so understanding. I didn't know any other man who would put up with my mega mood swings. He buried his face in my hair, inhaling deeply.

"You're smelling me again, aren't you?" I giggled.

"I can't help it," He mumbled into my hair.

"Do you think you can control yourself if we go out with your friends?" I asked.

"I make no promises when it comes to you. You sure you want to go out there? I can just tell them you need to rest. You did have a rough day today."

I pulled out of Rigid's arms and looked at him. I don't know what I did to deserve this man. He was the most handsome man I had ever seen, even if it was in the most unconventional way.

His pierced eyebrow and disc gauges in his ears gave him a look that most bikers I had met couldn't pull off. Pair his piercings with his blue Mohawk and he looked like he belonged in a punk rock band more than a motorcycle club. His massive muscles and sheer size are what made him so intimidating. The faint scar and the permanent scowl on his face just added to his intimidation factor.

"What happened?" I asked, running my fingers down the faint scar that ran from the corner of his left eye to the right corner of his mouth.

"Young and stupid," Rigid laughed. He caught my hand in his and pressed it to his lips.

"What happened?" I asked again.

"I can't even remember what the argument was about, but I got into it with a guy at a bar when I was twenty-two. This,' Rigid pointed to the scar, 'was his first and only hit he got in. He grabbed a broken beer bottle and took a swing at me, fucked up my face."

"What did you do to him?" I asked, not sure if I really wanted to know. I knew Rigid could kick ass, but I didn't really need to know the details.

"Just gave him what he had coming to him, babe."

"He still alive?"

"Yeah, he's sitting out in your backyard, beautiful."

My jaw dropped open, shocked that one of Rigid's brothers had done that to him. "Which one?"

Rigid shook his head and laughed. "Not telling you, babe. The past is the past."

"I'm so going to find out. How is he still a part of the Devil's Knights after he did that to you?" I said, gesturing to his scar.

"Because he wasn't a part of the Knights when he did it. He was just a young punk looking for a place to belong. The Knights were what he was looking for."

I was truly surprised by that response. I felt the Knights were a bunch of badass men who kicked ass and took names later. "Tell me who it is," I pleaded.

"Tell you what. Add it to the list of things we guess about each other."

"Not fair! Now I have to guess your name and who gave you that scar? Mine is easy to figure out. You just need to google it." I pouted.

"You're smart, babe. You'll figure it," Rigid smirked, wrapping me up in his arms.

"Not fair, Ansel," I mumbled into his chest.

"Where the fuck do you come up with these names babe? Fucking crazy." Rigid shook his head, laughing.

"I got an app on my phone. I pick the unpopular ones. I'm running low, though."

"You'll get it eventually. You ready to head out?" He asked, throwing his arm around my shoulder and steered me over where he set the drinks.

He grabbed the drinks but stayed connected to me. Opening the door, his hand slid down mine and gripped my hand. He tugged me out the door and pulled me over to a lawn chair.

"Sit. Relax," Rigid ordered as he took the seat next to the one he ordered me to take.

I looked around and only knew a couple of faces. King was sprawled out on one side of the picnic table, he nodded to me, and I waved at him. There were a couple of faces I remembered seeing at the hospital, but King was the only name I knew.

"Sit, beautiful. I'll introduce you," Rigid ordered again.

I plopped in the chair next to him, and he handed me my drink. I took a sip, realizing all eyes were on me.

"That scruffy-looking fucker over there is Gravel," Rigid said, pointing out a guy with a long gray beard and hair. His face was weathered from age, and his eyes were staring me down.

"Hi," I mumbled when he nodded his head at me.

"Those two fuckers over by the grill are Turtle and Hammer. Between the two of them they have a full brain," Rigid joked.

"Go fuck a squirrel," one of them shot back.

"Point made, Hammer," Rigid mumbled under his breath. I giggled, loving the comradery they had between them all.

"Now that asshole over there is Gambler. He's got an addiction to poker and fast woman. I'd stay far away from him," Rigid said, chuckling.

"Fuck you, man. I'm the nicest one of you fuckers. King's got his head so far up Meg's ass he can't see the sun anymore, and all you other fuckers are ornery assholes. You want nice, come see me, darlin'." Gambler said, winking at me.

"Reel it the fuck in, Gambler," Rigid growled. Rigid reached over, lacing his fingers with mine and pulled it into his lap.

"So it's like that, fucker?" Gambler asked, nodding his head at my hand clasped in Rigid's.

"It's most definitely like that, brother." Rigid's hand squeezed mine, and I looked up at his face. He was turned towards Gambler, they were staring each other down.

"Take care of what's yours, brother. Or someone else might," Gambler warned. I think it was a warning. Although I couldn't figure out why.

"I need a fucking platter or something. The brats are done," Turtle boomed from over by the grill.

"I'll get it," I said as I shot up from my chair. The stare down between Rigid and Gambler was freaking me the fuck out. I would have dashed to the kitchen, but Rigid was still holding on to my hand.

"Where you going?" Rigid asked.

"That guy, I think Turtle, needs a plate. I was going to get one for him," I explained as I tried twisting my hand from his.

"Turtle can get his own fucking plate."

"Please, Rigid. Let me go. I'll be right back," I pleaded.

"Right back here," he said as he let go of my hand.

I hightailed it to the kitchen, slamming the door behind me. I grabbed my phone and shot off a message to Meg begging her to ditch work and get her ass over to my house. I moved to the cabinet, grabbing down a plate and jumped when I heard the door open.

"You alright, darlin'?" King ask as he studied me.

"Uh, yeah. Just getting a plate," I said, waving it around.

"Don't mind Gambler, babe. He's just trying to get a rise out of Rigid. All those fuckers did it to me when they met Meg.

I'd have to ask Meg about that. I wasn't sure I liked it. "OK."

"You feeling better? Still in a lot of pain?"

"Um, just sore really. Nothing that really warrants me taking pills anymore. I... I want to... uh,...thank you for everything that, um... night. Thank you," I stuttered.

"No need to thank me. Don't take this the wrong way, but I did it for Meg. She needed to help you, and I was the best way to help. Now Rigid? Well, he didn't do it for Meg."

"Then why did he do it?" I asked. Unsure if I wanted to hear the answer.

"You. He did it because it was you. He would do anything for you." Lo walked to the fridge grabbing the whole case of beer, hoisting it under his arm. I suppose it was probably easier to bring the beer to the guys rather than having to come in the house all the time.

"I don't know what to do with that, King," I said, unsure if I wanted Rigid to do anything for me.

"Just go with it, darlin'. I've known Rigid a long time, and I have never seen him like this before," King said, heading back to the door.

"That's all the advice you have for me?" I asked.

"Cyn,' King said, turning back to me before he got to the door. 'I know you've been through a lot, we all know that darlin', but that man sitting out there wants to help you. He wants to make it all go away and give you back what you lost."

"I can't get back what I lost, King." I was broken and, although I knew I was slowly getting put back together, I was never going to be the same again.

"Then let him give you something new. Just don't shut him out."

"Your mom said the same thing. That I just needed to let him in, and everything would be alright."

"She's a smart woman, Cyn. She called that Meg and I would be together the day I met her." King walked out the back door, leaving it open for me to follow.

I walked back out, Rigid's eyes on me the second I stepped foot on the grass. Instead of sitting back in my chair, I headed over to Turtle and held the plate as he placed all the brats on it.

I could feel Rigid's eyes on me. I couldn't tell if he was still mad at Gambler or if he was over it.

King's words kept running through my mind. What kind of new was Rigid going to give me? Was this it? A motorcycle club sprawled around my lawn, drinking beer and shooting the shit.

The real question was, was this what I wanted?

Chapter 17

RIGID

Cyn was standing by the grill, talking with Ham and Turtle while they took the food off. I shot a look at Gambler, who was talking on his phone. I was ten seconds away from slugging the shit out of Gambler before Cyn got up to head to the house.

I didn't want to scare Cyn so I let it drop between Gambler and me.

"Come grab the rest of the shit with me." King motioned to me.

I followed King into the house and grabbed the buns and shit and headed back out the door.

Cyn was setting the overflowing platter full of brats on the table. She grabbed the three packs of buns I had dangling from my fingers and started opening them.

I heard the roar of motorcycles pull up the drive, knowing the rest of the guys had arrived.

Cyn's eyes darted to the front of the house, watchful of who was about to walk in.

"You ok, beautiful?" I asked, grabbing the spoons King had brought out and sticking them into the bowls of potato salad and cole slaw.

"Um, yeah. Still kind of tired but I'm good. How many people are coming?" She asked, watching the side of the house.

"There is eighteen of us total, but I doubt all the brothers are going to show. Probably only six or so more." I glanced to the side of the house and saw Crowbar, Demon, Slider, Python, and Roam walk in.

"Where's that gorgeous ol' lady of yours King?" Slider asked, grabbing two beers, opening both.

"Remember the last time you brought up Meg, douchebag?" King growled as he dropped the rest of the food on the picnic table.

"What'd I say? I asked a legitimate question. I've been in town for almost three weeks now, and I've only seen you a handful of times. All those times, by the way, Meg was with you." Slider gruffed, sitting on the other side of the picnic table.

"You jealous of Meg, Slider?" Gravel taunted.

"Fuck off, old man. Where's all the pussy?" Slider asked, looking around.

"Got to be fucking kidding me," Gravel mumbled under his breath.

Cyn's eyes bugged out of her head at Slider's words. Fuck me. Cyn was never going to be with me with these fucking idiots around. King was the first one of us to get an ol' lady, and there was obviously some adjustment going on.

"You want pussy, brother, you need to haul your ass back to the clubhouse. None of that shit is going on at Cyn's house," King growled.

"You Cyn?" Slider asked, his eyes traveling over Cyn. His eyes assessed her, taking in the fading bruises, cuts, and a broken arm.

"Yup," Cyn whispered.

"Sorry, babe," Slider said, losing the attitude he had seconds ago.

Cyn gave Slider a small smile. "You done being an ass?" I asked, pissed that Slider can never think before he fucking speaks.

"For the next couple of hours," Slider shot back.

"You guys are like little boys," Cyn said, opening the last pack of buns. Her broken arm slowing her down.

"They're worse," King chimed in.

"I am far from a little boy, babe." Slider said, winking at Cyn.

Fucker was God damn shameless. "Eat, assholes," I snapped, seeing all the food was ready.

Cyn walked over to the chair she was sitting in before and sat down, grabbing her drink. I walked over, standing over her, looking down. "You need to eat."

"I will when everyone else eats," she said.

"There might not be anything left with the way these fuckers eat. You'd swear it was their last meal half the time," I said, looking back at the picnic table seeing Crowbar shove half a brat in his face and Speed walking past with three brats and two hot dogs on one plate and another plate piled high with salads and chips.

"You might be right," Cyn said, looking amazed at the guys filling their plates.

"Come on, beautiful." I reached my hand out grabbing Cyn's, hoisting her out of the chair.

"I just need a brat," she mumbled as I dragged her over to the table.

"You need to eat more than that," I ordered, handing her a plate.

I grabbed two brats, sticking them in buns and put them on her plate. "Rigid, stop. I can't eat all this." I mounded two big piles of potato salad and cole slaw on her plate and threw some chips on top.

"Eat."

"Do we need to have another discussion about donut houses?" Cyn bitched, cocking her hip out, resting her hand on it.

"What the fuck is a donut house?" King asked as he filled his own plate.

"Long and stupid story, brother. Partly due to your ol' lady," I said, physically turning Cyn towards her chair, my hand on her lower back, guiding her back to her chair.

"You're just pissed that you can't come. Hell, none of you can come. Meg and I are the only ones who can go. You're all too hard and muscley," Cyn pouted, plopping down in her chair, munching on a chip.

"What the fuck does Meg have to do with it?" King wanted to know. He sat down next to Cyn leaving the chair on the other side of her open for me.

"Meg and I are going to live in a donut house so we can eat donuts anytime we want and not have to worry about anyone judging us. You guys are too hot to live in a donut house." Cyn replied. Acting like what she was saying made sense when it fucking didn't.

"Won't the donuts be stale before you got around to eating them?" Roam asked as if this made sense.

"Not if we shellac them with icing,' Cyn said, taking a bit of brat and swallowing. 'Who are you? Rigid introduced me to some of you, but some of you are new."

"That dipshit is Roam. He isn't around very much," I explained.

"Places to be, darlin'," Roam explained, winking at Cyn.

"Those two fuckers over by the table,' I said, pointing to the picnic table, 'are Demon and Crowbar. Demon is Crowbar's sponsor. Demon is the VP."

Cyn nodded at both of them, not speaking.

"Sitting at the picnic table are Python and Slider. Slider is a member of the Collinsworth chapter. He decided to come and bug the shit out of us up here."

"Fuck you. I actually came to scope shit out, see how things were going up here. Collinsworth is getting boring. Maybe I'll transfer up here," Slider said. I looked to King to see if he knew about that. He looked as surprised as the other brothers.

"We'll discuss that shit later," King said.

"Do you all have fake names?" Cyn asked.

"Not fake, darlin'. They're road names. We all earned them," Gravel explained.

"So who isn't here? I want to hear all these names," she said, finishing her first brat.

"Edge and Whiskey are scoping out venues for our new business venture. Swinger, Blade, Cowboy, Mickey, and Wheeler are at the garage. We had a couple last minute clients come in, and they had to stay late to finish them up," King said.

"How do you get a road name?" Cyn asked Gravel.

"They just kind of happen, darlin'. I got mine because I spent more time picking gravel out of my teeth than riding my motorcycle," Gravel chuckled.

"From the stories I heard, it took Gravel a good year before he stopped laying his bike down all the time," I laughed.

Cyn laughed, finally relaxing. "Ok. So how did you get your name Crowbar?"

All the brothers busted out laughing. "Well, you see,' Demon said after the laughing died down, 'Ol' Crowbar here was having a hell of a time on a run a few weeks after he became a prospect. One thing after another kept breaking on his bike. Well, he finally had enough of it when he ran over a crowbar someone had left on the road, and it popped his tire."

"So his name is Crowbar because he ran one over?" Cyn asked.

"No, darlin'. His name is Crowbar, because after he had run over the crowbar, he got off his bike, walked across two lanes of traffic, picked up the crowbar and beat the living shit out of his bike." We all roared with laughter remembering that day.

Cyn smiled, looking at Crowbar, who was blushing under her inspection. "So if you beat the shit out of your bike, how did you get back to the clubhouse?"

"Dumbass had to ride bitch with Demon. Funniest ninety miles of my fucking life." Speed snickered.

Cyn busted out laughing, throwing her head back. I watched her, loving that she was loosening up. "I can definitely see how that nickname came about," she joked.

"Cyn your real name, babe?" Slider asked.

"Cynthia. I hate it. I feel like a ninety-year-old when anyone calls me that. My parents have been calling me Cyn for forever,' she said, handing me her plate. 'I can't eat anymore, Augie," Cyn smirked.

"What the fuck did she call you?" Hammer asked around a mouthful of food.

"None of your fucking business," I bit out. Fucking Augie. Where the hell was she coming up with these names?

Cyn burst out laughing, thinking she was a regular fucking comedian. "Real funny, Cynthia," I mumbled under my breath.

She shot me an eat shit look, knowing we were even on the name front for now.

"If you would just tell me your name I wouldn't have to guess such ridiculous names." She shot back at me.

"You got to earn it, beautiful. No one has ever taken the time to earn it." I leaned into her, my face inches away from hers.

She grabbed a chip off the plate she handed me, shoving it into her mouth, crunching loudly. "I don't like playing games, Rigid. Someone always gets hurt."

"No games, beautiful. Just stick around and you'll find out. No running."

She looked me in the eye, studying me. "Maybe you're the one who's going to run, not me," Cyn whispered. I could tell she believed those words.

"I haven't run yet, babe." I leaned in closer till we were just a whisper apart.

She didn't back down, stood her ground, staring me down. "Yet," she whispered. She leaned the last half an inch and pressed her soft lips against mine. She parted her lips, waiting for me to react. I waited half a second till my tongue swiped her lip, giving me a taste of what I had been craving.

Her hand grasped my arm, and a whimper escaped. She wrapped her other arm around my neck, pulling herself even closer to me.

My tongue delved into her mouth, a groan I couldn't hold back rumbled out, and my need for Cyn took over. I dropped my plate, not giving a fuck about it. I framed her face with my hands and took what I needed.

I was seconds away from pulling her into my lap, desperate for her to straddle me, when I heard someone clear their throat, slamming me back into reality. I pulled away and looked into Cyn's eyes. They were clouded with desire and want, begging for more, her breath shallow.

Holy shit.

<<<<<<<<

Cyn

I was panting. Fucking panting. If Rigid wouldn't have pulled away, I'm pretty sure I would have been in his lap, begging for him to take me.

I had heard someone clearing their throat, but it hadn't registered. I was completely zoned out, only caring about what Rigid was doing to me.

"Beautiful," Rigid whispered, brushing his lips against mine, making me follow his retreating lips, wishing for more.

He sat back in his chair, staring at me.

"What the fuck is this?" Someone boomed, walking out of the house.

I tore my gaze away from Rigid, afraid if I stared any longer I would drag him back to my bed and beg for him to take me.

My gaze landed on Crowbar who was carrying the two pans of bars Meg and I had made. "Banana Cream bars and Snicker bars," I mumbled, still out of it from Rigid's kiss.

"Fuck yeah. Meg cooks like Betty fucking Crocker," Gravel said, grabbing a pan from Crowbar and setting it on the table. He grabbed the knife out of Crowbar's hand and cut a chunk off. He grabbed it out of the pan, shoving half of it in his mouth.

"You going to cut some for the rest of us, fucker, or you just going to feed your own face?" King asked, shaking his head at him.

"The only person who can even compete with Meg's cooking is your mom. So, fuck yeah, I'm going to feed myself before you fuckers get your god damn hands on it," Gravel said.

"I can cut them," I said, getting up and walking over to the table. Now that Rigid's lips weren't on mine, I was thinking clearly. I still wanted Rigid, I wasn't going to deny that, I just knew I shouldn't try to jump him with all his friends around.

The second I made the last cut, the pans were grabbed away from me and being passed around.

I glanced back at Rigid, his eyes staring me down and I felt my cheeks heat. I couldn't tear my eyes away from him.

"You got testicle toss, babe?" Slider asked, breaking me from my stare down with Rigid. I glanced at Slider, seeing him licking his fingers clean.

"Uh, you mean ladder golf?" I asked.

"Yeah, that too. You got it?"

"Garage," I replied. Slider wiped his hands on his jeans and headed in the direction of the garage with Turtle right behind him.

I grabbed my drink off the table and headed back to my chair. I grabbed the arm and scooted it away from Rigid. I heard him chuckle but didn't look at him. I knew I was ridiculous moving my chair three inches away from him, but damn it, he was driving me crazy.

My bruises were fading quickly, and the pain was tolerable now, but I knew I was still burying my head in the sand when it came to losing my baby and what Asshat had done to me.

"No running, Cyn," Rigid said, pulling the chair back to where it was.

"I'm not running. I just don't need to be sitting in your lap," I sniped, plopping down in the chair.

"Trust me, if I wanted you in my lap you'd be there," Rigid said, taking a drink from his beer and dropping it in the cup holder.

"Caveman Rigid is here, I see," I said.

"You've no idea, beautiful," Rigid said, winking at me.

"Alright fuckers, she's got testicle toss and corn hole," Slider said, walking back from the garage carrying the two ladders for testicle toss (since that was what Slider had renamed ladder golf). He had the balls hanging on his neck with Turtle following behind carrying the two boards for cornhole (also known as bean bag toss.).

"Fuck yeah. I'm in," Crowbar said throwing his empty plate in the garbage and helped Slider and Turtle set up.

"You want to be my partner, beautiful?" Rigid asked.

"Oh, so I actually get a choice? What if I wanted Slider to be my partner?"

"I'd say we need to get your head checked out again. You might still have a concussion if you'd rather be with Slider than me," Rigid said pointing to where Slider was gesturing for Turtle to suck his dick.

"I think I might be better on my own," I laughed, watching Turtle tackle Slider to the ground.

"Stick with me, beautiful. I'm the king at testicle ball," Rigid said, getting up from his chair. He wrapped his arm around my shoulders and pulled me to him.

"I guess if I have to be partners with you," I said, smirking at Rigid. I tucked my broken arm around his back, wrapping my good arm around his waist.

"Alright fuckers, divide up," King called.

"Come on, beautiful," Rigid said, guiding me over to one side of the Testicle Ball Toss.

Demon and Python teamed up, Slider and Turtle were still slugging it out on the ground so I assumed they were partnered together. Gravel was talking to Gambler about strategy (was there really any strategy to testicle toss and corn hole?), and Roam and Hammer were quickly chugging their beers, not making eye contact with King. King was the only one standing without a partner.

"King sucks at sports,' Rigid said, chuckling under his breath. 'No one ever wants to team up with him."

"You're all a bunch of fuckers," King grumped, walking over to the case of beer and pulling one out.

"He can't be that bad," I said, feeling sorry for King.

"Babe, every time we play testicle toss he somehow ends up losing at least two up in a tree or telephone wire." Rigid handed me the red set of balls and walked over to the other set of ladders.

I looked up at the telephone wires that ran across the back of my yard, wondering how the hell King could get them up that high.

"He tell you about the telephone wires?" Gambler asked, taking the blue set of balls off the ladder.

"Uh, yeah. I don't see how he can get them up that high. The ladders are only four feet high." I pondered, looking from the ladder to the sky.

"Neither do I, babe. But I've seen it happen." Gambler smirked.

I looked at King, who had moved his chair closer to the game, but I could still tell that he was pouting. "That man,' I pointed to King, 'can't get this,' I held up the two balls connected by a rope, 'on that?" I asked Gambler, nodding at the ladder in front of us, amazed.

"You don't want to know, darlin'." Gambler laughed.

"I'm assuming copious amounts of alcohol had to do with the telephone wire incident," I said, watching King chug his beer, pouting.

Gambler winked at me. "Don't all the good stories involve copious amounts of alcohol?"

"You're probably right," I muttered under my breath.

Gambler took the first turn, and I looked around my yard. Rigid and Gravel were on the other side from Gambler and me, while Demon and Python were playing corn hole against Roam and Hammer.

Slider and Turtle were off the ground and were pulling up chairs next to King to wait for their turn.

"You're turn, darlin'," Gambler mumbled to me.

I tore my gaze from the oddness that had taken over my yard and focused on the game.

Maybe this was going to be my new normal. Hanging out with a motorcycle club.

Oy.

Chapter 18

RIGID

"Knock it off or I'm going to knock you out with my cast," Cyn yelled across the yard.

"Bring it on, darlin'," Gambler goaded her as he threw the balls again, wrapping it around the wrung of the ladder.

"This is rigged. You rigged this!" Cyn bellowed.

Cyn and I were playing our third game against Gravel and Gambler. They had kicked our asses the last two times, and Cyn was determined to at least beat them once.

"Un-fucking-believable," Cyn said as Gambler wrapped the last one on the rung, ending the game and beating our asses again.

"Rigid, you suck!" Cyn said, pointing her finger at me.

"Beautiful, I did all I could," I laughed, enjoying the way Cyn had relaxed, throwing attitude around.

"You were supposed to make up for the fact I can't throw worth a shit thanks to this fucking cast.' Cyn said to me. 'Rematch in two weeks when I get this fucking thing off," Cyn said to Gravel, waving her cast around.

"It's a date, darlin'. I look forward to whipping your ass again," Slider said, grabbing the last beer from the case and throwing the empty box into the fire.

All the other brothers were sprawled out in lawn chairs surrounding the fire. It was going on eleven o'clock, and we had managed to finish that last game by the light of the campfire.

"You gave us a run for our money, sweetheart," Gravel said plopping down into a chair, and popping open a beer.

There was only one chair left open. I grabbed Cyn, pulling her over to the chair, sitting down on it and pulling her onto my lap. She had four wine coolers while we were playing so she was a bit on the tipsy side and willingly came to me.

I nestled her into the crook of my arm and wrapped my other arm around her waist. She had been close to me all night but just out of arms reach. I needed to touch her.

"Don't blow smoke up my ass, Gravel. You whipped our asses," Cyn said snuggling into me.

"Next time we should play for money," Gambler said from across the fire.

"I'm too poor for that shit," Cyn said as she drained her drink and threw it next to out chair.

"I won't let you lose too badly," Gambler winked at Cyn.

I let out a growl, warning Gambler to lay the fuck off Cyn. She elbowed me in the gut, giggling and whispered, "He's harmless."

"You mean shameless, beautiful." I nestled my nose in her hair, inhaling deeply. I would never get enough of her.

"What time is Meg going to get here?" Slider asked King.

"An hour. She was going to give me a call to see if the party was still going on when she got off work." King replied, getting up from his chair and stumbled to the edge of Cyn's lawn to take a piss.

"I think she's going to have to come pick up your drunk ass," Turtle chuckled.

"You fuckers wouldn't let me play fucking testicle toss, so I had to find something to do. Drinking and sexting Meg worked for me," King boomed across the yard.

"Oh jeez," Cyn mumbled, burying her face in my neck.

"Aren't you too old for that shit?" Hammer asked.

"Fuck no,' King said, zipping up his fly walking back to the fire. 'I feel like a goddamn teenager with Meg. Aren't you told old to not have common sense?" King shot back at Hammer.

"Fuck you," Hammer said.

"Nice comeback," King laughed, popping open another beer.

"I figured you had to have been texting Meg all night with that shit eating grin all over your face with your nose in your phone," Slider said as he threw another log on the fire.

"Jealous again?" King slurred. He really was drunk.

"Hmm." I heard Cyn hum. She nestled further into my arm, throwing her legs over mine and curled up in a ball.

"Tired?" I whispered into her ear.

"Yeah," She mumbled.

"Want to go in?"

"No, I want to wait for Meg to get here."

"You're going to be asleep before she gets here. You can see her later, beautiful."

"Just let me sleep here," Cyn whispered, her eyes fluttering closed.

I held Cyn close, enjoying the feel of her body in my arms and let her sleep. Her face was relaxed, a small smile playing on her lips.

"You know what you're doing with her?" Gravel asked from across the fire.

"Not a fucking clue. I just want her to trust me," I replied, talking low so not to wake Cyn.

"Keep doing what you're doing. She just needs you to be there for her," Gravel said.

"What, are you fucking Oprah now?" Slider joked.

Gravel flipped off Slider, shaking his head at him. "What are you even still doing here, Slider?" Gravel asked.

I glanced at King to see if he was listening. He had his phone out, clumsily texting or more than likely sexting.

"What are you doing here, Slider?" King asked, still staring at his phone.

"Collinsworth is getting old. I need some excitement." Slider said.

"You can always head out with me, brother," Roam suggested.

"Nah, I just need a fresh start. Collinsworth pussy is drying up. I've tapped everything there and don't want to go back for seconds." Slider crushed his can and threw it at the trash can, missing.

"They good with you leaving Collinsworth?" Demon asked.

"Yeah, they're down with it. They have five prospects that are going to be patched in in the next couple of months. They're trying to get some fresh blood in the chapter."

King nodded his head, finally looking up from his phone. "We'll have to vote on it, but I don't see why it'll be a problem. Plus, I won't be drunk off my ass. Demon, remind me about this shit tomorrow. I doubt I'm going to remember any of this shit. Shit." King tended to overuse the word shit when he was drunk. One time I counted him using it ten times in one sentence. He was definitely good entertainment when he drank.

"Fuck me. With King and Rigid off the market, I was finally getting my share of the pussy. Now if fucking Slider moves up here I'm back to getting sloppy seconds again," Turtle said.

All the brothers laughed, knowing Turtle was speaking the truth. Pussy wasn't into prospects too much. "You'll get patched in soon enough," Demon said, hinting at the fact that Turtle was due to become a full member. Turtle had passed his year of prospecting, and I knew it was only a matter of weeks till King brought the vote to the table of making Turtle full member.

Cyn shifted in my arms, curling her body around me. I leaned down, brushing her hair out of her face, and placed a kiss on her forehead.

"Endgame," King said, watching Cyn and me.

I looked up at him, knowing exactly what he was talking about. Cyn was my endgame. "Endgame," I said, agreeing with King.

Cyn was mine.

<<<<<<<<

Cyn

I woke up, nestled under my comforter and pressed against a colorful wall of hard, muscled, tattooed chest. I tilted my head up to Rigid but stopped when I felt wetness under my cheek.

Shit. I drooled all over Rigid in my sleep. Oops. I wiped my mouth and Rigid's chest with my hand, hoping for a hole to open up and swallow me. Drooling all over the guy you like isn't really the way to get him to notice you.

I finally tilted my head up all the way, thankful to see Rigid was still sleeping. I smiled, loving the fact he looked so content in his sleep. I felt the scar on my face, pulling the skin tight. I knew it was healing quickly by the fact my face felt tight and itchy around the stitches.

I lightly scratched around the scar, trying to relieve some of the itchiness.

"Careful, beautiful. You don't want to rip that back open," Rigid warned, surprising me that he was awake. His voice was scratchy and sexy from sleep, yum.

I stopped itching, laying my hand on his chest, tracing the rose he had over his heart. "Is this for your mom?" I asked.

"Yeah. I remember roses were her favorite, although she loved all flowers. She always had roses, though," Rigid said, placing his hand over mine.

"What was her name?" I asked.

"I've never talked to anyone about my mom, let alone told anyone her name," Rigid said, looking down at me.

"It's ok if you don't want to tell me," I whispered, afraid I had crossed a line, asking his mom's name.

"It's ok, beautiful,' Rigid said as he brushed my hair back. 'Her name was Charlotte."

"You should put her name right here." I drew a line under the rose with my finger.

"You think?" He asked.

"Yeah. I'll come with you. I can get my lotus flower when you go."

"There's another tattoo I want to get, too. Where are you going to put your lotus flower?" He asked.

"I was thinking on my right shoulder. What do you think?"

"Where ever you want it is good, beautiful," he said, running his fingers up my arm.

"Where the heck would you put another tattoo? You're basically covered," I said, looking at his chest.

"My neck. That way everyone can see it."

"What are you going to get?" I asked, curious what he would want everyone to see.

"You'll have to wait and see beautiful," he said, leaning down, pressing a kiss to my forehead.

"You're such a tease. You won't tell me your name, who gave you the scar, and now you won't tell me what tattoo you are going to get," I humphed, annoyed.

"I told you if you guessed the right name I would tell you if you were right. You keep guessing crazy, off the wall names."

"Well, you told me it was embarrassing. I figured it wasn't anything typical like Adam or Alex."

"Keep guessing, beautiful," Rigid smirked.

"Axel?" I guessed.

"No," he said, chuckling at me,

"Abraham?"

"Nope."

"Adonis?"

"Wasn't he a god?"

"Yes."

"You calling me a god?" Rigid laughed.

"No. Not at all. Me just suggesting that name has gone straight to your head, Augustus."

"Nada."

"Alfredo?"

"Isn't that food?"

"Maybe. I blame the fact I'm hungry for that one," I giggled.

"Negative on the Alfredo,' Rigid chuckled. 'Although I will feed you, beautiful."

"Arrick?"

"No. Now get up so I can feed you," Rigid said, spanking me on the ass and slid out from underneath me.

I laid my head on the pillow, watching Rigid stretch, enjoying the show.

"Why is my chest wet?" Rigid asked, wiping his chest with his hand.

I busted out laughing, as Rigid screwed his face into a grimace. I apparently didn't wipe all my drool off him. Whoops…

"This is you, isn't it?" Rigid asked, holding his hand up to me.

All I could do was nod my head, laughing too hard to answer.

"Classy, beautiful," Rigid said, winking at me. He grabbed his pants from the back of my chair where he must have put them on last night, and shimmed into them.

"I'm the classiest chick you know. Well, besides Meg," I said.

"You got that right. You and Meg are definitely in a class of your own. Now, up. I'm starving." Rigid ordered.

I slid out of bed, my feet touching the floor and I realize I don't have any pants on. I looked down, realizing I didn't have the same shirt on either. "Give yourself a little show last night, Rigid?" I asked, shaking my head at him.

"Hey, in my defense, you were lucid, somewhat. I asked if you wanted me to change your clothes and you said yes. I can't help it if you were too drunk and tired to remember," Rigid held his arms up in the air in innocence.

"Mhmph.' I shook my head at him, laughing. 'Did Meg ever make it last night?"

"Yeah, the second she got here King was all over her. She basically opened the door to her truck, and King was on top of her. She shoved him over to the passenger side, and they took off. I'm sure they'll be back today to get his bike."

"Good. It's Friday, right?" I asked, pulling on a pair of capris.

"Yeah, beautiful."

"Yay! I'm starting to remember what day it is.' I giggled, grabbing my favorite tee. 'Turn around."

"Cyn, really? I fucking undressed you last night." Rigid ran his hand through his hair, his fingers getting stuck in the gunk he put in it every day.

"I was passed out when you undressed me, even though you say I was lucid.' I rolled my eyes at him. 'Go do your hair or something." I ordered, shooing him away.

"Fucking crazy, beautiful," Rigid said, walking out of my room headed for the bathroom.

I yanked my tee over my head, my cast getting tangled in it. I yanked it the rest of the way off and threw it in the hamper. I shoved my casted arm through my vintage Betty Boop tee when my phone started blaring "Honky Tonk Bodonka Donk", also known as Meg's ringtone.

"What's up, chica?" I asked, wedging the phone in-between my head and shoulder.

"You need to come over, like ten minutes ago." Meg frantically shouted into the phone.

I rammed my other arm through my tee and pulled it over my head quickly, knocking the phone to the floor. I quick picked it up holding it up to my ear "What? Why?"

"Remy is on the way home, and Lo is in the shower. I tried to shove Lo out the door when Remy texted saying he was on the way home, but Lo said no and jumped in the shower. Hello! You need to come over. NOW!" Meg shouted.

"Meg, calm down. You knew this was going to eventually happen. You love Remy, you love Lo, and they'll love each other."

"No. You don't understand. Lo is the furthest thing from Hunter.' I cringed. Ugh, Hunter. Douche canoe supreme. 'Remy has never been around someone like Lo. Remy hunts and fishes and you know, I can't think of anything else, but you get the point. Lo doesn't do any of those things. What are they going to have in common? You have to come over and be a buffer. Distract Remy. Bring Rigid. He can distract Lo. Come now."

"Meg, I don't think -." All I heard was a dial tone. I threw my phone on the bed. I grabbed a pair of shorts out of my dresser and tugged them on. Digging through my closet,

I found a pair of flip flops, shoved my feet into them and headed to the bathroom to get Rigid.

"Open up!' I yelled, banging on the bathroom door. 'We have a rescue mission."

Rigid threw open the door, his shirtlessness taking my breath away. My gaze traveled up his chest, stopping at his nipple piercings. Oh, those nipple piercings. I licked my lips, imaging what they would feel like against my tongue.

"Beautiful, keep licking your lips like that and the only rescue mission you are going on is the one to free my dick from my pants," Rigid growled.

My eyes snapped to Rigid's, my thoughts interrupted. "We need to rescue Meg," I said.

"Why? What trouble did she get herself into now? King can help her."

"King is her problem. Well, Remy too," I mumbled.

"Explain," Rigid said, stepping out of the bathroom, grabbing my hand and pulling me down the hallway to the kitchen.

"Remy is on the way home from his dad's to Meg's house, and King is there. She's freaking out."

"Why is she freaking out? Is she hiding King from her kid?" Rigid asked as he filled the coffee pot with water.

I shut the water off and grabbed the coffee pot out of his hand. "Not time for that. We can hit the drive through on the way. Remy knows about King, but Meg is freaking out because King is the complete opposite of Hunter, her ex, and Remy's dad. We need to go." I walked back to the bedroom with Rigid following me.

I grabbed a shirt from his bag with the Devil's Knights insignia on it and threw it at him.

"I want breakfast too," Rigid grumbled as he pulled his shirt on.

"Deal. Can we take your bike?" I asked, secretly begging he said yes.

"You think you can hold on with a broken arm?" Rigid asked as he shoved his feet into his boots.

"Yeah. I can manage."

"OK. Change your shoes first, beautiful. Sandals aren't good on a motorcycle," Rigid ordered.

I shot to my closet, totally ok with Rigid making me change my shoes and grabbed my white canvas sneakers out. I quickly put them on and tied them up.

"Little excited about riding on my bike, beautiful?" Rigid asked, smirking at me.

"Just a little," I giggled. I grabbed his hand and pulled him down the hall and out the front door.

"We can't stop and get coffee on the bike unless you are up for drinking it there which will delay your rescue mission." Rigid handed me a helmet and swung a leg over the bike.

I quickly snapped the helmet on and climbed on behind Rigid. "Meg has coffee. Plus she can cook us breakfast for making us come over so early."

"It's ten-thirty," Rigid laughed.

"Oh, well. Whatever. Just drive," I said, excited for my first ride on Rigid's bike.

"Hold on, beautiful," Rigid said right before he cranked up the bike.

The bike rumbled to life, vibrating through me. I wrapped my arms around Rigid, holding on tight.

He kicked the kickstand up, and we rocketed out of the driveway. "Take the long way!" I yelled over the roar of the engine.

Rigid shook his head, and I knew he had a big smile on his face. He gunned the throttle, and we took off.

I really didn't care where we were headed as long as I was on the back of Rigid's bike, I would go anywhere.

Chapter 19

RIGID

I was camped out on Meg's couch with Cyn snuggled under my arm while Meg and King were making breakfast.

Having Cyn wrapped around me on the back of my bike was beyond fucking heaven. I took the long way to Meg's house, and it was still too short. For a split second, I seriously considered driving past Meg's house and driving till I ran out of gas or the nearest hotel.

The second we pulled into the driveway, Meg shot out of her house, frantic. Remy still hadn't shown up yet because Meg had texted him with a bogus list of things she needed from the store to hold him up.

"Who wants a mimosa?" Meg yelled from the kitchen. Although she really didn't need to yell, there was only a half wall between the living room and the kitchen.

"I'll take one," Cyn said.

"Beer,' I grunted. 'None of that girly shit."

I heard a car pull into the driveway and knew the show was about to start. I know King heard the car, but neither of the girls did.

King smirked at me, also anticipating what Meg was going to do.

Meg was clinking ice cubes into wine glasses when the front door opened, and her kid walked in.

"Remy!" Meg shouted, as her dog, Blue, bellowed and ran into the bedroom. That mutt was definitely not a good guard dog.

"Hey, mom. What the hell was up with that list you texted me? Toothpaste, Pringles, chicken livers, and beer nuts?" Remy mumbled as he juggled the bags in his hands.

"Oh, you know. Just trying to think of things we need around the house," Meg lied.

"Lord knows you can't be without chicken livers and Pringles," Cyn snickered. I turned my head to the side, smothering my laugh into my shoulder.

"Hey, Cyn. How ya feeling?" Remy asked as Meg grabbed the bags out of his hands and took them into the kitchen.

"A lot better. I basically slept the past two weeks." Cyn said, smiling up at Remy.

"How's the arm? I still remember when I broke mine when I was seven," Remy said as he sat in the big ass puffy chair across from us.

"I remember when you broke your arm. I can't believe that was ten years ago already," Cyn said.

Meg walked in the living room with King behind her. She handed Cyn and me our drinks and turned to Remy. Fuck, this was going to be entertaining.

"Uh, Remy, there's someone I want you to meet.' Meg held her hand out to King, and he stepped to her, taking her hand. 'This is Lo, or you can call him King. Lo, this is Remy, my son." Meg held her breath like she was waiting for the end of the earth.

"Hey," Remy said to King.

"Hey, good to meet you," King replied.

"You're dating my mom?"

"Yeah."

"Cool. That you're bike out front?" Remy asked.

"Nah, I had too much to drink last night, and your mom had to come pick me up. My bike is over at Cyn's. That's Rigid's bike out front." King said, pointing to me.

Meg elbowed King in the gut. "Don't tell him you drank too much," she hissed at him.

"Babe." King rumbled at her, shaking his head, smirking.

"So you're dating Cyn?" Remy asked me.

"No," Cyn said.

"Yes," I said at the same time as Cyn.

Remy laughed at us. Apparently, Cyn and I were the entertainment now.

"We're just hanging out," Cyn said, taking a drink of her mimosa.

"I didn't know sleeping in your bed with you was just hanging out now," I whispered so only Cyn could hear me.

She choked on her drink and started hacking up a lung. "Asshole," she hissed back.

"You making breakfast, mom?" Remy asked.

I sniffed the air and smelt something burning. "Shit!" Meg shrieked as she ran back to the kitchen.

"Well, that went better than I thought," Cyn said.

"She was freaking out about this wasn't she?" Remy asked.

"I don't think freaking out is the right word. Panic attack might better describe how your mom has been for the past hour since you texted," King laughed.

"I figured out something was up when she texted me the shopping list," Remy said, looking at King.

I could tell the kid was sizing up King, figuring out if he was good enough for his mom.

"You part of that new motorcycle club in town?" Remy asked.

"Yeah. I'm the president, and Rigid is my Sgt. at Arms. We just moved here a couple of months ago," King said, leaning against the wall by the TV.

"Nice. You guys opened up the new body shop, right?" Remy leaned forward, resting his elbows on his knees.

"Yeah. King runs the front end, and I see over the back end. I'm one of the master painters." I said.

"Awesome. I remember when mom was restoring her truck, and she let me help, I really liked doing it. You guys need any help? Mom has been on me about getting a job."

"I can't let you do any painting or anything like that, but you could help with all the prep work," King said, as he grabbed the beer Meg brought him. She stood next to King, leaning into him.

"Did you just get a job in the two minutes I wasn't in the room?" Meg asked.

"Hell yeah," Remy said, sitting back in his chair with a shit eating grin on his face.

"Are you sure? You don't have to so this," Meg said, facing King.

"Babe, remember what I said? Nobody makes me do something I don't want to."

"As long as you're sure, it sounds good to me," Meg said, beaming at King.

King leaned down, brushing a kiss against Meg's lips and she froze. Her eyes bugged out, quickly looked around the room and booked it back to the kitchen.

"Mom!" Remy yelled.

"Uh, yeah?" Meg said.

"You know I'm seventeen, right?" Remy called.

"I think I was there when you were born, Remy. I can count how old you are," Meg sassed back. Even talking to her own kid, she threw sass. King definitely had his hands full with her.

"Then you should know I've kissed my fair share of girls, and I've seen dad kiss his girlfriends in front of me. You don't need to run in the kitchen, freaking out. I'm fine."

"Babe, come here," King called.

I could see Meg, her back turned to us as she shook her head, no. "I want a redo on this whole day, Lo," Meg whined.

"Meg, come here, please," King asked. I could tell he was getting annoyed.

Meg walked in the living room, her arms crossed over her chest pouting. King wrapped his arms around her, holding her close.

"Remy, you ok with me dating your mom?" King asked.

"Treat her good and I don't have a problem with it," Remy replied.

Cyn snickered next to me. "Meg is the child right now. I love this," Cyn snorted.

I press her close, kissing the side of her head. "Shhh, beautiful," I whispered.

"Hurting your mom is the last thing I would ever do. We good?"

"Dude, we never had a problem, but, yeah, we're good," Remy replied. He picked up the TV remote and turned the TV on, obviously done with the conversation.

"Go make breakfast, babe.' King turned Meg in the direction of the kitchen, giving her a little pat on the ass. 'Cyn needs to eat."

"I'll help," Cyn offered, hopping up off the couch. From what I could see from the couch, Cyn wrapped her arms around Meg, talking low so only Meg could hear her.

"Fucking worried about nothing," King grunted, sitting on the other end of the couch.

"What did she think was going to happen? Chicks are crazy," I muttered.

"Not a fucking clue, brother," King said, shaking his head.

"Is this what I have to look forward to with Cyn?" I questioned.

"More than likely. Like you said, brother, chicks are crazy.' King took a long drink from his beer, propping the bottle on his leg. 'I wouldn't change anything about her, though. All the crazy talk about donut houses and worrying about her kid liking me makes Meg, who she is."

"Do you guys want pancakes or waffles?" Meg asked from the kitchen.

"Waffles!" Remy shouted.

Meg looked at King and me over the half wall of the kitchen, her hand propped on her hip. "What about you two? Waffles ok?"

"Good with me," I answered.

"Whatever you want to make, babe, I'll eat. You know that." King rumbled at Meg.

"K," Meg whispered, turning back to the stove.

Cyn had hopped up on the island and smiled at Meg. Those two really did have each other's backs. I was happy that Cyn had a friend like Meg.

Being around the clubhouse pussy all the time, I never really saw chicks sticking up for the other pussy in the clubhouse. It was basically a dog eat dog world when it came to women in the clubhouse. Maybe Meg and Cyn would change that.

I know the parties would never stop, but maybe with Cyn and Meg around, more of the brothers would start to settle down.

I knew Cyn had settled me down, and I had barely touched her. I couldn't imagine what would happen once I nailed Cyn down and made her mine. She had gone through a lot of shit with her ex, but I really don't think that it broke her as much as she thought. With the support of her friends and me around, there was no way she was going to get lost.

I had found her, and I wasn't going to let her go.

Chapter 20

Cyn

"When do you think you are going to come back to work? You think you can drive a forklift with a broken arm?" Meg asked as we walked out onto her front porch.

We had eaten breakfast, and it was now going on three. After breakfast, we all sat around shooting the shit. Meg had finally relaxed about King meeting Remy and was back to acting like her quirky self.

"I have to get a checkup tomorrow, so I am hoping the doctor will be able to tell me when I can come back. I'm sure Cal is freaking out without me there." I replied as I grabbed the helmet Rigid handed me.

"*I* need you back. Especially without Troy being there, I'm all alone." Meg pouted.

I strapped the helmet on and climbed on behind Rigid. "I'll call you tomorrow and let you know what I find out. Who knows, I might be back Sunday."

Rigid nodded to King and Remy and cranked the bike up. "Come over and get your bike whenever. Cyn and I won't be home for a bit."

"Where are we going?" I asked.

"You'll see, beautiful," Rigid said. He backed up the bike, and we rocketed out of Meg's driveway in the opposite direction of my house.

I awkwardly wrapped my arms tighter around Rigid, leaning in. "Tell me where we are going," I said again.

"Just enjoy the ride. It's going to take about an hour to get there." Rigid said. He grabbed my good arm and laced his fingers through mine. I relaxed into him, my casted arm resting on his thigh.

We glided along country roads, neither of us talking. Partly because I would have to scream over the roar of the bike for Rigid to hear me and also because I loved surprises.

After forty-five minutes of driving, we pulled over for gas. While Rigid was filling up, he told me to run to the bathroom because he didn't think there was a bathroom where we were headed.

As I was walking out of the bathroom, Rigid met me half way and held out his hand for me to take.

"What's in the bag?" I asked, looking at the plastic bag he had dangling from the fingertips of his other hand.

"Dinner. Not as good as anything you can make, but it will do." Rigid assured me as we walked to the bike. I grabbed the helmet that was dangling from the handlebars.

Rigid stuffed the bag into his saddle bag, and we both climbed on. "How much longer till we get where ever the hell it is that you are taking me?" I asked as Rigid started up the bike.

"Twenty minutes," Rigid replied as he kicked the kickstand up and we took off down the road again.

I held on tight, snaking my hand under his shirt, stroking his firm stomach. I leaned forward, placing a kiss on the back of Rigid's neck. He stiffened, and placed his hand on mine, holding it in place. "Be careful of what you're doing, beautiful," Rigid called over the roar of the wind and engine.

I placed another kiss on his neck, telling him I knew what I was doing. He grabbed my hand, placing it high up on his thigh so I could feel his growing cock underneath his jeans.

I stroked his cock, the bulge growing bigger with every touch. Kissing his neck more, I pressed my breasts fully against his back, enjoying the solidness of him against my body.

"Beautiful,' Rigid growled, 'keep that up and we're not going to make it where I really want to take you. I'm going to find the nearest hotel and let you do that the proper way without going sixty miles an hour down the road." He grabbed my hand, resting far away from my fun.

"To be continued," I whispered in his ear.

I felt his body shake with laughter and smiled. We turned down a two-lane road lined with trees and I enjoyed the shade from the sun.

I thought back over the three weeks, and my grin got even bigger. Spending all the time with Rigid had made me realize Rigid was more than what he seemed.

Sure, he was a big, hunk of an intimidating man, who knew what he wanted and did whatever he wanted, but there was more to him than that.

He never left my side when I was in the hospital. He let me cry all over him not once, but three times when I couldn't tell which way was which and the only thing that made sense was to cry.

It had been almost two months since Nick had cheated on me. Almost a month since he left me on my living room floor broken and alone, but Rigid had come along and put the pieces together without me really noticing.

Except there was one piece that was still missing and I didn't think that one would ever be put back. I had lost my baby. I had only known for two weeks that I was pregnant and had never gotten to the doctor before Nick had hurt me.

It had never really sunk in that I was going to have a baby, but it still hurt.

Tomorrow I had a doctor's appointment set up and planned to talk to the doctor about losing the baby and if I had any lasting effects from what Nick had done to me. I may not be ready to have another baby right now, but I did want to have kids one day.

We turned down a dirt road that opened up to a lake at the end. Rigid parked next to the shore and swung off the bike. "Does this thing have a radio?" I asked.

"Yeah, beautiful. Take this,' Rigid said handing me the bag of food and a folded up blanket, 'and I'll turn it on."

I swung my leg over the bike and grabbed the bag and blanket from Rigid. I spread the blanket out closer to the shore and started taking out the food Rigid had picked up from the gas station.

Laying out the two prepackaged sandwiches, two bags of chips, and a couple of candy bars, when a twangy country came pouring out of the speakers from Rigid's bike. "I never figured you for liking country," I said, sitting on the blanket, watching Rigid walk towards me.

"It's the only thing that I could get to come in half way decent. I normally have Black Stone Cherry or Pop Evil playing when I paint." Rigid laid out on the blanket and leaned back on his elbows with his legs stretched out.

"Hmm, you and Meg would get along well when it comes to music. She listens to all those plus some." I sat on my knees, my hands resting on my thighs, looking down at Rigid. God, he was gorgeous. His sunglasses were propped up on the top of his head, a lazy smile playing on his lips.

His black tee was stretched across his chest, his cut hanging open and the bottom of his shirt riding up, exposing a glimpse of is stomach.

"That's good, beautiful, but Meg isn't really what I want to talk about right now," Rigid said.

"So what do you want to talk about then?" I questioned.

"You," Rigid smirked.

"What about me?"

"You've never really talked about that night, beautiful. I'm worried that you're keeping it all locked inside you." Concern laced his voice.

"I told you everything that happened."

Rigid grabbed my hand, tugging me closer. "I need to know that you're ok. You're healing on the outside, but what about on the inside?"

"I'm not sure what you want to hear? I guess I'm ok. I hate Asshat. I never thought he would do anything like that to me. I planned on spending the rest of my life with him. It's shocking to think that you know someone, and then you realize you don't."

"You told me that night what he said to you.' I nodded my head, remembering how pissed I was at Rigid that night. 'Did you know he felt that way about you?"

"No. I mean, he never really fawned over me about my looks, but it wasn't like he talked shit to me or anything. I thought we had a good relationship while we were together. Looking back on it now, I did all the work to keep us together, and he just did whatever he wanted. He didn't like Meg or Troy either. That should have been my first clue that he wasn't any good. Meg tried to warn me off from him, telling me that he reminded her of her ex, but I was too young and stupid to listen to her. I thought I knew better. Obviously not," I humphed.

"Do you care what happens to him?" He asked me.

"No. I hope I never see him again. His sister was a complete bitch. I heard she just got a job at the same place Meg, Troy and I work. That is going to be interesting. Hopefully, she won't be on my shift." Bree from work had texted me this morning letting me in on that little gem of information. I was looking forward to going back to work until I heard that.

"You think she will give you any problems?"

"Lord knows. We got along, for the most part, but I saw what she would do if you were not on her good side. Cherry is not someone you want to mess with."

"Cherry?" Rigid asked.

"Yeah. Tall blonde, big ass tits, and, unfortunately gorgeous." She really was pretty. Bitch.

"Fuck. You got to be fucking kidding me."

"What? You know her?" Please don't let her be someone from Rigid's past. I know with him being part of the club, there were always available girls around, but I didn't know Cherry hung around the club.

"She just started hanging out at the club the past month. King had a little run in with her the night Meg ran away from him." Rigid recalled.

"Oh my god! King slept with Cherry!" I shrilled horrified.

"I'm not saying, darlin'. If it happened, it was before he met Meg. I know he didn't the night Meg saw them. It was all a misunderstanding that night." Rigid tugged my arm, and I fell down next to him, my head resting on his shoulder.

Fuck. I didn't want to know, but I needed to ask. I know if he had slept with her, I couldn't hold it against him because we weren't dating or anything, but it was still going to hurt if he had slept with Cherry. "Did you ever, you know, um, sleep with Cherry?" I timidly asked.

"No.' I breathed a sigh of relief, grateful. 'But I'm not a saint, beautiful. If you ever come to the clubhouse for a party, you are more than likely going to end up meeting women I've been with."

I didn't say anything. I felt my chest tighten, hurt from the fact I would meet women from his past. I was confused, though. Did I have a right to be hurt when I wasn't Rigid's girlfriend? Were we dating? Or were we just a hookup?

Rigid had said he wasn't going anywhere, but for how long? That was the same problem Meg had when she had first met King.

She waited for the day he would leave her because she didn't think she was good enough.

Meg had issues that I don't have, though. I knew who I was and, although I knew I wasn't the most beautiful woman, I knew that I looked good. At least, I would when all my bruises faded. My face was basically healed and unless you saw me naked, you couldn't tell that I had been beaten. My stomach was taking longer to heal, but even those bruises were fading more and more each day.

"What are we, Rigid?" I hesitantly asked.

"Honestly?"

I tilted my head back to look at him. His eyes were pointed down at me, and we just stared at each other.

"Are we anything at all?" I whispered, afraid of the answer.

"We're more than I've ever had."

"Does that mean we're dating?" I guessed, shocked by his words.

"It means you're mine. That first night I saw you at your anti-bachelorette party, I wanted you. It may have only been that I only wanted you in my bed, but I still wanted you. Knowing you now and seeing everything you've been through and how you somehow made it out stronger than you've ever been, has made me want you forever."

"What if I'm not ready for that?" I admitted.

"Then we do whatever you are ready for. If all you want is a friend right now, that's all I'll be."

"What if I want more than a friend?" I whispered, afraid to say the words out loud.

"I'll be whatever you want, Cyn. Just tell me."

"I want you to kiss me." I didn't hesitate. I knew exactly what I wanted from Rigid. He wanted me to be his and I wanted him to be mine.

We leaned into each other, meeting halfway. His lips brushed against mine, the breath I had been holding rushed out, relieved to finally feel his lips on mine again.

He gently pushed me onto my back, his hand coming up, caressing my face. "I don't want to hurt you, Cyn. If you want me to stop, all you have to do it tell me. I promise," Rigid vowed.

"You couldn't hurt me if you tried, Rigid. You may be rough around the edges sometimes, but I know deep down, under all this muscle, badassery, and blue hair, you'd die before you would hurt me.' I snaked my hand up his arm, grasping the back of his neck and pulled his lips down to mine. 'Kiss me." I whispered, my lips a breath away from his.

Rigid gazed down at me, not moving. "What did I do to deserve you?" He asked, his eyes going lazy.

"You were there when I needed you, even though I didn't know I needed anything," I whispered.

"I'll always be there," he vowed.

"Prove it." I closed the gap, pressing my lips to his.

Rigid took over instantly, his lips hard and demanding. I ran my hand down his back, grasping the hem of his tee and tugged it up.

"Fuck, you taste so good," Rigid rumbled against my lips. I whimpered, missing the touch of his lips even for a second.

I reached up with my broken arm, trying to reach his face and I can't bend it enough to touch him. "Put your arm down, beautiful. You'll knock me out with that thing," Rigid grunted as he lowered his lips back to mine.

"I want to touch you," I mumbled against his lips.

"Shh," he whispered, silencing me with his kiss. His kiss was demanding, taking everything I had to give. His tongue slipping in my mouth, tasting and teasing.

I heard Rigid growl, his hand sliding down my neck, caressing my breast, making my body arch up, begging for more.

"More,' Rigid rumbled, ripping his lips from mine. Leaning back on his knees, he ripped his shirt off, throwing it towards our dinner that had been forgotten. 'I need to feel more of you."

I sat up, running my hand over his rock hard abs, traveling up, flicking his nipple. I moaned, wanting more too. I quickly folded my legs under me, so I was mirroring Rigid, both of our hands resting on out thighs, not touching.

"I want to taste you. I need to feel you on my tongue," I confessed as I leaned forward, my fingertips touching his nipple piercing.

I hesitantly snaked my tongue, taking a taste of Rigid. The instant my tongue touched the hard metal, I know I never wanted to touch another man. Rigid growled above me, and goose bumps sprang up all over his body.

Reaching up with my hand, I played with his other piercing as I licked and sucked, enjoying the control I had over Rigid with just a few touches.

"Fuck me, I've been praying for the day you would do that." Rigid moaned, his hands caressing my back, pulling my shirt up, bunching it up in his hands.

Breaking contact with Rigid, I grabbed the hem of my shirt and ripped it over my head, throwing it behind us. "Yes," Rigid said as he eyes went liquid with desire, his hands clenched at his sides.

"Touch me, Rigid. I need to know you want me," I pleaded, knowing if he looked at me for one more second, I would combust from the desire and need he stirred up inside me.

Rigid unclenched his fists, flexing his fingers as his eyes continued to devour me. He touched my shoulders, trailing his fingers down my arms. "Two more weeks till this comes off?" Rigid asked as he grabbed my fingers that were sticking out of the cast and lifted them to his mouth, kissing them.

I nodded my head yes, unable to form a coherent sentence. I couldn't wait till I got the fucking thing off. It had been driving me insane. I couldn't tie my shoes, along with about fifty other things and now I just added touching Rigid to the list of things it was fucking with.

I pushed on Rigid's chest, knocking him onto his back, crawled on top of him and straddled his waist. I heard the sounds of birds chirping, and it pulled me out of the moment. "Shit, Rigid! What if someone comes down here?" I shrilled, panicked as I tried to cover myself with my arms. I twisted around reaching for my shirt that I had just tossed off. Jesus, what the hell was I thinking? Whenever I was around Rigid, it was like I forgot about everything else and only saw him.

"Beautiful, stop. No one is going to come down here. It's a private drive and lake," Rigid said as he grabbed my hand and pulled me back to him.

"How do you know that? The owner might come down here or fuck, I don't know, drive-by on his boat.' Rigid laughed, his body shaking underneath me. 'Stop! I'm serious!" I shouted.

"Babe, Gravel owns this. I texted him, asking if I could come up here for a little bit. He barely comes up here since we've gotten the garage going and now with working on the strip club, it'll be awhile till he gets up here. He plans on building a house here in a couple years. We're the only ones here. Promise," Rigid assured me.

I looked around, noticing there was no house in sight, and you couldn't see the main road from where we were. "How the hell does Gravel own a whole fucking lake?" I asked.

"Something about it being family property. We never believed him till he showed it to us when we moved up here. It's pretty fucking amazing here."

"It is,' I agreed, as I gazed down at Rigid. 'You're sure we are alone?"

"Yes. Gravel is the only one who knows we are here,' he said as he placed his hands on my hips, his hands spanning my side and held me in place.

"So what are you going to do with me?" I asked as I ran my fingers down his chest, flicking his nipple.

"Ever been skinny dipping, beautiful?" Rigid asked as I tweaked his nipple piercing.

"No.' I said as I leaned down and kissed my way up his stomach, my final destination his piercings I couldn't get enough of. I ran my tongue over them, hearing Rigid's breathing get shallow with every flick of my tongue. 'Is that why you brought me here?"

"I brought you here because I wanted to be with you away from everyone. I love that you have Meg in your life, beautiful, but fuck me, I just want you to myself sometimes." He ran his fingers through my hair, cupping the back of my head and pulled my lips to his.

"My sweet Rigid," I whispered against his lips.

"Ashly," he mumbled.

"What?" I asked pulling away from him. What the hell was he talking about?

"Ashly. That's my name, beautiful," he said again.

I sat back on his legs and looked down at him. Rigid just told me his name. After a month of guessing and playing around with it, he just spits it out, surprising the hell out of. "Ashly?" I ask.

"Yeah. Ashly," he smirked at me. He could tell I was in shock that he had just told me his name. Asshole.

"Why did you tell me?" Yup, Rigid finally tells me his name, and I ask him why he told me. I don't know what was wrong with me.

"I wanted to hear that out of your lips when you asked me to kiss you."

"What's your last name?" Probably something I should have found out sooner but hell, I didn't know his first name all this time.

"Marks."

"Middle name?"

"Nathan."

"Ashly Nathan Marks. I like it. Why don't you?"

"It's not exactly a guy name, babe. At least not the Ashly part," he grumbled under his breath.

"Can I call you Ash instead? Ash kicks ass." I smiled.

"Ash, huh?" He rubbed his chin, his eyes locked on mine.

"Please," I pleaded. I wanted a name for Rigid that was all mine. I loved how King only let Meg call him Lo. I wanted that with Rigid.

"All the guys are going to give me shit about my name if you call me Ash in front of them," he reasoned.

"Punch them. That will shut them up." I giggled.

Rigid laughed, his body shaking undermine. "Call me Ash, beautiful. If it makes you happy I can live with the shit, they'll give me."

"Thanks, Ash," I said, testing his name out. I smiled, loving that I knew his name. Finally.

"You're welcome Cyn."

"I'm kind of going to miss guessing your name. Although I was going to have to just start naming objects that started with A. Apple was going to be my next guess." I laughed, leaning down, placing a quick kiss on his lips.

"You're fucking loony, beautiful." He followed my retreating lips, threading his hands through my hair and pulled me down, flush on top of him.

"I'm happy," I whispered before his lips touched mine. He claimed me with that kiss. Branding me, making me never want to feel anyone's lips beside his. His tongue danced with mine, begging for more. I moaned, wrapping my arm behind his neck, threading my fingers in the back of his Mohawk.

I pulled on his hair, wanting more. He growled, his hands sliding to my ass, squeezing and pulling me closer. "I can't get enough of you," he mumbled in between kisses.

I ran my lips down his neck, nibbling on his ear. "Neither can I, Ash," I whispered in his ear.

"Only you, Cyn. Only you," he vowed. He rolled us over, my lips sealed to his.

"I think I'm lying on a sandwich." I giggled against his lips, feeling a lump underneath my ass.

Rigid rolled me onto my side, pulling the squished sandwich from underneath me, throwing it to the edge of the blanket, and rolled me back on my back. His lips devouring me. I moaned, running my hands down his back, hooking my fingers into the waistband of his jeans.

"You have too many clothes on," I said, thrusting my hips up, begging for more.

"So do you, beautiful, but you need to put your shirt back on. The first time I sink into your lush body, I want it to be in your bed, not on a blanket in the middle of nowhere." He placed one more kiss on my lips and pulled away. He grabbed his shirt, pulling it over his head.

I laid frozen, wondering how the hell he just switched it off like that. One minute we were both going crazy and the next he's pulling his shirt on, telling me we were going to wait. Really? "What just happened?"

"I realized you're better than a roll in the hay, or grass, I guess. We eat and then we go back to your house. Just putting our plans on hold for an hour or two, beautiful." He grabbed my hand, pulling me up.

I sat there staring at him. "Two hours, tops. That's all you've got till I jump you and take what I know you want to give me."

"Deal, darlin'.' He handed me my shirt and a sandwich. He sat back, grabbing the chips, ripping them open and set them in between us.

I awkwardly pulled my shirt over my head, once again praying for the day that I would have this fucking cast off.

Sitting Indian style, I opened my sandwich and took a big bite of it. "Eat fast," I said, my mouth full.

Rigid laughed and shook his head at me. "Try that again without your mouth full." He chuckled.

I swallowed and grabbed one of the sodas. I popped the top and took a drink. "Fuck, that shit is dry,' I grimaced. 'I said eat fast."

Rigid also grimaced as he took a bite of his sandwich. I laughed as he twisted around and spit it out. "How the fuck did you swallow that?" He asked, grabbing my soda, downing half of it.

"It wasn't easy," I laughed.

"Pack this shit up. We'll stop and get something on the way home." He grabbed the plastic bag, holding it open and I threw everything inside. He stood up, looking down at me. Fuck, he was gorgeous.

"Did we really just almost have sex with our shoes and pants still on?" I giggled, taking in what had just happened between Rigid and me.

"Yeah, I think so. I was about ten seconds from coming in my jeans, just from having your hands on me." Rigid marveled, running his hands through his Mohawk.

"Why a Mohawk and why blue?" I asked, handing him the bag, standing up and started folding the blanket.

"Fuck if I know. Just cut it that way one day and decided I liked it.' He ran his hand through his hair, ruffling it. 'Why blue? Hell, all last year it was green. I just pick a color and go with it."

I tucked the blanket under my arm and looked at Rigid. I couldn't picture him with a green Mohawk. Hell, I couldn't picture him with a regular haircut. "I like it," I stated as if my opinion mattered.

"Good to know, beautiful." He smirked and grabbed the blanket and headed back to the bike. He tucked everything in the saddle bags and swung onto the bike and held the helmet out to me. I grabbed it, quickly strapped it on and climbed on behind him.

"We can just eat at home," I suggested, wrapping my arms around him.

"Eager to get home?" He laughed as he cranked up the bike.

"Just a little." I giggled.

"A little over an hour and you're mine, beautiful," Rigid promised before heading back the way we came.

I held on tight the whole way home, realizing things had changed. I guess Rigid hadn't said the exact words that we were together, but what else could 'mine' mean?

I watched the fields and houses fly by as when cruised down the country roads and never felt more content or safe in my life. I might just have found my happy ending.

Chapter 21

RIGID

I pulled up to Cyn's house, and King was leaning on his bike, arms crossed over his chest with a pissed off look on his face. Fuck, what the hell had happened now?

I parked next to him, and Cyn hopped off quickly, taking her helmet off and handed it to me. I hung it on the handlebars and swung off the bike.

"What's up?" I asked.

"Well, I tried calling you about twenty minutes after you left Meg's house.' I reached into my pocket where I always had my phone and felt nothing. I patted down my other pockets not finding it either. Fuck. 'Called you about twenty times until Remy walked out of the house holding your fucking phone, saying the damn thing was going off like crazy." He tossed it to me, and I snatched it out of the air.

"Shit, sorry, brother. It must have fallen out of my pocket earlier." I shoved it in my pocket and folded my arms over my chest. I knew something must be up for King to come and track me down.

"Meg's in the house if you want to go inside, Cyn. Mickey and Crowbar should be here in a couple minutes." He said to Cyn, dismissing her.

Fuck, this was not good. Cyn threw me a concerned look and then headed to the house. The screen door slammed shut behind her, leaving King to tell me what the hell was going on.

"Got a call from Troy," he said.

"What did he have to say? Something going on with the Assassins?"

"Yeah. He said from the rumblings he's been hearing around town, it sounds like something is going to go down tonight. He thinks they might be trying to move Asshat. He's not for sure, but he feels like if we are going to make out move, now is the time," King said.

"We leave tonight?" I asked.

"As soon as Mick and Crow get here, we head to the clubhouse. While you were off the fucking grid with your woman, I've been getting things ready. Gravel, Ham, Demon, and Gambler are waiting for us to get there. Slider headed up as soon as I got the phone call from Troy. He just called, said things definitely felt off up there. Pack some shit and let's head out." King turned to the house and headed in.

Son of a fucking bitch. Of course, just when I almost get things nailed down with Cyn, I have to leave town. I ran my fingers through my hair and looked at the house. Cyn was standing at the screen door, looking out at me. I motioned to her to come out and watched her walk to me. She walked straight into my arms, wrapping herself around me. "You have to leave, don't you?" She whispered.

"Yeah, beautiful. I need to take care of things," I mumbled into her hair. I inhaled deep, burying my nose in her sweet smell.

"Be careful. I think we just found each other, Rigid, and now I'm afraid I'm going to lose you before I really get to be with you."

"Nothing is going to happen to me. I promise," I vowed, hearing the concern in her voice.

"There goes our plans for tonight." She pouted.

"Raincheck, beautiful," I said, holding her tight. She relaxed in my arms, tucking her head under my chin. I didn't want to leave, but I didn't have a choice. The sooner I knew Asshat was taken care of, the sooner I could breathe easier.

"How long are you going to be gone?" She asked.

"Hopefully only a day or two."

"I plan on cashing that raincheck right away," She whispered into my chest.

"I'll text you when I'm ten minutes away so you can get ready." Her body shook in my arms as she laughed.

"OK.' She leaned back, looking me in the eye, smiling. 'You pack, and I'll make you something to eat. Your attempt at dinner before didn't really hit the spot."

I kept my arm slung over her shoulder, her body tucked under my arm, and we walked into the house. I headed down the hall to her bedroom to pack my bag. I shut the door behind me and leaned up against it.

Looking around her room, I could see that it had become our room. My things were mixed in with hers. The last time we had gone to the grocery store, she had insisted on picking up a box of blue hair color and had planned on dyeing my hair for me. She was crazy. I told her I just mixed it up, smashed it into my hair and took a shower twenty minutes later. After she had wiped the horrified look off her face, she informed me I was doing it the wrong way and insisted she would do it from now on.

There was a basket of clean clothes Cyn had brought in the bedroom two days ago that had not been put away yet. I really doubt it ever would. We both had just been digging through it, finding what we wanted and left the rest.

I rummaged through the basket, pulling out three black tees and tossed them on the bed. I grabbed two pairs of jeans out of the closet, tossing them on the bed next to the tees and grabbed some socks and shit out of the drawer and quickly filled my bag.

I headed to the bathroom, grabbing my toothbrush and hair shit, tossed it on the top of my clothes and zipped the bag up.

"Rigid! It's done," Cyn called from the kitchen.

I slung my bag over my shoulder and headed down the hall towards Cyn. Stopping by the bedroom door, I took one more look at the bed, wishing I didn't have to leave Cyn. This was the first time in my life that something was more important than The Devil's Knights.

Cyn had become more important than anything in my life. Cyn was my rock, my desire, and religion. I was nothing without her. She became my compass in the dark, my everlasting light. She was mine.

Cyn

I had two big roast beef sandwiches on a plate, and a bag of chips open next to it. I had been nibbling on the chips, trying not to worry about the fact that I wasn't going to be with Rigid. He was leaving me. The longest he had left me since the attack had only been hours at a time, with him texting me numerous times.

I had just called to him that it was done. I grabbed the bag of chips and hopped up on the counter.

After my tenth chip and telling myself that I wasn't really hungry and was only eating because I had no idea what else to do, Rigid walked into the living room, tossing his bag by the door and made his way into the kitchen.

I pushed the bag of chips away and wiped my hands on my pants. He grabbed his plate I had set on the kitchen counter and walked over to me. He pushed my legs apart and stepped in between them. Setting his plate next to me, he rested his hands on my thighs and looked at me.

"You going to be ok while I'm gone?" He asked, concern in his voice.

How did he know that I was worried about him leaving? I thought that I had hidden my disappointment well when he had told me outside. I grabbed the edges if his vest and pulled them together. "I'll be fine.' I lied, plastering a smile on my face. He had enough to worry about with going after Asshat, he didn't need to worry about me on top of that. "I'm sure Meg will be here a lot. Don't worry about me. You need to concentrate on what you need to do."

"Call me if you need anything, beautiful. I'll always answer if I can. Leave a message if I don't answer. I don't want you to worry about me at all," he said softly as he ran his hands up my thighs, cupping my waist with his hands and gave me a gentle squeeze.

"I won't worry about you, as long as you promise you won't worry about me." I offered, knowing that I would totally worry about him until he was back.

"Deal," he said as he pressed a kiss to my forehead.

I relaxed into his embrace, loving the feel of his arms wrapped around me, making me feel safe.

"Ready?" King asked as he came slamming back into the house with Meg following close behind him.

"Yeah," Rigid croaked, his voice sounding like he was trying to hold on so he didn't break. I knew exactly how he felt. He was only going to be gone for a couple of days, but it felt like my heart was going to be taking off down the driveway with him. This was crazy. How could I feel so strongly for someone I had only known for a couple of months?

"Mick and Crow are outside," King said. He pulled Meg into his arms, ravaging her with a quick kiss and headed back out the door.

"I'll be back," Meg mumbled as she walked down the hallway. I heard the bathroom door shut and Meg quietly sobbing. Fuck. I didn't want Meg to be sad. King was leaving her all because of me. I wished I had never met Asshat. Things would have turned out so differently.

Rigid glided his hand up my arm and caressed my neck, turning my focus back to him. "I've got to go. Be careful while I'm gone. Take Crow or Mick with you wherever you go until I tell you things are taken care of. I don't want anything else to happen to you."

"I will." I leaned forward, pressing my lips to his, wanting to taste him one more time before he left.

He threaded his fingers through my hair, coaxing my lips to open with a swipe of his tongue. I held into his biceps, savoring the feel and taste of Rigid. "Ash," I moaned out, as he pulled away from me.

"I love when you call me that, only you can ever call me that," he growled as he claimed my lips again, brutally branding me. I ran my hands down his back, pulling the hem of his shirt up so I could feel the warm flesh of his back.

I pressed myself tight against him, not wanting to let go. I heard a bike crank up outside and knew it was only a matter of time before King or one of the other guys came in, wondering where the hell Rigid was.

He pulled away from me, gently placing kisses down my neck and finally pulled away. "Say it again, say my name," he growled at me.

"Ash," I whispered, loving the sound of his name.

"Only Ash from now on. You have Ash, no one has ever had him before. He's all yours," he vowed.

All I could do was nod my head and feel the tears stream down my cheeks. He wiped them away with his thumb and placed one last kiss on my forehead. He turned away, grabbed his bag from by the door and looked back at me. There was so much I wanted to say, but none of it would come out. It felt too soon to be feeling these feelings, but yet they were still there, begging me to say them.

"Bye, beautiful," Rigid said and walked out the door. I heard his bike crank up, joining the roar of King's. I ran to the screen door, hoping to get one last glimpse of Rigid before he left.

King and Rigid roared down the driveway with Mick and Crow watching. "I love you," I said to the glass of the door. It was too soon for me to feel that, but it felt right. I turned away from the door and walked over to the couch.

Crow and Mick walked up to the door and knocked. I laughed, finding it hilarious there were two bikers on my front step, politely knocking, asking to be let in. "It's open," I yelled as I flipped the TV on.

"You hungry?" Meg asked as she walked past the couch and into the kitchen.

Mickey and Crowbar grunted yes as they both pulled up stools to the island, watching Meg dig in the fridge. They each grabbed one of the sandwiches I had made for Rigid and finished them in four bites each. It was amazing how much food these guys were able to put away.

"What about you, Cyn? Hungry?" Meg asked as she pulled cheese, milk, and more cheese out of the fridge. She walked to my tiny pantry and pulled out a box of elbow noodles.

"Mac and cheese?" I replied as I got up from the couch and headed to the kitchen to help her cook.

"Yeah. You know I cook when I need a distraction," Meg mumbled as she grabbed a big pot out of the cabinet.

"What else are you going to make?" Crowbar asked.

"Pork chops?" I suggested as I looked in the freezer.

"Fuck yeah," Mickey said, wiping the crumbs off is chest from the sandwich he had just demolished. I grabbed the pork chops out and set them in the microwave to defrost.

Turning away from the microwave, all eyes were on me. "What?" I asked.

"You ok?" Meg asked, as she turned to the sink and filled the pot with water.

"Um, I think so?"

"Don't worry about King and Rigid, babes. They know what they are doing. They shouldn't be gone for more than a couple of days," Crowbar said as he got up from his stool and headed for the fridge. He grabbed two beers and sat back down. Crowbar and Mickey popped the tops to their beers and looked at Meg and me.

"Has this happened before?" Meg asked.

"You know I can't tell you anything, darlin'. King told us you were going to try and pump us for any information," Mickey chuckled.

"Asshole," Meg mumbled under her breath. Both guys burst out laughing, and I smiled at Meg.

"I'm sure you know more than I do," I said, trying to pacify her.

"Humph, doubtful. Fucking Lo distracted me, and I was too far gone in the Lo Daze to remember that I was supposed to be pissed at him.' Meg slammed the pot full of water on the stove, sloshing water over the sides. 'I don't know shit."

Crow, Mickey, and I burst out laughing as Meg flipped us all off and turned back to the stove, ignoring us.

"It'll all be ok, darlin'. Nothing either of you needs to worry about," Crowbar said, reassuring Meg and me.

My phone dinged with a new text message, and I pulled it out of my pocket. It was Rigid.

Miss me yet? He asked.

I smiled, loving the fact he had not even been gone an hour and he was already texting me.

Who is this? I texted back, laughing as I punched the letters.

The last man you'll ever kiss.

Oh, now I remember. ;) I wrote back, thinking he couldn't be more right.

Don't ever forget, beautiful. I'm headed to church. I'll text you when I get to Fall's City.

Be careful. I like you the way you are. Are you sure you can't come home? I walked over to the couch and plopped down, helping Meg forgotten.

Shit needs to be done. I'll see you soon. Miss me.

It's hard not to. <3

I waited five minutes to see he would text back, but he didn't. I tucked my phone into my front pocket and flipped the TV to Sons of Anarchy. Crowbar and Mickey ambled into the living room, Mickey taking the recliner and Crowbar sitting on the opposite end of the couch.

"I've watched this whole series, at least, three times. Shit never gets old," Mickey said, popping up the chair, kicking his feet up and reclining back.

"Beat ya!' Meg yelled from the kitchen. 'I think I've watched them all, at least, ten times."

"Whatever, babe," Mickey chuckled.

I grabbed the blanket off the back of the couch and wrapped it around me. I laid down at the end of the couch, curling up into a ball, my eyes trained on the TV, but I didn't see the show. I thought back on the last month, wondering when I feel in love with Rigid.

Was it when he bought me my new boots? When he let Meg and I tease him about his name and not get upset with us for making fun of him? Or was it that first night back in my house when he had woken me up from my nightmare and stayed with me the whole night? Could you really fall in love with someone that fast?

I pulled the blanket up to my chin and tucked it under my arms, my head the only thing sticking out. I scanned my living room, noticing the small changes since Rigid had been staying with me.

His spare pair of motorcycle boots were sitting by the door, my motorcycle helmet was hanging off a coat hook hanging on the wall, and one of his tees were hanging on the back of the kitchen chair.

Rigid had somehow worked his way into my life and house. He was everywhere, and I hoped he never left.

Chapter 22

RIGID

I shoved my phone in my pocket, shaking my head. Fucking Cyn. She thought it was hard not to miss me, she had no idea what I was going through.

All I wanted to do was hop on my bike, shoot up to Fall's City, take care of Asshat and be back in Cyn's bed before dawn. Except I knew that wasn't going to happen.

"Church, now," King yelled from the clubhouse door.

I walked through the door and straight to my chair to the right of King. All the other brothers filed in and took their chairs.

"Alright. I just talked to Troy. He said Slider just got into town, and they are both keeping their eyes on the Assassins. Troy has been talking to people around town who have seen Nick around town. He doesn't come out often, but he has been seen. Troy has only physically seen him once."

"So what makes Troy think that they are planning on making a move tonight?" I asked.

"For the past three days, there has been a lot of traffic going in and out of their compound, more so than usual. Word has it that they are planning on moving further up north and expanding their operation west. Troy said if they move Nick, it's going to take a lot to find him again. It took Troy almost three weeks to find out this much. We need to make a move now or wait even longer to figure out where they are moving to," King informed us, his hands steepled in front of him, his eyes looking over everyone.

"Alright, so, what's the plan?" Gravel asked.

"We leave now. I left Crowbar and Mickey with Cyn and Meg. I want Python, Whiskey, and Hammer to stay here and look over the clubhouse and shop. Everyone else is headed to Fall's City. Edge called ahead and found us a place to stay. It's off the beaten path so that the Assassins won't know we are there until we want them to know. Pack light, brothers. I don't plan on this taking more than a day or two." King walked out of church, headed straight to his room. Everyone filed out, either to pack a bag or to the bar.

I headed to my room, shutting the door behind me and walked to my closet. I opened the doors and moved a pile of clothes and three boxes out of the way and reached up to the back of the shelf and pulled down a small, black case. I unlocked it, and pulled out my .40 cal, and grabbed an extra clip. I checked to make sure it was loaded and put it in the waistband of my jeans at my back. I pulled my cut and shirt over it, making sure it wasn't visible.

I grabbed two extra white tees out of the dresser and headed back out to my bike. I walked past the bar, watching some of the brothers taking a shot before we hit the road. Normally I would be there right alongside them, but I wanted my head clear.

Walking out the door, I saw King and Swinger filling their saddlebags and making sure they had everything. I shoved my tees and extra clip into my saddlebag and swung my leg over my bike.

I waited, sitting on my bike, counting the minutes till we left.

It had taken ten minutes before all the brothers were ready to go and on their bikes. I flipped my glasses down off the top of my head, and we all cranked up our bikes. It was like thunder was attacking our little town. I revved my bike, ready to get this done. King motioned, raising his hand above his head, circling his hand for us to head out.

King took off first with Demon and I following behind. The rest of the brothers fell in line behind us, riding alongside each other two by two.

It was time to fix a wrong that had been done to Cyn, and then I was heading home to her, right where I belonged.

<<<<<<<<

Cyn

"Cyn! Wake up!" I heard as my body was being shaken violently. I quickly snapped out of my sleepy fog and saw Meg above me, frantically trying to wake me up.

"Knock it off, Meg," I grumped, wrenching her hands off of me.

"Jesus Christ, Cyn, you were fucking screaming like the god damn house was on fire. I've been trying to wake you up for the last ten minutes." Meg sighed as she plopped down on the bed next to me.

"Sorry," I muttered.

"Are you ok?" She asked as she shoved a pillow under her head.

"Just a bad dream. I haven't had one like that since the night I came home from the hospital. Maybe watching all that Sons before bed wasn't the best idea," I said, trying to downplay the fact that my dream had scared the living shit out of me.

"Hmm, when I watch Sons before bed, all it does is give me sweet Opie dreams." Meg hummed, a goofy smile on her lips.

"You're crazy.' I laughed. 'You can head back to bed, I promise not to scream anymore. I'm exhausted," I lied. I was wide awake and sure that I wasn't going to be able to fall back asleep, at least not tonight.

"Ok, I'll leave your door open. Just holler if you need me," she mumbled as she got up, flipped the lights off and headed out the door and back to the guest bedroom.

I reached over and turned on my bedside lamp, illuminating the room with a soft glow. I leaned back into my pillows and tried to calm my heart that was still racing.

Nick had been strangling me in my dream, and I hadn't been able to get up. I saw Rigid behind Nick's back, but he just stood there, watching Nick hurt me. I kept screaming in my dream for Rigid to help me, but he never moved closer to me, just watched, an impassive look on his face. I had no idea what the hell the dream meant, other than the fact that I obviously wasn't over what Nick had done to me.

I grabbed my phone, looking to see if Rigid had texted me. He had texted me at nine thirty 'Here' and that was it. I had texted him back, asking him where he was staying, but he had never answered. I would have been worried except for the fact that Meg had gotten a call from King, and she had asked me if Rigid was OK. King had told her he was fine but busy. She didn't ask any more questions so that was all I knew.

I threw my phone on the bedside table, seeing that Rigid hadn't texted and grabbed the TV remote. I turned on a mindless infomercial about the newest rage in cleaning and hoped that sleep would come, or Rigid would call.

Rigid never called, and sleep never came.

Chapter 23

RIGID

I was in a smoky bar, sitting next to Troy, wishing I was back in Rockton with Cyn. My phone had died right after I had texted Cyn we had made it and it was now back at the hotel charging.

Troy had heard that some of the Assassins men were going to be at The Wet Seal tonight so that lead me to now, having to act friendly with Troy while keeping an eye out for anyone who looked like an Assassin.

I was at a disadvantage not knowing what Nick looked like, so that was why Troy was with me so he could spot him if he came in.

"Hey, there handsome, you looking for some fun tonight?" A blonde asked as she crowded her way into my space, trying to climb into my lap. Normally I would be all for this chick, but now that I had Cyn and knew what she tasted like, nothing would do but her.

Blondie wrapped her arms around my neck and pressed her tits into me. I looked over her shoulder and saw Troy laughing at me and tipped his bottle at me. Douchebag.

"Not interested," I grunted, grabbing her arms and set her away from me.

"One dance, please." She pouted, swaying her hips to the music.

I shook my head no at her and turned my attention to the other side of the bar, hoping she would get the point I wasn't interested. I finished off my beer and motioned to the bartender for another. I saw the blonde flounce off and breathed a sigh of relief she didn't put up a fuss.

"Man, hard life with chicks just throwing themselves at you," Troy chuckled.

"Yeah, except when you aren't interested. Then it's just fucking annoying," I said as I grabbed me a new beer.

"So, what's the deal with you and Cyn?" He asked as he peeled the label off the bottle of his beer.

"I think the better question is what is between you and Cyn?" I countered. That fucking hug he gave her a couple of weeks ago still bugged the shit out of me.

"Nothing to tell. Fuck, there's more to tell between Meg and me, then there is Cyn and I. Cyn liked me when she first started working at the plant. I wasn't into her, and she got over it pretty quick. I'm more close to Meg than I am Cyn, but I still care for her," he said as he chugged down half of his beer.

"That was then, what about now?"

He laughed, setting his beer down and wiped his mouth with the back of his hand. "Still nothing."

"Keep it that way," I growled.

"So now answer my question. What is going on with you two? She's been through a lot, she doesn't need any more shit in her life."

"She's mine. That's all you need to know."

"For how long?" He scoffed.

"Till I fucking die," I bit off, glancing around the bar, noticing a few newcomers in the bar.

"Not him," Troy said.

"What the hell does this fucker look like?" I asked.

Troy smirked, finishing the rest of his beer. "The complete fucking opposite of you. I think the only thing ya'll have in common is that you're both tall fuckers."

"So I'm looking for someone tall. That's about three-quarters of the guys in here," I mumbled, annoyed with Troy's less than stellar description.

"Brown hair, light tan skin, skinny like a fucking pole. Not a fucking clue what Cyn saw in him."

I set my empty beer down and turned my stool towards the door. There was a bouncer at the door checking

ID's and scoping out the chicks as they walked through the door.

A bachelorette party was making its way into the bar, all of them digging through their purses, looking for their wallets. They had dick necklaces and straws sticking out of their shirts, and the bride was wearing a veil and had some banner thing stretched across her chest announcing she was the bride.

"Fuck me. Is that what Cyn and Meg looked like the night of her party?" Troy asked as turned his stool to watch the same show that I was.

"Fuck no. They just looked like a bunch of chicks out for the night, this looks like a fucking circus." I said, watching the bride dump her purse out on the floor, looking for her ID.

"Jesus Christ. Did she really just sit down?" Troy asked, smothering his laugh with the back of his hand.

"Got it!" She screamed as she jumped up from the floor, jumping all over the shit she had just poured out.

A group of guys was behind the bachelorette party, impatiently waiting to get in. I looked them all over, trying to tell if any of them were Asshat, but even with Troy's somewhat better description, it was hard to tell who he was.

"That's him," Troy hissed at the bachelorette party walked past us and the group behind them filed in.

"Which one?" I asked, eyeing them all up. Knowing I was in the same room as the fucker who had hurt Cyn made my blood boil.

"Blue shirt, white hat."

My eyes instantly focused on him, taking in every detail about him. He was a little over six foot, skinny frame with barely any muscle and a buzz cut from what I could see with the hat he had on his head. He looked like your average guy, but I knew what a piece of shit he was.

Troy turned around, facing the bar so Asshat wouldn't see him, but I stayed facing him, staring him down as walked past me. I hadn't worn my cut tonight, knowing the instant he saw it he would know we were here for him.

I had made eye contact with him for a second before the pussy looked away, nervously looking around.

"Call King," I ordered, not taking my eyes off his retreating back as he took a seat at the other end of the bar.

Troy pulled his phone out quickly telling King we had found Asshat and listened as King told him what to do next.

"They'll be here in fifteen minutes. He said to just keep an eye on him and to stay with him if he leaves."

I nodded my head, unable to speak as I saw Asshat grab one of the girls from the bachelorette party and pull her into his lap. She willingly went, too drunk to realize she had her arms wrapped around a douche canoe.

"I'm going to hit the head," Troy said, keeping his back to the other side of the bar and headed to the bathroom.

I looked at the clock above the bar, seeing that it was already past midnight and hoped Cyn was fast asleep.

Asshat let the girl go, slapping her on the ass as she walked back over to her friends. I shook my head, wondering if I was ever like this douchebag. I had had my fair share of the club pussy, but I never treated them wrong. This guy was just a fucking sleazebag.

I cursed myself for letting my phone die. I wanted to check in on Cyn and make sure was ok, but I couldn't. I planned on asking Troy to borrow his phone when he came back to check in on her.

I kept my eye on asshat but took in the other guys he had come in with. They were obviously Assassins. They all wore baggy pants that hung halfway down their asses and shirts two sizes too big.

I made eye contact with one of them and watched him size me up. His gaze traveling over me, taking in my scuffed boots and ripped jeans. I knew that I was intimidating. It was something I loved. One look at me could send a punk running in the other direction without a second glance.

The guy who was sizing me up, spread his legs out, widening his stance, making himself look bigger than he was. I wasn't worried about any of the tools that were in the Assassins. I could take them all and still have enough to take out Asshat.

Troy came back, keeping his back to the Assassins and ordered another beer. I shook my head no to the bartender when he asked if I wanted another. I had already had two. I wanted my head to be clear.

Troy's phone chimed, and he pulled it out of his pocket. "They're here. Parked in the back."

"Good. Now we need to get Asshat out of here and in the back. Any ideas?" I asked.

"I think I got something that might work," Troy said with a sinister smile spread across his face.

"Fuck yeah," I said, eager to get this shit done. Time to take the trash out.

Chapter 24

RIGID

"She was such a fucking bitch in bed, man. I had to beg for her to ever give me head. Fucking Punta," Asshat slurred as he walked arm and arm out the back door with Troy.

Troy's bright idea had been to act as a stumbling drunk and 'accidently' run into Asshat and tell him what an awesome job he had done on Cyn and act like he hated her.

It had worked. Some people were fucking idiots. I had stayed back, not really joining in on the conversation, just acting like a friend of Troy's.

Troy had convinced him to head out back for a smoke. I cracked my knuckles, anticipating what was waiting for him behind the door.

"You slept with her, right?" Nick mumbled as Troy opened the door and they stumbled out. Troy was pretty good at acting drunk.

"Nah, dude. I was never that lucky," Troy said, instantly pulling away from Nick and pushed him into the back alley.

Nick stumbled, one knee going to the ground before he found his balance and stood up straight. He looked around, his eyes growing wide as he took in the circle of Devil's Knights members that were closing in on him.

He tried barging through the circle, but Slider stuck his arm out, clotheslining him, knocking him to the ground. He scrambled backward like a crab, frantically looking around for an escape.

"What the fuck?!" He shrilled like a little girl.

"We are here on behalf of Cyn," King said, his voice a low growl.

"I didn't mean to hurt her. I swear. She told me about the baby and I just lost it. I'm not ready to be a dad,' he babbled. 'She kicked me in the fucking nuts, she asked for it, man. You know how it is."

"No. I don't know how it is,' I said as I walked forward, closing in on him. 'I don't know how it is to beat a woman so badly that she loses her baby, and it takes almost a month for her bruises to heal. Why don't you explain to me how a woman you got pregnant, deserves to have the living shit beat out of her?" I spit out, my fists clenched at my sides.

"You can't do this. I've got the Assassins on my side. You won't get away with it if something happens to me. They've been waiting for you to come."

I laughed, like the fucking threat of the Assassins was going to scare me. "I don't give a fucking shit if you've got the fucking pope on your fucking side. No one hurts Cyn and gets away with it."

"Please, please. I'll do anything that you ask. Just please don't hurt me."

"Please don't hurt me. Please, please," Hammer mimicked, all the brothers laughing.

"The time for begging is over. Now it's time to pay the price for hurting my woman," I said as I grabbed the collar of his shirt, hauling him up and planted my fist in his face.

He grunted out as my fist connected with his face three more times, blood gushing from him nose and mouth.

"The Devil's Knights do not take kindly to any man who hurts a woman. Now, throw in the fact that you hurt one of my brother's woman, well, things are not looking good for you, Nick," King said as he stepped next to me.

I dropped Nick to the ground with a thud, his head smacking the concrete. "Everyone gets a turn, and then you are mine," I walked out of the circle and leaned against the brick wall.

Troy was first, making Nick stand up and then leveled him with one punch. "You were never worth the air she breathed, Troy said and spit in his face.

Each member took their turn, letting Nick know he wasn't worth the air he breathed, let alone Cyn's.

King was the last one, punching him in the stomach lifting him off his feet with the force of his fist, Nick crumbling at his feet.

He groaned low, whimpering in pain. I walked slowly over to him, anticipation rolling through me. I had been waiting what felt like forever for this moment.

I crouched down next to him, his shallow breathing the only audible noise. "This is what Cyn looked like when you left her in her house, beaten and broken. You took away her future with every kick you landed to her stomach. There is one difference between Cyn then and you in this moment right now. You want to know what that is?" I asked.

Nick didn't answer, his breath evening out. "Answer him!" King screamed.

Nick cracked open one bloodshot eye and closed it quickly. "What?" He breathed out.

"She found a new future with me. You, your future ends right now," I vowed.

I stood up and grabbed my cut that Hammer was holding out to me and shrugged it on. I circled around Nick, watching the slow rise and fall of his chest.

I looked around at my brothers, each of them nodding their heads at me, letting me know it was time. "Look at me," I ordered to Nick.

He cracked his eyes open a slit and looked at me. "This is for Cyn," I said as I raised my foot up and stomped it down on his head, his skull cracking against the hard cement.

"This is for her baby you took away from her," I stomped again on his face, my boot crushing his skull even more.

His lifeless eyes were still open, staring up at me, but I knew he was gone. "This doesn't come back on the Knights.' I said, looking around again. 'His death is on my hands."

"No one is even going to know we were here, let alone what you just did. The Devil's Knights have your back, no matter what, brother. You know that.' King said. 'Let's head out."

I looked down at Nick, realizing Cyn was finally safe, and she could put this all behind her. We could all put it behind us.

Chapter 25

Cyn

"Please! Just for a little bit!" Meg pleaded as I filled my coffee cup and sat at the kitchen island.

"Meg, I don't feel like going anywhere. Why don't you just go and then come back here when you are done?" I asked as I stirred my coffee and took a hesitant sip.

"Because you need to get out of the house and I don't want to go by myself. I'd drag Remy along, but he's off with King at the garage working. Please, please, please." She begged.

I rolled my eyes and looked at Meg. Everything was back to normal for her. She told me that Nick would never bother me again, and I had nothing to worry about. She told me the guys had gotten back into town two days ago; two days after they had left.

I hadn't seen Rigid in four days. He had texted me when he had gotten into to town, telling me had some shit to take care of, and he would see me later. I still haven't seen him.

I had no idea what was going on. When he had left, I thought we were a couple or whatever. Now, with Nick taken care of, I didn't see him. Was he just with me before out of pity and to make sure I was ok? Or did he really have things to do? I know for the past month he had really neglected his job and the club so maybe he had a lot of things to check up on.

Last night, I had broken down and texted him, asking when he was going to come over. He didn't answer until I had finally fallen into a fitful sleep with one word, 'Soon.'

That was another thing. I had been sleeping like shit since Rigid had left. I could only sleep for a couple of hours before a nightmare would wake me up and then not be able to fall back asleep. I was living off two to four hours of sleep a night.

"I'm going to try to take a nap. Maybe another time." I lied. I knew I wouldn't be able to fall asleep. The dream that had woken me up at four o'clock this morning was still haunting me, and it was already nine o'clock. This one was sticking with me. I had dreamed the same dream I do every night about Rigid watching Nick hurt me, but this time, it was different. Rigid had disappeared half way through, and Nick had managed to get my pants off. I had woken up, screaming at the top of my lungs as he had slid his hand into my underwear. It felt so real that I felt it had really happened.

Shaking my head, trying to get the lingering dream out of my mind, I closed my eyes and took a sip of my coffee.

"You just woke up. You can take a nap later. I'm just running to the dollar store and then the hardware store. Go get dressed, I'm not taking no for an answer. You need to get out of the house," Meg said as she spun around and filled her coffee cup, essentially ending our conversation.

There was no point in arguing with Meg, so I grabbed my cup and headed to the bathroom and started dragging my brush through my hair.

All the bruises were gone from my face, and I only had a faint scar on my face. I had gone to the doctor a couple of days ago, and he had cleared me to go back to work and told me everything had looked ok.

I had asked him if I would be able to have kids again and he had said there wasn't any obvious reason as to why I wouldn't be able to. He had asked me if I was trying to get pregnant again and I had shaken my head vehemently no, saying I just wanted to know for the future.

My cast was scheduled to come off in a week and then everything from the past six weeks of healing and recovery would be gone, Rigid too apparently. I don't know what had scared him off, but maybe it was for the best. He would have broken my heart eventually so maybe now was a better time for it to happen then a month or a year down the road.

I threw my hair up into a ponytail, knowing Rigid hated when I had it up, which made me put my hair up every day since he hadn't talked to me.

I grabbed a pair of cutoff shorts and my black tank top with the words 'Liar' splashed across the chest, and quickly pulled them on. I shoved my feet into a pair of sparkly flip flops and headed back to the kitchen. "This is as good as it's going to get today," I said, looking around for my cup of coffee. Remembering I had taken it into the bathroom with me, I turned around and quickly grabbed it and headed back to the kitchen for a refill.

"Has he called you at all?" Meg asked as I stirred in creamer and sugar.

"No."

"Has he come over?"

"No." I looked up to see Meg staring at me. Damn pity. I hated it. I didn't want it.

"I saw him yesterday," she said cautiously.

"At least, that's one of us," I whispered.

"I'm sorry, honey. If it makes you feel any better, he looked like hell. King won't tell me anything, but he says that's because he doesn't know anything. Rigid isn't talking to anyone. King said he was fine heading back to the hotel and when they left. But he said something was different when they got back to clubhouse," Meg said, I know trying to make me feel better.

"Well, I guess whatever it is, he's not telling anyone. Let's go." I dumped my coffee into a travel mug and screwed the cover on.

"Maybe he just needs time," Meg said as she slipped her flip flops on.

"Or, maybe it just wasn't meant to be. After taking care of Asshat for me, maybe he realized I wasn't what he wanted. We got thrown together so quickly because of what happened to me.' I opened the front door and headed to Meg's truck. 'You got lucky with King. I honestly don't think there can be too many people like him. Rigid and I just aren't meant to be."

"Stop,' Meg ordered, grabbing my hand. 'You can't believe that. I saw the way he looked at you. He looked just like King does at me. Something had to have happened when they were gone."

I gently pulled my hand out from hers and ran my fingers through my hair. "Maybe, Meg. But I can't help him or make him be with me if he doesn't want me too. He knows where I live, I haven't gone anywhere, he has." I felt a tear run down my cheek and quickly wiped it away. I had been fighting crying over him the past couple of days. He didn't want me anymore. He was done with me, and now I had to figure out how to be done with him.

"Give it time. Please," Meg pleaded.

I nodded my head, wanting the conversation to be over. Meg pulled me into a quick hug and then we both climbed into her truck.

I buckled up and looked out the side window. I wanted Rigid so badly that it hurt, but I didn't think he was going to be there to help ease the pain anymore. The only person I had left to rely on was myself. I was going to fix myself, this time, I just didn't know if I would be able to recognize myself anymore. Cyn might be gone for good.

RIGID

"That Chevelle needs to be done by the end of the week," King said as he walked past me as I was mixing up paint.

"Yeah," I said, screwing the cap back on the Candy Apple red color and put it back on the paint shelf.

"That all you got to say?" King asked, pissed off.

"Not much else to say. You want it done by Friday, it'll be done." I knew what King was talking about, but I seriously didn't want to talk about it.

"You're a fucking ass, you know that right? What the fuck crawled up your ass and changed your mind about Cyn? I got Meg breathing down my fucking neck wanting to know why you dropped Cyn like she was nothing." King threw his clipboard at me, hitting me right in the chest.

"She's not nothing," I said, picking up the clipboard and handed it back to him. King grabbed it and threw it across the paint room.

"What the fuck is your deal?! All you've done since we've gotten back is stay in your room and work. You don't fucking talk to anyone unless it's about work and anyone that does try to talk to you about the club or Cyn you act like you're going to rip their fucking heads off. WHAT THE FUCK IS GOING ON WITH YOU?!" King yelled at me.

I scrubbed my hands down my face, trying to wipe the fatigue and sleeplessness away. I looked at King, his arms crossed over his chest, waiting for an answer. I didn't have an answer that was good enough, though.

After we had climbed on our bikes and back to Rockton, all I had was time to think on the way home. I wanted to go home to Cyn, climb into bed with her and never get out. Something stopped me, though.

"She deserves something better than what I am," I said, finally saying the words out loud.

King threw his head back and laughed. "You're fucking kidding me with this bullshit, right?"

I shook my head and grabbed the color I had just mixed up and headed for the paint booth. I know I sounded like a fucking pussy, but I just couldn't go to Cyn.

"You think she won't want you now that you've got blood on your hands?" King asked.

I stopped in my tracks, my head falling down. "She deserves better."

"Better? What, some douchebag that beats the shit out of her and leaves her for dead is better than you? Or maybe she can find some douche canoe who can be her little whipping boy. You think that's what she deserves?"

"No."

"Then who should she be with, Rigid? If not you, who? You think you can handle her being with someone else? Knowing there is someone else sleeping in her bed at night, giving all those smiles you love to someone else. You can handle that?"

"No!" I yelled, my heart being ripped out of my chest just at the thought of Cyn even thinking about someone else, let alone being with them.

"Then get your fucking head out of your ass and go get your woman before she realizes she can live without you. That's the only thing you're not there is showing her. The more you're not around, the more she'll realize she can make it on her own without you there."

"I'll go over there tonight. I got shit to catch up on around here," I said as I walked into the paint booth and shut the door behind me. I walked over to the bench along the wall and set the paint down, leaning against the workbench, putting my full weight on my arms as I thought about the ass chewing King had just given me. I hung my head down and stared vacantly at my boots, thinking of Cyn.

King was right, but I still felt that Cyn deserved something better. She deserved to be worshiped for the rest of her life. Put up on a pedestal and never be let down.

But son of a bitch, I wanted her more than anything. The past four days had been torture. I would work all day until my hands wouldn't work anymore and then I would go to my room and drink till I passed out. I had thought about getting some pussy to come to me room, but I knew that wouldn't take away the craving and want I had for Cyn. There was only one thing that was going to make me feel better, and that was Cyn.

There was only one thing to do. I had to be what she deserved. I would be the one to worship her and put her on the pedestal she deserved. I would be everything she deserved and more.

She was mine, and no one was going to get her but me.

Chapter 26

Cyn

"I'm starving. Let's hit the drive thru and then we can head back to your house," Meg said as she slammed her door shut and started the truck up.

"Sounds good to me," I mumbled as I buckled my seat belt.

We had hit up the Dollar Store where Meg had reenacted the meeting of Lo and Ethel. She had cracked me up as she imitated Lo's gravelly voice and Ethel's bossy persistence for Meg to come over for lunch. After the dollar store, we headed to the hardware store where Meg picked up a shovel, garbage bags, and a sledgehammer. After the cashier gave us a concerned look and asked us what our plans were for the night, we stumbled out to the truck laughing our asses off thinking the cashier thought we had murder planned for the night, or, at least, burying a body.

"What the hell do you need a sledgehammer for anyway?" I asked as we crossed traffic and got in line at the drive-thru.

"King wants to put a privacy fence up at the house. We picked up all the wood and stuff yesterday, but forgot to get something to help pound the shit into the ground. I told him I would pick something up today," Meg explained as she rolled down her window and rattled off our usual order of tacos and burritos.

"You should put a pool in," I said as I grabbed the exact change out of her ashtray and handed it to her.

"Ugh, are you going to come over every day and put chemicals and shit in it?" She asked as she counted out the change in her hand.

"Um, no. I'm just going to come over and sun my ass and then jump in the pool." I giggled.

"Mmhmm. Just like Remy. There will be no pool, other than the little kiddy one I put out for Blue to plop his butt into." Meg said as she handed the cashier the money.

"Shit," Meg said as I heard change drop onto the ground.

"Let me see if you have any more," I said as I rummaged through her truck.

"How much did I drop?" Meg asked the cashier.

"Looks like two quarters and a dime," The cashier said, obviously not amused by Meg and me.

"All you have is two nickels and a penny," I said as I looked into her glove box and found none.

"I'll just grab this," Meg said as she swung her door open and hit the wall of the restaurant with a sickening thud.

"Oh fuck," I said, watching Meg's eyes bug out of her head.

"Holy shit! I didn't just do that! Oh my God, my dad is going to kill me!" Meg screeched.

"Aren't you like fifty or something?' The cashier asked. 'You seem too old to be worrying about what your dad is going to say."

"Why you little fucking twerp. I ought to grab you-.' I threw my hand over Meg's mouth, interrupting her rant.

"Here,' I said, grabbing a dollar out of my purse. 'Take this." I thrust the dollar at the cashier and removed my hand from Meg's mouth.

"I'm thirty-six you little pencil dick," Meg shouted through the window.

I busted out laughing at the fact that Meg just called a seventeen-year-old a pencil dick.

"Shut up,' Meg snapped as she looked at her door. She slammed it shut, and the latch didn't catch. 'Fuck me. I can't even shut the fucking door." Meg moaned as she tried shutting it again.

"Stop trying, you're just going to wreck it more." I gasped, laughing as she tried again.

"Oh my god! How the hell am I even going to drive! I'm going to fall out," Meg whined as she held the door shut.

"Here's your change and your food," The cashier said, holding the food and change out to Meg.

Meg grabbed the change, handing it to me and then the food, setting it on the seat in between us.

"You might want to get that looked at," The cashier said as he slid the window shut, a smirk on his face.

"Pencil dick!" Meg screamed at the now closed drive-thru window.

"Oh my god. Stop, please," I pleaded through the laughter and tears running down my face.

"I'm a fucking idiot.' Meg said as she held her door shut with her left arm and shifted the truck into drive and slowly drove forward. 'I have to take this to the shop. Hopefully, I can make it that far." Meg said as her left arm slipped on the door and it popped open.

"Oh my god!" I screamed as Meg leaned out to grab the door and swerved, almost hitting a parked car.

"I got it, I got it," Meg said as she barely missed the parked car and held the door shut.

"Maybe you should call King to come and get us.' I giggled, watching Meg steer with her knee and trying to grab food out of the bag. 'Or at least, wait until we get to the garage to eat." I grabbed the bag out of her hand and set it by my feet.

"But I'm hungry, and I just messed up my precious truck, I need to eat. Please!"

I shook my head, still laughing. "Nope. Concentrate on the road old lady."

"Ugh, now I really need to eat. I don't look fifty do I?" Meg asked, flipping down her visor and looking at herself in the small mirror.

"Stop,' I said, flipping her visor back up. 'I don't know how you even managed to flip that thing down without killing us. The garage is five miles from here. Can you control yourself that long so you don't kill us?" I scolded. Meg was a freaking nutbag. One minute ranting about her truck and the next checking herself out in the mirror.

"Only if you feed me, at least, one bite of my burrito. Otherwise, I make no promise not to crash this truck out of hunger pains."

"You're such a pain in my ass, you know that," I said as I grabbed a burrito, unwrapped it and held it up to Meg's mouth. She ripped off a big chunk and smiled at me.

"Ye ke lev wit o ma," Meg said around a mouthful.

"Try chewing and then talking," I suggested as I grabbed my bottle of water and handed it to her.

She swallowed and grabbed the bottle of water as she steered with her knee. "I said, you can't live without me."

"Mmhmm, sure," I said as I held the burrito out for her to take another bite.

In a matter of minutes, Meg had devoured the burrito and my whole bottle of water. "Lo is going to shit bricks when he sees what I did to the truck." Meg worried as she pulled on the main road that headed to the body shop.

"Tell him to take a pill. It was an accident.' I said, digging through my bag looking for a piece of gum for Meg. 'Here," I said, handing the unwrapped piece of gum to her mouth.

"Thanks. I'm sure Lo doesn't want to taste my lunch while I distract him by kissing him when I tell him about my door."

"Solid plan.' I said. 'Jump him and he probably won't even notice you can't shut the door." I joked as we pulled into the parking lot. It was filled with various cars and bikes.

I saw Hammer and Crowbar by the entrance to the clubhouse and gave them a little wave as Meg and I got out of the truck. "Shit, Rigid is here, isn't he?" I said scurrying over to Meg.

"More than likely. Come on, I'll protect you," Meg said, throwing her arm over my shoulder.

"Hey, babe,' King said walking out of the front office of the body shop. 'You pick that shit up I asked you to?" He said, wiping his hands on a blue shop towel and stuck it in the back pocket of his jeans.

"Um, yeah. Except there was a bit of an accident,' Meg mumbled as she walked over to King and placed her hands on his chest and looked up at him.

"You ok?" He asked, concerned. So sweet with Meg. I sighed, wishing I had what they had.

"I'm fine and so is Cyn,' Meg said, throwing a look my way. 'I can't really say the same about my truck, though." Meg mumbled.

I smothered my giggle with my hand as King's gaze travel over Meg's truck, his eyes stopping on the door that Meg had left open. "What happened?" He asked as he walked over to the door.

"Well, I was trying to hand this little pencil dick my change when I dropped it on the ground. Cyn and I couldn't find any more in the truck, so I kind of opened my door, not thinking, and smacked the hell out of it against the building.

Then that pencil dick had the freaking nerve to tell me I was fifty! Can you believe that shit?" Meg shrilled, more outraged over being called fifty then messing up her truck.

"Why did he say you looked fifty?" King asked as he ran his hand over the edge of the door.

"She said, and I quote, 'My dad is going to kill me.' I think he thought she was a little too old to be worried about what her dad was going to say." I laughed.

"Babe, you're a fucking nut," King said shaking his head at Meg. She flipped him off, and he laughed even harder.

"Can you fix it?" Meg said, her hands propped on her hips.

"Yeah, hold on,' King said as he walked back into the office.

"I got to pee,' Meg said, hopping back and forth. 'I'll be right back," she said as she dashed into the office, following King.

I leaned against the front fender of Meg's truck and leaned my head up to look at the sky. It was a beautiful clear day with no clouds in sight. I heard a garage door open, and a car pulled out. The car door slamming and a person walking towards me.

"Cyn."

I knew that voice. I had been praying to hear that voice again. I tilted my head down and came face to face with the man I thought had left me behind.

"Rigid." I breathed out. Fuck.

Chapter 27

RIGID

I saw her tanned legs the second I pulled the car out of the garage bay. She was leaning against Meg's truck looking like a fucking goddess with her head tilted back, looking up at the sky. I was supposed to be pulling the Chevelle out of the body shop bay and into the paint booth, but the instant I saw Cyn, I had stopped the car and gotten out.

I had called her name before I got to her and her eyes connected with mine.

"Rigid." She almost sighed out. I forgot how beautiful she was. She had her hair tied up, and all I wanted to do was tug that fucking tie out of her hair and bury my face in her sweet scent.

"You ok?" I asked, wondering why she was here in Meg's truck.

"Um, yeah. Meg kind of hurt her truck and we had to bring it here. She can't shut the door so it's really not safe to drive it right now," She said as she motioned to the open driver's side door.

I walked past her, moving to the open door and crouched down to look at it.

"There you are," King said as he walked out of the office door.

"Yeah, here I am," I said as I ran my hand over the bent edge and chipped paint of Meg's door. She really had done a fucking number on it.

"Fixable or you think I'm going to have to find a new door?"

"I should be able to bend it back and touch up the clear coat. That's the one good thing about having a patina paint job; dents and scratched kind of blend in." I chuckled as clear coat peeled off in my hand.

"Shit,' Meg said as she walked out of the office door. "You're not supposed to be here," Meg said to me.

"I kind of work here," I replied as I stood up, brushing my hands off on the overalls I had on. It had gotten hot in the paint booth, so I had peeled the arms off and wrapped them around my waist.

Meg curled her lip at me, snarling. "Ass," she spit out at me. Apparently, Meg was still Cyn's pit-bull.

"Babe," King said as he curled his arm around Meg's shoulder, pulling her to him. 'Let's go check the books and see when I can fit you in."

"I know the owner, there shouldn't have to be any fitting me in," she said as she let King steer her back into the office, thrown an eat shit look at me.

"She's a little feisty today," Cyn said as I turned my head towards her, our eyes connecting.   "Just a little." I chuckled.

"Um, I'll just go wait in the office. I don't want to interrupt you at work," she mumbled as she made her way past me, headed for the office.

"Wait,' I said as I grabbed her wrist, stopping her. 'Can we talk for a second?" I asked, hoping she wouldn't tell me no.

Her eyes darted back and forth between the office and me. "Um, just for a second," she said, finally deciding.

"Come on," I said as I pulled her wrist, my hand traveling down so I could intertwine my fingers with hers.

I lead her to the body shop bay I had just pulled the Chevelle out of and hit the button to close the overhead door behind us.

"Do we really have to shut the door?" She asked, watching the door slid down.

"Yeah, there's AC piped into each bay. King throws a shit fit whenever we leave the doors open longer than needed," I explained.

"Oh. So this is where you work?" Cyn asked as she looked around.

I was the only one who had their own work bay that was sectioned off from the other bays. King gave me all the important jobs that needed extra attention. There were two other brothers who painted, but they weren't as good as I was. Whenever there needed to be a mural or special graphics painted, I was the one which King went to. After being off for a month, there was a huge backup of cars that were waiting for me.

"Yeah. Here and the paint booth is where I spend most of my days,' I said as I walked over and grabbed a rolling chair I used when painting pin striping. 'Sit, beautiful," I said, pushing the chair towards her.

She grabbed the chair, sitting in it and rested her feet on the top rung. "What did you want to talk about?" She asked as she bite her finger nails.

"I missed you." I had to say it. She looked so unsure, I had to say the one thing I knew would make her feel better.

"I've missed you too," she whispered.

"Thank God." I breathed out, relieved I hadn't been too late.

"Is that all?" She asked.

"No, beautiful. There is so much more."

"Tell me then," she ordered, crossing her arms over her chest.

"I missed you and the reason I stayed away from you is because you deserve so much more than who I am and the things I've done."

"Shouldn't I be the one who decides what's best for me?" She asked.

"Yes, but you don't know everything I've done Cyn. You don't know the man I used to be." I said as I grabbed an empty bucket and turned it upside down and sat down on it.

"Well, then tell me. That is why you wanted me to come in here so you can talk, so talk. Tell me all the reasons you think that you aren't good enough, and then I can decide if you are what I need."

I rested my head in my hands and looked down at the floor. Fuck, where to even begin. "Nick isn't the first man I've killed."

I heard her suck a breath in, my words shocking her. "Did they all deserve it?" She asked.

"Yes. I've never killed a man who didn't deserve it. But that doesn't make it ok, Cyn. I have blood on my hands that will never wash away."

"Nick is dead," she said, more like a question.

I raised my head up and looked her in the eye. "Yes. I watched the life drain from his eyes, and I would do it over again in a second for the things he did to you. I will never regret taking his life," I said truthfully. Nick was the one who deserved to die the most.

"I'll never hold it against you. I would never feel safe if I knew he was alive somewhere, possibly hurting someone else. I understand why you did it, Rigid. Don't beat yourself over it. King or any of the other guys would have done the same thing."

"How can you be so understanding? I'm a murderer, Cyn," I said, shaking my head. I couldn't believe she was so understanding.

"You're not, Rigid. You are someone who righted a wrong. That is the only way I will ever see you in that situation. You might as well stop trying to convince me otherwise," she said as she crossed her arms over her chest, pushing her tits up.

I ripped my eyes from her chest, trying to concentrate on things I needed to say. "I'm no virgin, Cyn. I've been around the block more times than I can count. I can't guarantee that you won't ever run into a chick that I had been with."

"When was the last time you had sex?" She asked.

"The night before your un-bachelorette thing." Not for a lack of trying, but no one was going to fill the void Cyn had created.

"Seriously?" She asked, shocked.

"Yeah, beautiful."

"Rigid, that's like six weeks. Fuck that's more than six weeks!"

"Trust me, I know," I said as I scrubbed my hands down my face.

"You waited for me," she stated, her voice shaky.

"Fuck yeah, I waited for you, Cyn. I knew you were worth it all after that first night. Even though I fought it, I knew you were the only one."

"I'm not the same girl I was that first night you met me. Nick broke me in ways that are still haunting me. I haven't been able to sleep the past four days," she said as tears streamed down her face.

"Fuck me. Cyn, why didn't you tell me? I would have been over in five minutes. You never had nightmares when I slept with you."

"That's because you held them at bay, you kept them away. You left and that first night you were gone, I woke up screaming and scared the shit out of Meg. I can only sleep for a couple of hours before his face haunts me in my dreams.

I don't know how you did it, but I need you even in my sleep."

"Son of a bitch." I bit out as I dropped my head down, my vision going blurry from the tears I knew were threatening to fall. She said the words that cut right through to my heart. She needed me. Even in her sleep, she needed me.

I heard the wheels of her chair roll and looked up to see Cyn standing over me. "We deserve each other, Ash. I'm not going to let you talk yourself out of being with me. You're not perfect and neither am I. We all have flaws, it's all about how you move on and become the person you were meant to be. I want to move on with you by my side."

"I love when you call me Ash," I said, standing up, instantly wrapping my arms around her.

"I love that you trusted me enough to tell me your name, although I do like calling you Rigid, too. Maybe I'll just call you Ash when you make me extra happy." I giggled.

"I make you extra happy, beautiful?" I asked, leaning back to look into her amazing green eyes.

"Yes, Ash. You make me the happiest I've ever been in my life," she whispered as she leaned up and pressed her lips to mine.

"You're mine," I mumbled against her lips, savoring the taste of her I had missed.

"I'm yours," She whispered back.

I grabbed her ass, hauling her body fully against me, hoisting her up as she wrapped her legs around me. Her fingers delved into my hair, holding my lips to hers. She nipped at my bottom lip, and I opened my lips, letting out tongues dance.

"I need you," she whispered.

I wrapped my arms tight around her and spun around, headed for the work bench. I set her ass on the counter, keeping her legs wrapped around me.

"We can go to my room," I said in between kisses and nips along her neck. Her hands were roaming all over my body, trying to feel everything at once.

"I need you now," she whimpered as her hands grabbed the bottom hem of my tee and pulled it over my head. She threw it behind me and ran her hands up and down my back.

"Are you sure, beautiful?" I asked as she rained kisses down my chest, her hot mouth covering the bar I had running through my nipple, her tongue playing with it.

She raised her head, her face inches away from mine. Her eyes were clouded with desire and lust. I had never seen a more beautiful woman in my life. I grabbed the hair tie she had in her hair and tugged it out. Her hair cascaded down, framing her face.

"I've never been surer of anything in my life," she said, her hands gliding up my chest, her fingers toying with my piercings.

I lowered my lips to hers, claiming her with one kiss.

Fuck me, she was mine.

Cyn

I couldn't get enough of Rigid. His amazing kisses and roaming hands were driving me insane. "Ash." I whimpered, as he trailed kisses down my neck, his head buried in my hair.

"God dammit, Cyn. You taste so good. I need to see you," he groaned as he pulled my shirt over my head tossing it over my shoulder.

He cupped my breasts through my bra, his lips trailing kisses along my collarbone and over the tops of my breasts.

I threw my head back, trying to give him better access. I leaned back on my arms, thrusting my breasts in his face. He reached behind me, unhooking my bra with a skill that I didn't want to know where he got. All that mattered was right now.

He pulled the straps down my arms, and I leaned forward, pulling it off completely and threw it in the same direction as his shirt.

"Yes." Rigid groaned as he lowered his lips to my breasts, raining kisses all over them.

I leaned forward, working the coveralls he still had on, down his legs. He stepped out them, his lips never leaving my skin. Popping the button on his jeans, I slid down the zipper and tugged his pants down.

"Mmhmm, slow down, beautiful," he groaned as I slipped my hand into the waistband of his underwear. He grabbed my hand, stopping my delicious journey.

"Fuck slow. We can do that later. I just want to feel you, please," I begged, as I leaned in, kissing him, trying to distract him.

I sucked his bottom lip into my mouth, loving the taste of him. Nipping his lip, I ran my tongue over it, as he released my hand and drove his fingers into my hair.

I slid my hand all the way in his underwear and cupped his cock. He groaned deep in his throat and thrust his hips into my hand. Stroking him, I felt three hard ridges on the shaft of his cock. I ran my fingertips over them, realizing Rigid had a Jacob's ladder.

"You like, beautiful?" He asked as I pulled away.

"I want to see," I whimpered, as I pushed him away. I hopped off the workbench and kneeled in front of him.

I pulled his pants down to his knees and looked up at him. "A little help," I said as I gestured at his boots he had on.

He stepped back, toeing them off. I grabbed him by the waist and pulled him back to me. I worked his pants all the way off as he stepped out of them and threw them over by our growing pile of clothes.

I sat back and reached up to the waistband of his underwear and tugged them down. His dick sprang out, bobbing in front of me. "Wow." I marveled as I stroked my hand up and down his shaft. My fingers trailed over the three bars he had, the feel of his soft skin and cold metal begging for me to taste him.

Rigid chuckled, throwing his head back. "Stand up," he ordered.

"Not yet," I said, licking my lips as I watched a drop of precum seep out of the head of his rock hard dick. I leaned forward, licking the drop up.

"Son of a bitch," Rigid groaned. I looked up, his eyes on me.

"I want to taste you," I said as I leaned forward, licking up his shaft. I heard him suck in a breath and his stomach tighten.

I scooted forward on my knees, so his dick was inches away from my lips. I gripped his dick at the base and stroked him up and down. Lining his dick up with my mouth I leaned forward, twirling my tongue around the head and sucked it into my mouth.

"Yeah, beautiful. Take it," Rigid groaned, thrusting his hips at me.

I opened my mouth, slowly working him down my throat and stroking the base of him with my hand. He was too big to fit all the way down my throat, but that doesn't mean I didn't try.

"Hold still," Rigid said. I stopping bobbing up and down his shaft, still holding him in my mouth.

He threaded his fingers through hair and held my head tight. He thrust forward, held my head firmly, and fucked my mouth. I loved the feel of him pulling my hair while his rock hard dick slid in and out of my mouth.

I could hear his breath pick up and knew he was close to coming. I opened my throat and swallowed the next time he thrust. He shuddered above me and pulled his dick all the way out.

I whimpered at the loss of him and wiped my mouth on the back of my hand. "Why did you stop?" I pouted.

"The first time I cum is going to be in that sweet pussy, not down your throat," he grunted, trying to get his breathing under control.

"I want you to come in my mouth. I want to taste all of you." I said, leaning back and looked up at him.

"You will, just not now. Up," he ordered, holding his hand out to me.

I grabbed his hand, and he pulled me to my feet. Reaching down, he popped the button on my shorts and pulled them down. I was standing in just my underwear in the middle of a body shop with Rigid, who was completely naked. Definitely not how I thought the day was going to go.

He wrapped his arm around my waist and pulled me to him. He slid his other hand down the front of my soaking wet panties and cup my mound. "This is mine," he growled, parting my folds and stroking my clit.

I whimpered, loving the feel of his rough, calloused finger against my soft flesh. "Please," I pleaded, wanting more.

"So needy," he teased, speeding up the flicking of my clit. I braced my arms on Rigid's shoulders, holding on as he drove me to the brink of ecstasy. I thrust my hips into his hand, reaching for more.

He claimed my lips with his while his fingers brought me closer and closer to my release. His warm, soft tongue stroked mine, out tastes mingling together creating an intoxicating taste I wanted more of.

"I want you to come on my hand, and then you are going to come all over my dick," he rumbled, as a rush of wetness soaked his hand.

"Rigid," I moaned, wanting more.

"Say my name," he growled. One finger entered me, pumping in and out as his thumb continued to stroke my clit.

"Ash." I breathed out, as lights burst behind my eyes as I fell over the edge, moaning in pleasure.

He slowed his hand as my limp body clung to him, to wrung out to stand on my own two feet anymore. "That was the most beautiful thing I have ever seen," Rigid growled in my ear.

He pulled his hand out of my panties, lifting it to his mouth, and licked his finger. I shivered as he sucked it clean, moaning around his finger.

"I want more," I said, not even recognizing the words coming out of my mouth. He had ignited a fire inside me that I didn't want to go out. I would never get enough of this man.

"Panties off," he ordered, watching me.

I quickly shimmied them off, his eyes watching me the whole time. I tossed them into the pile of clothes and waited. I crossed my arms over my chest, feeling self-conscious standing naked in front of him as his eyes traveled over me.

"Arms down,' he ordered. I slowly lowered my arms, wanting to please him. 'Don't ever hide from me, Cyn. When we start hiding from each is when things change. You get all of me, and I want all of you. Nothing between us. Ever."

I nodded my head, agreeing with him. He stepped towards me and wrapped me up in his arms. "Don't leave me again," I whispered, the words out of my mouth before I had a chance to think about them.

"I'm sorry, beautiful. I just needed to figure things out," he confessed.

"Next time talk to me, don't run away. I'm scared to, Rigid. I don't know what I'm doing, but I do know that I want you there with me," I said, pulling back, looking him in the eye.

"I promise, beautiful. You get all of me from now on. Even when I act like a fucking pussy." He smirked, lowering his lips to mine. I threaded my fingers through his hair, craving his taste.

"Wrap your legs around me," he growled, his hands traveling down my back and cupping my ass. He lifted me up and my legs snaked around him.

His dick was cradled in between the folds of my pussy. "I need you," I pleaded.

He walked back over to the workbench, holding me with one arm, and grabbed a stack of clean rags and laid a couple down. He set me down, his arms still wrapped around me.

"Scoot your ass to the edge."

I scooted forward and leaned back on my arms. "Take me," I whispered, anticipation coursing through me.

"Keep your legs spread wide," He said, lining his cock up with my pussy. He nudged the folds open with the head of his dick, and I held my breath.

"Please," I moaned as he slid his dick over my clit.

"So fucking wet. All for me," he rumbled.

I threw my head back as he thrust into me. He slowly pulled out, leaving just the head in. I groaned as he slowly thrust back inside me. "Harder," I moaned as he slowly worked me up.

"No. I want you to feel me inside you and know that no one can ever make you feel this good," he grunted as he continued his slow torture.

Every time he pulled out, his Jacob's ladder drove me insane. Touching places I never knew existed. "Ash," I gasped out as I felt my desire building.

He moaned at the sound of his name and speed up a little faster. "I love when you call me that. No one but you, Cyn. No one," he growled.

"Faster, Ash, please. Take me, hard," I begged.

"Son of a bitch," he growled as he slammed into me. He picked up the pace, his hips slapping against mine.

"Yes!" I shouted, finally getting what I had been craving.

"Such a tight, fucking pussy. God damn milking me," he said as he slammed his lips down on mine, his tongue delving inside my mouth, taking and giving.

"I'm gonna cum," I moaned against his lips. He sucked my bottom lip into his mouth, and I shattered all around him.

"Mine!" He shouted as he slammed into me one last time and his release filled me, as we held onto one another.

I buried my head in the crook of his neck and held on as tremors worked through my body. "You're smelling me again, aren't you?" I giggled as I felt Rigid bury his nose in my hair.

"You're like a fucking drug. I've gone four days without you, that's three and a half days too long." He chuckled, keeping his face buried in my hair.

"That's your own fault. I stayed right where you left me, waiting for you. I'm always waiting for you."

"And I'll always come back to you, Cyn. I promise," he said, threading his fingers through my hair and tilting my head back.

"Just don't leave and I won't have to wait," I teased, stroking his cheek, smiling at him.

"You're pretty feisty today," He stated, grabbing my hand and kissing my palm.

I shivered, feeling the AC pouring out of the ceiling above us. "I need to keep you in line," I purred as I leaned into him, stealing his warmth.

Rigid slowly pulled out of me and I let my legs drop to the floor. "You're cold, beautiful. I'll grab your clothes," he said, steadying me as he pulled away. I tested my legs to see if they would hold and wobbled a little. I leaned against the workbench and laughed at the fact that Rigid had fucked me so good that I couldn't even stand anymore.

"What's so funny?" He asked, handing me my clothes. He pulled his boxers on, followed by his shirt and pants.

"I can't even stand. What did you do to me?" I asked.

"Get used to it, beautiful. I plan on doing that to you again once we get back to your house." He pulled on his boots and looked me over. I hadn't gotten any of my clothes on yet, but he was already fully dressed. Apparently, I didn't have the same effect on him as he did to me.

"That's not fair that you are completely fine, and I'm just a naked mess, not even able to stand up." I pouted as I pulled my bra out of the pile of clothes he handed me and fumbled putting it on.

He reached behind me, swatted my hands away and hooked my bra in seconds. "Trust me, beautiful. You drove me just as crazy, I'm just eager to get you home and do it again." He pulled my shirt over my head, and I stuck my arms in. He crouched down, holding my shorts out and I stepped into them. He pulled them up my legs, snapped the button and zipped them up. He grabbed my flip flops placing them at my feet and slid my feet into them.

"You could, at least, look a little rattled," I pouted, pulling my hair up into a high ponytail.

He grabbed my hand, stopping me from putting my hair up, and put it on his dick. It was still hard, ready to go. "My dick is about five minutes away from punching through my jeans, beautiful. I am anything from ok," he growled.

I licked my lips, my hand cupping him, wanting more. "We can always go to your room," I purred, biting my lip.

"Deal," he said as he bent down, throwing me over his shoulder.

"Rigid!' I yelled. 'Put me down! I can walk now!"

He slapped my ass, making me squeal in surprise. "No." He walked through an open door and out into a huge area that had five car lifts and various guys milling around, working on cars.

"Oh my God," I mumbled into Rigid's back, realizing all these guys had just heard us having sex.

"Ain't nothing they've never heard before," I heard Rigid rumble, knowing what I was thinking.

"About fucking time!" Someone shouted at us as we walked by.

"Fuck off," Rigid snapped as we made our way through the shop. He ducked through another door, and I heard Meg squeal.

"Put her down!" She yelled.

"She's mine," Rigid said.

"Yeah, well. You going all caveman on her ass sure doesn't look like she agrees if you have to carry where ever the hell you are headed," Meg said. I couldn't see her (all I could see was Rigid's ass, but what a fine ass it was) and knew she was throwing some major sass.

"Out of the way, Meg," Rigid growled, his patience wearing thin.

"I don't know where you think you are going. Cyn and I have to be to work in an hour. That is unless I should start calling you Minute Man if you plan on being done with Cyn in fifteen minutes." Meg cackled and burst out laughing.

"Can't you control your woman?" Rigid said I'm assuming to King.

"I like her the way she is," King rumbled.

"Ha!" Meg shouted.

"She isn't going to work. Tell 'em she's sick or something." Rigid declared as he made his way around Meg.

"Um, Rigid. I kind of have to go to work. I've missed so much the past month and now that I'm not on medical leave, they're watching me closely," I said, totally raining on both of our parades. I had totally forgotten that I had to work tonight. I used to enjoy going to work, but ever since Asshat's sister had started working at the plant, she had been making my life a living hell. I had only been back for three days, but it was three days too many.

"Son of a bitch. I finally get you back, and now you got to leave?" Rigid growled, setting me on my feet.

"You're own damn fault you haven't been with her," King said from the desk he was sitting behind.

I looked around, taking in the office. Meg was blocking the doorway that I'm assuming lead to the clubhouse, with her arms propped up on her hips, scowling at Rigid. "She hasn't slept, you know?" Meg said accusingly at Rigid.

I gasped. I hadn't realized that Meg knew I wasn't sleeping. The night after they had taken care of Nick, Meg had gone back to her house, and things had gone back to normal. She had only been around that first night I had the nightmare. Apparently, I wasn't hiding my lack of sleep very well.

"I know. I'll make it better," He vowed, throwing his arm over my shoulder and pulled me to him.

"You better." Meg huffed as she walked over to King's desk and sat on the edge, crossing her arms over her chest.

"You really got to work tonight, beautiful?" Rigid asked.

"Yeah. As much as I dread going, I have to. Bills to pay and all that shit," I said.

"I'm going to throat punch Cherry tonight if she says one word to you," Meg said vehemently.

"Easy tiger," King chuckled from his desk, shaking his head.

"What the hell are you talking about?" Rigid asked.

"I told you, Cherry, Nick's sister, started working at the plant while I was out on medical leave. She's been a raging bitch the past three days since I came back. She's gunning to get me fired and take my job," I explained.

"Why didn't you tell me?" Rigid growled.

"You kind of weren't talking to me, and we were kind of busy just now." I snapped back. Ignorant man, I thought he was done with me an hour ago. Like I was going to go running to him about someone calling me names and giving me a little bit of trouble? Oy.

"You should have told me," He repeated.

I shook my head at him, annoyed that he was pissed off. "It's nothing. She'll get tired of messing with me and move onto someone else to mess with. I'm just keeping my head down and doing my job. I talked to Cal about it, and he is aware of the situation," I explained, trying to pacify him.

"Who the hell is Cal? Why the fuck would you tell him and not me?" Rigid accused.

"Jesus Christ, man. Cal is out fucking supervisor!" Meg shouted. King busted out laughing, his whole body shaking.

"How the hell am I supposed to know that?" Rigid huffed, crossing his arms over his chest, throwing an eat shit look at King, who was still laughing.

"Ok, now that everyone is up to date with my life,' I exclaimed, 'I need to run home quickly and get ready for work." I looked at Meg expectantly, seeing as she was my ride.

"I'll take you home and then to work," Rigid stated, grabbing my hand and threading his fingers with mine.

"Good,' Meg said, jumping off of King's desk. 'I still have to run home, change, and take Blue out before I go to work. We totally would have been late if I had to take you home."

"Are you sure?" I asked, looking up at Rigid.

"Yeah, beautiful. I can take a break for a little bit and then I can work on the Chevelle while you are working," Rigid explained as he tugged me to the door.

"I'll see you later!" Meg called as Rigid pulled me out the door and on his bike.

"I've got sandals on," I said looking back and forth between my flip flops and Rigid's bike.

"It's a short ride, beautiful, and I'll be careful," he promised, handing me my helmet.

I strapped it on and climbed on behind Rigid. "Hurry up, I still need to take a shower and find some clothes to wear tonight," I bossed, wrapping my arms around him, missing the feel of being on his bike behind him.

"I can help you with the shower," Rigid said as he cranked up his bike.

"I'm trying to not be late for work, Rigid. You can stay outside, cause I'm pretty sure you walk through my door, neither one of us will be getting back to work," I countered.

Rigid shook his head, laughing and we rocketed out of the parking lot.

I was back where I belonged, wind blowing in my hair and my arms wrapped around the man I loved. Life was finally starting to look up.

<<<<<<<<<

Chapter 27

RIGID

"Yo! I'm heading out to pick up Meg, you coming with?" King shouted from the office.

I looked at the clock, seeing it was almost eleven and grabbed a rag to wipe my hands off. I had managed to get the Chevelle painted and just needed to clear coat it in the morning.

I threw the rag into the dirty bin and made my way to the office. King was waiting by the door, ready to lock up. King and I were in the same boat now. Both of our women worked nights, so we needed to find things to do to fill the time when they were gone.

It looked like King and I were going to be doing a lot of work in the evening hours from now on. "Get all your paperwork taken care of?" I asked, eyeing his desk that was now clear of all the papers that were littering it eight hours before.

"Yeah, till it fills up again tomorrow." King joked as he held the door open for me.

I walked over to my bike, waiting for King to climb onto his. I cranked mine up, anxious to get to Cyn. I watched King, lock the door and pocket the keys. He swung onto his bike, and we headed out.

It had been eight hours too long since I had held Cyn.

<<<<<<<<<<

Cyn

"Just give me the fucking word and I'll twat punch her," Meg snarled, her fists balled at her side.

"She's not worth it, Meg," I said, trying to sooth her.

I looked across the parking lot, watching Cherry and her small gang of friends that she had managed to make in the short time she had started working at the plant. They were gathered around her car, talking loudly about how Cherry had banged Meg's man and how she was going take Rigid away from me. I really wasn't concerned about it.

Meg, on the other hand, was about to go apeshit on her ass. I heard bikes roar in the parking lot, thankful I wouldn't have to be pulling Meg off of Cherry.

Meg and I both turned to watch our men pull in and appreciated all their sexy goodness.

"And here comes my new man right now." I heard Cherry call. I looked over my shoulder and watched her making her way over to Meg and I stood.

Son of a bitch. Maybe we weren't out of the drama woods yet.

King and Rigid pulled their bikes right next to us and killed the engines. By the time King and Rigid had gotten off and were standing next to us, Cherry was by us.

"Hey, King," she purred, her voice overly sweet.

All he did was nod his head at her and pull Meg into his arms. Meg melted into him, wrapping herself around him.

Cherry huffed at his blatant refusal of her and shifted her sights on Rigid.

"Hey, Rigid," she purred, batting her eyelashes at him.

I rolled my eyes, totally over Cherry and all the bullshit that came with her.

"'Sup," Rigid said to her. He draped his arm over my shoulder and curled me into his body. He pressed a kiss to the side of my head, and I melted a little bit at his sweet kiss.

"You guys looking to have some fun tonight?" Cherry asked, completely oblivious to the fact that King was with Meg and Rigid was mine.

"My schedule is full right now. I think King's is too." Rigid replied, politely rebutting her.

"What, with these two? Please, I can show you a much better time than they can," She said, popping her hip out and tossing back her hair. I don't know how she looked so good after working an eight-hour shift.

No offense to Meg, but we both looked like we had run ten miles and needed a good night sleep. Cherry, on the other hand, looked like she had just stepped out of the beauty salon. If she weren't such a bitch, I would have asked her what her secret was.

"We're not interested, Cherry. Try somewhere else. You're not going to get anything from us other than a cold shoulder and possibly being banned from the club if you keep messing with our women," King replied. Meg had turned around, trying to kill Cherry with a death glare, while King had his arm wrapped around her waist.

"We'll see about that. If what my brother says is true, it won't be long till you start stepping out on that one, Rigid,' she said pointing her finger at me. 'Heard she's shit in the sack. You know where to find me," Cherry said with a parting wink at Rigid and sauntered away.

"Let me go, King. Just one good punch to her junk that's all I want. One twat punch." Meg fumed, trying to pull out of King's arms.

I looked up at Rigid, his eyes watching Cherry walk back to her car and friends. "I'm assuming she doesn't know about her brother?" I questioned.

Rigid's eyes fell to me, and he shook his head. "We took care of it, or should I say Slider took care of it. He knows some messed up shit that has helped us out in a pinch."

"I'm not sure I want to know," I said, guessing how Slider had gotten rid of Nick.

"I don't ask either, beautiful," Rigid chuckled, a grin spreading across his lips.

"Can we go home now?" I asked, suddenly really tired. I still wasn't used to working yet. I used to be able to work my full shift and stay up until four AM before I felt tired. Now, midnight hit and it was a miracle I made it home before I fell into a fitful sleep filled with nightmares and tossing and turning.

"Yeah, beautiful." He grabbed my hand, lacing his fingers through mine and walked us over to his bike.

King had managed to calm down Meg, and they were also getting ready to leave.

I grabbed the helmet Rigid held out for me and strapped it on. I watched Meg do the same thing while neither of the guys put one on. "How come we have to wear helmets and ya'll don't?" I asked.

"Cause you guys are more important than we are. Got to keep you safe," Rigid said, leaning down, placing a swift kiss on my lips and swung his leg over the bike.

I looked at Meg, who was flipping on King as he climbed onto his bike, his back to Meg. "Fucking men," Meg ranted as she climbed on behind King.

I shook my head, laughing, and scurried on behind Rigid. "I'll see you tomorrow!" I yelled at Meg as Rigid and King cranked up their bikes.

She threw a quick wave at me, and they rocketed out of the parking lot, headed to Meg's house. Rigid and I pulled out after them, headed to my house. I loved being on the back of Rigid's bike at night. The stars above us, the moon shining bright, lighting the sky.

I felt so at home and safe riding with Rigid. He drove like the bike was a part of him, smoothly making turns and curves, our bodies becoming one as we leaned together. I loved it. If it were possible, I would never ride in another car, ever. I think I was made for the biker bitch life.

Most of all, I was made to be Rigid's.

Chapter 28

RIGID

Cyn was passed out next to me, her breath lightly drifting over my chest. As soon as we had gotten off the bike and walked into her house, I took one look at her and knew she needed sleep more than the long, hard, fuck I had wanted to give her.

I pulled her down the hall, to her room, and quickly stripped her clothes off her. I pulled one of my tees out that she still had in the top drawer of her dresser and pulled it over her head. She wrapped her arms around me, snuggling into me. I lifted her up, cradling in my arms, and laid her down on her bed. I pulled the covers over her and walked back out, locking the door and turning off all the lights.

By the time I made it back to bed, she was out, her hands tucked under her head, softly snoring away. Quickly taking off my clothes, I slid into bed with her and just enjoyed having her back in my arms.

She had slept all through the night, not even a whimper from her lips. I slept light, making sure I would wake up if she had a nightmare.

It was just past nine o'clock, and my dick was ready for her to wake up. I had woken up an hour earlier, and it had taken all my will power not to wake her up and fuck her till she couldn't walk.

She stretched out next to me, her eyes flickering as she woke up. "Morning," she said sleepily.

"Good morning, beautiful," I replied, my hand cupping her chin and leaning down, placing a kiss on her lips.

"I could get used to waking up this way," she confessed, wrapping her arms around my neck, pulling me on top of her.

"I'll be here every morning as long as you'll have me," I smiled, placing kisses up and down her neck.

"I guess, I'll have to get you a key so you can come over while I'm at work. I'll expect you waiting in bed, naked for me every night." She giggled, her hands traveling down my back.

"I'm pretty sure that can be arranged," I quipped, nipping her neck.

She squealed, pulling away from me. "No biting." She laughed, her eyes filled with the light I had seen the first night I had met her.

I cupped her jaw with my hand and ran my thumb over her bottom lip. "What about sucking?" I asked, pushing my thumb into her mouth.

She licked my thumb, swirling her tongue around it and sucked on it. "Fuck me, you are amazing," I marveled, watching her eyes fill with desire.

I slid my hand down her body, gliding over her firm breasts, her nipples puckering at my light caress.

"I want you, Rigid," she moaned, bucking her hips at me. My hand kept sliding down her body, grazing her curvy stomach and I cupped her mound, her panties soaked through from her need for me.

"Is this for me?" I asked, stroking her.

"Yes, I'm all yours," she whimpered.

I tugged the band on her panties down, exposing her glistening mound. I parted her folds, my finger flicking her clit, making her body shiver. "So wet," I growled.

"Stop teasing me, Rigid. I need you."

"I've been waiting forever for you to say those words. There's only one thing that could make them better." I said, hoping she knew what I was talking about. I loved when she called me Ash. She had only been doing it for a short time, but I already knew it was something I wanted to hear all the time.

She leaned up, bracing herself on her elbows and whispered, "I need you, Ash."

I crashed my lips down on hers, taking what was mine and what she was giving. I never imagined I would find a woman like Cyn. I was never letting her go.

"We have too many clothes on," she mumbled against my lips.

I grabbed the bottom of her tee and ripped it over her head and tossed it on the floor. I cupped her tits, my thumbs flicking over her puckered nipples. She grabbed the waistband of my boxers and pulled them down, and grabbed my dick that was bobbing in between us. "Is this for me?" She taunted, throwing my words back at me.

"Only for you, beautiful." I chuckled, loving how playful she was with me.

She stroked my cock, my arms on either side of her head, holding me up to give her more room to play. "Why did you do this?" She asked as she ran her fingertips over my piercings.

"Honestly?' I asked. She nodded her head and went back to stroking me. I took a calming breath, trying to get my dick under control. 'I was young and stupid and heard it made sex for the girl unbelievable."

"So you did this just for the girl?" She asked, not believing me, a smirk playing on her lips.

"Well, that and I thought it looked pretty badass," I joked.

"You're such an arrogant ass sometimes, you know that?" She said and burst out laughing.

I lowered my lips to hers, inches away and whispered, 'You're not supposed to laugh when my dick is in your hand. You might give me a complex." I teased.

"A complex? Really, you?" She questioned as she laughed.

"Yeah. I think I know how you can fix it, though."

"Oh yeah? How?" She asked.

"Flip over, get on your hands and knees," I ordered, sliding off of her. I sat back on my haunches, waiting for her to follow my orders.

She looked me over, her eyes lingering on my raging hard on and rolled over to her stomach and got on her hands and knees. "I'll deny this five minutes from now, but I love when you get all bossy on me," she said, lifting her ass directly in front of me.

I ran my hands over her firm ass, loving the extra padding she had back there. Cyn was made for me. She was soft and curvy in all the right places.

My hands parted her ass, seeing the beautiful rose of her ass. "Have you ever been played with back here?" I asked as my fingertip circled her puckered hole.

"No," she said as a shiver ran through her body.

"One day, I'm going to make this mine, too."

"Rigid," she moaned as I continued my exploration. I lightly probed her tight hole, and another shudder racked through her body.

I moved my other hand down the crack of her ass and found her sweet, wet pussy. "I'm going to take this today," I growled, her hips thrusting into my hand as I found her clit.

"You're driving me crazy, Ash," she whimpered, begging me for more with each thrust of her hips.

I held on to her hips and leaned down, swiping my tongue through her drenched pussy. She moaned out, making my dick even harder than it was. "You want to come on my tongue or my dick, baby?" I asked. I swiped my tongue through her wet pussy again, flicking her clit.

"Your dick. Please, I want your dick!" She called out.

I flicked her clit one more time and leaned back, lining my dick up with her sweet pussy. I thrust all the way in, her pussy milking me. I reached around, finding her clit and stroked it.

"Ash," she groaned as I moved in and out of her.

She tossed her head back, her hair cascading down her back. I grabbed her hair, bunching it up in my hand, and tugged on her hair. I slammed into her, loving the feel of her pussy squeezing my dick and her silky hair in my hand.

I pulled on her hair again, a groan of pleasure breaking free from her lips. "Harder," she begged.

I tugged on her hair again and slammed my dick deep into her. "Again!" She screamed.

Son of a bitch, I loved this woman. I thrust even harder, slamming into her and yanked on her hair. I held her head back as I pounded into her. I felt my balls tighten, knowing it was only a matter of seconds before I exploded inside of her.

I reached around and flicked her clit, and she came, squeezing my dick with each tremor that rocked through her body. I plunged all the way into her and filled her with my cum.

Flicking her clit one more time, I wrung the last of her orgasm out of her, and she collapsed onto the bed. I laid down next to her, my arms giving out.

"I think you broke me," she mumbled into the pillow.

"Ditto, beautiful. I don't think I have ever cum that hard in my life," I confessed as I pulled her hair out of her face and set it off to the side.

I leaned over and placed a kiss on the side of her head. She cuddled closer to me, laying her head on my arm. "We need to do that again, but you know, like in a couple of hours." She giggled.

"Agreed. I'm fucking starving right now," I said, laying my head down.

"I don't feel like cooking,' she whined. 'Call Meg and tell her to come over and cook for us," she joked.

"We could head to the clubhouse. Mickey always makes a shit ton for breakfast, and it passes for edible." I suggested.

"Good idea, except then we have to put clothes on."

"Yes, beautiful, you'll need to put clothes and decent shoes on since we'll take my bike."

"Ugh, that all sounds good except for the whole getting up part." She giggled, a grin spreading across her face.

"Up. You've got ten minutes to get your sexy ass dressed and out to my bike. I need to eat to keep up my stamina with you, baby," I said as I slid out of bed and looked around for my boxers.

"Hmm, I like this show," Cyn purred as she threw her arms behind her head, watching me pick up all our clothes.

I picked up my pants, and a condom fell out of the pocket. "Son of a bitch. We didn't use a condom yesterday or today. Shit," I said, looking at Cyn.

"I'm on the pill. We should be fine. I know I'm clean, and I assume you are, too," she said calmly.

"I'm clean. I got checked a month ago. You're on the pill?" I asked.

"Yeah, I got back on it that first checkup three weeks ago. I told the doctor I wasn't sexually active, but he said it was a good idea to be on the pill just in case," she explained.

"So, does that mean you could get pregnant again?" I asked, afraid to know the answer but also wanting to know.

"Yeah. The doctor didn't see a reason why I wouldn't be able to get pregnant again. Not that I'm going to try shortly to get pregnant, but it's nice to know when I decide to try to that it's hopefully possible." She divulged. I could tell that she was extremely happy with that little bit of news.

"Good, beautiful,' I said, pausing in my search for my boxers and leaned over her laying a kiss on her lips. 'Now you've got eight minutes to get that sexy ass on my bike," I teased, ducking as she threw her pillow at me.

"You're an ass," she pouted as she crawled out of bed. She grabbed her robe from the back of her desk chair and threw it on.

"You planning on riding my bike in just your robe?"
I teased.

She flipped me off and walked out the door towards the bathroom mumbling about cavemen and assholes.

I shook my head and continued my search for my boxers when I looked out her window and saw them hanging from the frame. I pulled them on and grabbed a clean shirt out of her dresser and pulled on my jeans I had worn last night. I was going to have to bring more clothes over if I planned on spending the night here more.

I pulled on my socks and boots and headed to the kitchen to make Cyn a cup of coffee I knew she was craving.

"Is that for me?" I heard her ask as I filled her cup, adding sugar and creamer.

I turned around, holding it out to her and looked her over. She had on a white tank top, faded blue jeans and the boots that I had bought her. She had her thick, black hair piled on top of her head and it made my fingers itch, wanting to tug out the tie and watch her hair cascade all around her.

I handed her the cup and shoved my hands in my pockets, trying to control myself. She held the cup up to her nose and inhaled deeply. "Oh my god that's good," she said after she took a sip.

"You have exactly three minutes to drink that and be on my bike," I said, flipping the coffee machine off and headed to the front door.

"You're not going to stay in here and talk to me?" She pouted.

"If I stay in here with you, beautiful, I'm going to do a whole lot more then watch you drink your coffee," I replied as I walked out the door. I heard her quick intake of breath and knew she agreed.

I walked to my bike and threw my leg over her, waiting for Cyn. I looked up at the sky and knew things could only get better from here on. I had Cyn, and nothing was going to change that. She was mine.

Chapter 29

Cyn

"How come you took the short way here?" I asked as I swung my leg off Rigid's bike and took my helmet off.

"Because, as much as I love having your sweet body wrapped around me, I'm fucking starving, beautiful," Rigid said as he grabbed the helmet from me and hung it from the handlebars.

"Hmm, I see where I rank," I teased. Rigid rolled his eyes and pulled me into a hug.

"Cyn! I didn't know you guys were going to be here this morning," Meg said as she walked out of the office, two cups of coffee in her hands. Gravel followed behind her gnawing on a piece of bacon and a cup of coffee in his hand.

"Rigid and I were hungry but didn't feel like cooking," I explained as I grabbed a cup from her. I inhaled deeply, smelling the hazelnut creamer Meg always used. Yum.

"You going to finish up the Chevelle today?" Gravel asked Rigid.

"That's the plan old man, you feel up to helping?" Rigid asked.

Meg tugged my hand and pulled me away from Rigid. "Over here," she whispered, moving us a couple of feet away from Rigid and Gravel.

"What's up?" I asked as I took a sip of coffee. Heavenly.

"So I assume you and Rigid are all good now?" She asked, digging for details.

"Yeah. We're good," I said, a goofy smile spreading across my face.

"Oh geez, I know that look all too well. It's always on my face whenever Lo is around." Meg joked.

"What's up with Troy, I haven't seen him around lately except for a couple of glimpses of him at work?" I asked.

"Eh, he's been pissy lately. That chick he was dating dumped him when he was up in Fall's City those couple of weeks. I say good riddance, but he seems pretty bummed about it."

"What was her name again?" I asked, unable to remember it.

"Not a clue. I never even met her. We need to find a chick to hook him up with. What do you say?" She asked.

"Meg, we've tried that like ten times before and each time they end in a disaster. I think we should just let Troy find his own girl," I chided, remembering all the horrible dates we had set Troy up on.

"Humph, alright. I'll listen to you for now." Meg pouted, upset she couldn't hook Troy up.

"Let's go get-.' I started but was interrupted by screaming and yelling.

"Get down!" Rigid yelled. Just as the words left his mouth, gunfire went off. Meg and I dove to the ground, huddled together.

I heard three more shots and then squealing tires and a car taking off.

"Are you ok?" Meg and I said at the same time.

We both looked each other over making sure we were ok when we heard someone yell, "Clear."

I looked over to where Rigid and Gravel had been standing and saw Rigid, kneeling on the ground, covered in blood next to Gravel, who was laid out on the ground.

"Rigid," I screamed as Meg and I scrambled over to him. Rigid had his hands pressed firmly into Gravel's shoulder, putting pressure on the bleeding.

"King! Call an ambulance," Rigid ordered.

"Meg, go get a blanket or something to put over Gravel. He's losing a lot of blood," he said. Meg ran into the clubhouse the door slapping shut behind her.

"Are you ok, Gravel?" I asked as I kneeled next to his head.

"I'm fine. Just hurts like a son of a bitch," Gravel grunted.

His eyes fluttered, threatening to close. "Stay with me, Gravel. The ambulance will be here in no time. I happen to know they have the good drugs on board," I joked, trying to keep him awake.

"I'm gonna… need 'em," he groaned.

"Do you need me to do anything?" I asked Rigid.

"Just keep doing what you're doing. We need to keep him awake," Rigid calmly ordered.

I gave Rigid a small smile and looked back at Gravel, who had his eyes shut. "Hey, Gravel, no going to sleep on me. You need to get better so you and Gambler can play Rigid and me in a rematch of testicle toss."

Gravel opened his eyes and gave me a half smile. "Huh, we'll whip your asses all over… again, girl. You might… want to practice before… you call out such a … crazy challenge."

"We'll see about that." I laughed. I heard sirens in the distance and breathed a sigh of relief that they were close.

"Can you hold on for five more minutes?" I asked Gravel.

"Only if you show me your tits," he teased while grimacing at me.

"Just because you're bleeding all over me, old man, doesn't mean I won't punch your fucking lights out," Rigid growled.

Gravel laughed but ended up coughing, jerking his hurt shoulder, causing more pain. "Son of a … bitch. This fucking … hurts," he groaned out.

I looked up at Rigid, concerned about Gravel. He read my look and nodded his head, telling me it would be ok.

Looking up I saw the ambulance pull into the parking lot in a cloud of dust and flying gravel. The two paramedics burst out of the ambulance and started firing questions off to Rigid. Rigid answered them all calmly, telling the paramedics what happened and everything he could think of that would pertain to Gravel.

They loaded him up on the gurney and into the back of the ambulance. "Call Ethel," Gravel shouted before the doors shut.

I looked to my left and saw King standing there with his arms wrapped around Meg. I was so focused on Gravel that I hadn't even notice Meg and King come out of the office before. We all watched the ambulance drive away, Gravel hopefully ok in the back.

"Come here, beautiful," Rigid said as he cradled me in his arms. I went willingly, needing to feel him in my arms.

It could have been Rigid in the back of the ambulance. He was standing right next to Gravel when he had gotten shot.

"Who would want to hurt Gravel?" Meg asked.

"They weren't aiming for Gravel," King said.

"Then who the hell were they aiming for?" I asked, confused.

"Me," Rigid replied, quietly. My body went rock solid by that one word.

"Why you? Who the hell were they?" Meg demanded to know.

"The Assassins. Payback for what we did to Nick," King explained.

"No, Nick's death is on me, and no one else in this club. I told you that before we left the hotel. All of this is on me," Rigid snarled.

"You think the Assassins care about who gave the final blow? They know it was Devil's Knights, and now they are out for blood. They don't care who's they spill as long as it's a Knight.' King barked. 'Church in an hour. Crowbar and Hammer, you follow the ambulance. Someone stays at Gravel's door at all times. I'll be up after church,' King commanded and herded Meg into the clubhouse as she shot question after question at him.

"I... I'm scared," I stuttered, my arms tightening around Rigid. The events of what just happened sinking in.

"Come on," Rigid said as he grabbed my hand and pulled me into the clubhouse. As we were walking in the door, I saw two police cars pull up and wondered if anyone was going to get into trouble.

"Do we have to talk to them?" I asked, tipping my head at the two police cruisers.

"We will, first I want to change and make sure you are ok," Rigid said, tugging me in the door and down the hallway to his room.

He pulled his set of keys out of his pocket and opened the door. I stepped inside, and he shut the door behind us.

He pulled his bloody shirt over his head and tossed it into the corner. He pulled a clean one out of his dresser and tugged it over his head. "Sit down," he ordered, as he walked into to an open door and flipped on the light. I saw it was a bathroom before he shut the door behind him.

I sat down on the bed, looking down at my hands that were shaking. I heard the bathroom door click open, and I jumped. Son of a bitch.

Rigid sat down next to me and pulled me into his lap. "Look at me," he ordered.

I looked him in the eye and felt the tears threatening to fall. "I almost lost you again," I whispered, as I let the tears fall.

"I know, beautiful, but I'm still here. It's going to take a lot more than a bunch of idiots and a trigger happy idiot to take me away from you. I promise," he vowed.

I shook my head no. "You can't promise that, Rigid. If you had been standing two feet to the left, you could be the one in the back of that ambulance, not Gravel. I can't lose you again," I wailed, becoming hysterical. The man I loved was almost taken away from me again. Holy shit, the man I love. I love Rigid.

"I love you," I blurted out, unable to keep it in. I had just realized it, but if what had just happened taught me anything, it was to not wait for later. I loved Rigid, and he needed to know.

"Just calm down, you're ok. You're just in shock right now, take a deep breath and just take a minute to breathe, beautiful," he calmly said, ignoring what I had just blurted out.

"No!' I yelled, knocking his hand away from my face. 'I mean, yes I'm in shock, but no, I love you. I know you think I don't mean it, but I do. I don't want to live without you. I can't live without you. I love you with everything I am Rigid. I'm not going to change my mind or take it back when this all wears off, I love you," I babbled.

"Cyn, this is crazy," he reasoned.

"I know it's crazy, but I love you. There will never be another person who makes me feel the way you do. I love you!" I yelled.

"Jesus Christ,' Rigid said, rubbing his hands down his face. He looked me in the eye and just stared at me. 'I love you, too." he whispered.

"You love me?" I asked like an idiot.

"I love you," he declared, louder.

"Holy shit, you love me," I cackled, a grin spreading across my face. I tackled him, pushing him onto his back and straddled him.

He placed his hands on my hips, his fingers spanning my waist. "I love you, Cyn," he repeated.

"I love you, too, Ash," I whispered, leaning down, placing a kiss on his lips.

"Now what?" He asked against my lips.

"Um, you need to go to church and then we need to go to the hospital and make sure Gravel is ok."

"Then what about after that? This isn't over yet, Cyn. We are going to have to take care of the Assassins." Rigid said somberly.

I took my eyes off Rigid and glanced around his room. This was where Rigid had stayed when he wasn't with me. This room and the club were his life before me. "You do what needs to be done, and you come home to me, no matter what, you come home to me. Promise me."

"No matter what, I will always come home to you, Cyn. You're all I need. If I don't have you to come home to, I have nothing. I love you with all that I am. I'm yours," he vowed.

"No matter what,' I agreed, 'I love you too," I laid a kiss on his lips and laid my head down over his heart.

The steady beating of his heart calmed me, and I knew no matter what happened next, Rigid and I would make it through together. We would always come home to each other.

The End (For Now)

Coming Soon...

Gravel's Road

A Devil's Knights Novella

Ethel had her happily ever after. It may have ended too soon, but it was more than some people got. After Gravel gets hurt, it's Ethel to the rescue, nursing him back to health, and unearthing feelings she had tried to hide for so long.

Gravel doesn't want to settle down. He's lived his life his way for the past forty years, why mess with something that isn't broke? Except Ethel manages to sneak her way in, making Gravel second guess his plan, wondering if maybe there has been something missing all along.

About the Author

WINTER TRAVERS is a devoted wife, mother, and book lover who lives in Wisconsin. Winter spends her days writing, cooking, baking, and daydreaming of the day a Motorcycle Club rolls into town and decides to set up shop. (Fingers Crossed.)

Stay up to date with everything Winter Travers.

www.facebook.com/wintertravers

64968496R00202

Made in the USA
Charleston, SC
12 December 2016